THE LAST SUTTA

THE LAST SUTTA

VISHESH DUBEY

Anecdote
Publishing House
For the love of quality reading!

Anecdote
Publishing House
For the love of quality reading!

anecdotepublishinghouse.com
champreaders.com

Anecdote Publishing House
2nd Floor 2/15 Lane no. 2 Ansari Road, Daryaganj-110002
Email: info@anecdotepublishinghouse.com
Website: anecdotepublishinghouse.com

Published by Anecdote Publishing House

First Edition 2025
ISBN 978-81-982589-9-1
MRP ₹ 399

Book Promoted and Marketed by Champ Readers Pvt. Ltd.
Edited by Meraki
Cover design by The Book Bakers
Layout by Graphic Tailor
Printed by Thomson Press (India) Ltd, New Delhi

"हार वो चरस है जिसे फूंके बिना,
जीत का नशा नहीं चढ़ता..."

CONTENTS

ACKNOWLEDGMENT

I would have never written this book, had it not been for that one day, when I had no money, no job, no one to love, no one to share my feelings with, and no intent to keep on fighting whatever life threw at me.

So, I sat in a temple for five hours, in front of Mahadev, writing down my pain in a diary, wondering if someone would even have enough time to read a ten pager suicide note.

By the time I was done, I had written 50 pages, of a story that I wanted to live. I looked up, and he was still there, smiling. I left home with a new lifeline that day and never looked back after that. To Mahadev, to Maa, Papa and Bhai.

PROLOGUE
LOVE IS NOT ENOUGH

"You don't even have a house of your own, you travel on a bike and your salary isn't even enough to meet your expenses. Listen to me Abhay, love will fade away after a few years, what will be left is just struggle. I can't marry you. I feel bad for you, but please try to understand, my parents have kept me like a princess all these years, and I want to live the rest of my life the same way. I am seeing someone and would most probably marry him. I wanted to tell you about us but then I was scared you'd behave immaturely. This is the last time we are meeting; please don't bother me by texting or calling. Ok?"

Nandita waited for me to give a reaction while I blankly kept staring at her face.

She still looked beautiful, with those ruthless yet pretty eyes, those perfect lips, that perfume she wore, every moment that I spent with her, those flashbacks of how I proposed to her and how much she loved me until she discovered that I wasn't rich and that my parents didn't have any other assets apart from their two kids.

"Oh, please don't start that drama all over again. Crying is not going to change anything." She looked at me, irritated and disappointed. I instead turned my attention towards the fresh *'mehndi'* on her hands.

There was so much I wanted to tell her that day, but I chose to stay silent.

I was in pain, of course, but it was more of a disappointment.

I took out my wallet and signaled the waiter for the bill. Nandita and I used to be regulars at this café. We were now a familiar face for the staff working there.

"No, you need the money, keep it. I'll pay the bill, as such, most of the time; it's me who pays the bills." She took out her debit card. I signaled her to remain seated and picking up my laptop bag, walked up to the counter.

"How much?" I asked the girl at the counter.

"475 sir," she replied.

I handed her over a 500-rupee note as she looked straight into my eyes.

"Here's your change sir and please take care." She smiled reassuringly.

I realized something that day, you don't need to have to be rich to have a good soul. Sometimes, the best people come from the darkest corners of the world.

"Abhay, we are not finished." Nandita interrupted from behind.

I looked back at her knowing that it was the last time we both were seeing each other.

"Goodbye," passing a smile, I walked away.

It was one of those nostalgic winter evenings in Delhi. The thick white fog had slowly begun setting in and a cold light breeze further enhanced the drama. I walked towards the parking lot.

From a distance, I saw Nandita walking up to her car. She was talking to someone over the phone and I could hear her voice. It was quarter past eleven and the streets had gone quiet.

"Yes Dad, I will be home in the next twenty minutes. Yes, I asked him to buzz off. Imagine he paid the bill this time." She broke into a hearty laugh.

I never felt inferior about being a middle-class guy but that day, Nandita made me realize the difference between the rich and the average.

A couple of minutes later, she drove past me while I stood there, watching her leave. All these months I kept ignoring the fact that life is not a film story and that practicality exists, even in love.

I discovered an important aspect of human relationships. Money is the fuel you need to run your relationship successfully. Love does not thrive if you are poor. A strong wave of struggle and your ship of romance would hit the seabed of hopelessness even before you know it.

Money buys out every flaw, be it caste, religion, ethnicity, age difference, disability, etc. If you are not rich or at least decently well off, then the only time you become important to another human being is during elections or if the rich guy/girl needs someone to satisfy his/her physical/ mental or emotional needs, for a while.

For me as a guy hailing from a middle-class family, Nandita showed me the mirror. She made me realize that your status decides your partner. The hard reality, but then the truth must be spoken.

I checked my watch, it was almost midnight. Did not even realize how a breezy evening changed into a cold winter night. I had been sitting in that empty parking lot for three hours.

The Tibetan prayer flag tied on my bike slowly fluttered as the cold breeze silently swept through the desolated parking lot.

I reached for my pocket and pulled out a pack of cigarettes I had bought after meeting Nandita.

"Seventeen, eighteen, nineteen, twenty." I counted the number of cigarettes in the pack. Then pulling out one cigarette, I wrote Nandita's name on it.

This was not the first time I was facing rejection; however, this was the first time I felt ashamed for being born into a middle-class family.

How does someone wealthy get an automatic right to insult and overpower people who are not of the same standard? Why do children born in a middle-class family have aspirations limited to getting a decent job, buying a 2 BHK flat, marrying a simple girl (of the same caste and getting some dowry if possible), having kids, growing old, withdrawing from PF savings and then one day, just die?

The answer is the society we all live in. The 'aunties' and 'uncles' in their late forties or early fifties have their rulebooks and constitutions on what is wrong or right in the way their children are living. Most Indian parents are afraid of being judged by the society they live in because of how their children look, behave, and perform in academics. Their kids would be judged for keeping long hair, growing a beard, wearing short clothes, tattoos or piercings and God knows everything normal and trendy for a rich kid to do.

I decided to give it back to this rich kid, to show her that middle-class guys might not have dad/mom's money to spend blindly, but what they do have is a soul that feels, a mind that thinks, and a heart that knows how to control its needs.

Nandita was now a goal, and crushing her ego was my only motive.

More than revenge, it is about daring to dream, daring to punch above one's weight, and most importantly, changing the way I looked at myself in the very mirror that Nandita showed me.

There is a point in your life where you simply decide, irrespective of the circumstances, irrespective of the noises in your head, you just decide.

This is my story. Those 20 cigarettes to answering a girl who thought I was nothing more than a loser.

MOMENT OF TRUTH

I woke up late the next morning. There are times when you open your eyes and it feels as if you had survived an apocalypse yesterday. It seemed as if I had woken up amongst the debris of my glorious past. All these months, I had a habit of texting Nandita as soon as I woke up, today was however different.

"You look troubled. Are you fine?" Maa handed me a cup of tea and waited for my answer. She could sense that something was wrong with me.

"Nothing, just a minor headache," I smiled reassuringly.

I wanted to tell her everything, but I knew she wouldn't understand.

"Whatever it is, everything will be fine. Start trusting in God." Maa left without saying more, she understood that I needed some time alone.

Halfway through the day, I checked my phone almost a hundred times. There were times when I would type a text, begging her to come back, and almost send it to her.

By evening, all my courage, goal, and anger were overpowered by my desperateness to get a text from her. I was struggling to come to terms with the fact that she had moved on without looking back.

So I kick-started my bike and drove towards her house. Reality is not for the weak-hearted. You might want to know the truth but only a few would have the courage to stand and look into its eyes when it stares at you.

I reached her place and parked my bike at some distance, careful enough not to be noticed. Everything except my emotions seemed to be calm that day. Half an hour later, Nandita stepped out of the front gate.

Wrapping herself in a peach-colored stole, untied hair, a white suit with a pair of contrasting bangles, and carefully placed small black *bindi*, she calmly walked towards a BMW car.

At that precise moment, a guy stepped out of the car. He looked like a model. Honestly, I was no match for the guy. The way he waved at Nandita's parents, the way he opened the car door for her, I could have only dreamt of a life like that.

I did not react at all. In fact, to my surprise, I felt at peace. It was as if the love within me took its last few breaths.

Something died within me at that moment.

The thing about truth is that when you finally face it, there is no escape from the purest form of emotions you would experience. It might rip apart your life or leave you crying out of happiness, but in that one single moment, you have absolute clarity. That exact moment is called the moment of truth. I had just experienced mine.

A week later, Nandita made her engagement official. A lot of people had lots of questions for me, most of them intended to hear me crib, cry, or maybe just enjoy the weakest moment of my life. In return, all I did was just smile and walk away.

Sometimes, you just have to hold back your hardest punch and keep taking blows instead. When the time comes, one punch is enough. For all those who were trying to have fun at my cost, I just knew that it wasn't them whom I had to answer. I was chasing something far more impossible.

Until now, I had accepted a mediocre life for myself. Nandita had only given me a taste of what this life was about to throw at me. However, life is not a two-hour inspiration film where you become the richest guy in India while you were once struggling for a proper meal.

I did not have a high-paying job; moreover, I worked as a relationship manager with a bank. If there was ever a list of worst jobs published, a relationship manager with a bank would top the list for sure.

A non-existent love life, a blood-sucking job, a messed-up mind, no friends, no money, what else do you need to reach the lowest point in your life?

Well, it is exactly here that my life changed.

The only thing that holds you from taking a leap of faith and discovering the purpose you are born for is fear. Fear is a big word; it doesn't let you take risks. It creates more self-doubts about your abilities even before you begin.

Most of the people who struggle with depression are those afraid to accept the reality about themselves and work towards changing it. At just twenty-six years old, I was utterly broken, staring at life as a complete failure.

I felt as if I had nothing else to lose. Hence, my fear of losing went away as well. What else could go wrong from here? Everything was already messed up.

I decided to rebuild as it was the only option I hadn't explored for a while.

Rebuilding yourself generally involves a focus on three things, health (mental and physical), career, and money.

It isn't easy to stay happy all the time. For that, you need to have a no fucks given attitude. It should be to the point that you almost convince your brain that everything you think about yourself is the truth, the rest is all noise. Nothing else should matter then. Opinions, feedback, points of view, etc., need to become irrelevant to you and the only thing that matters is what makes you feel happy.

This is where your friends come into the picture. Those few people whom you'd go to war with. I had not spoken to my best friend for seven years. Today, after all these years, I decided to finally turn and look at my abandoned past.

I picked up my phone and typed a name. I wasn't even sure if he would remember me anymore, but I needed him more than ever today.

"Hello," a smooth and polished voice answered the phone.

"Hi, Mr. Bhagat Saroha?" I tried to be as formal as I could.

"Yes, who am I speaking to?" Bhagat replied in a curious tone.

"This is your dad, son." I waited for his reaction.

"That is not how you talk to your grandfather?" Seven

years of radio silence between us and it took Bhagat less than seven seconds to recognize me.

For the next fifteen minutes, we were abusing and accusing each other of staying out of touch for so long. Childhood friends, they don't forget you.

"My parents shifted to Jalandhar a few years back. I am taking care of my dad's business," Bhagat informed.

"How is Anisha? When are you guys getting married?" I asked Bhagat excitedly.

"I'll tell you all when we meet Abhay. Everyone has a story to tell," Bhagat replied.

"See you soon," I smiled and hung up the call.

It felt good as if I had just removed a stone from my chest. Talking to your best friend after ages and getting to know that they still remember you, that feeling is priceless. Bhagat was my recall to the life I had decided to quit long back. A flashback of memories blanked me out for a few minutes.

Faces of a few people flashed in front of my eyes — Bhagat, Anisha, Aanchal, Neeraj, and the girl with whom my relationship remained undefined, Palak. Today, I missed each one of them. I had cut the cord with these friends some ten years ago. But now, for some reason, I felt they were going to be an important part of my life and future.

Things were still far from normal. A one BHK flat with four people living in it, an education loan on my head, a brother who was searching for a job, leaving aside his dream of pursuing an MBA from IIM, tons of broken dreams and hopelessness, all of us living together.

How do you get out of something like that? If struggle had a definition, I guess my situation would have aptly described it.

It was important for me to change my mindset even before changing my situation. Your mental health has a lot to do with the way you look at things. The only source of income I had was my job. Leaving the job was not an option. I realized that I needed to accept the fact that no matter how bad my job was, it was all I got.

There was nothing I could do about it apart from performing well in it. If you are going through shit, keep going unless you are out of it. Shit cannot be forever. The only way was to move forward.

I had a clear roadmap in my mind. Staying sharp at work, spending less, and saving as much as I could. Parallelly, keep looking for those small chances that would take me ahead of the rest, and commit myself to becoming so rich that Nandita gets to know about me, not from her friends but the news itself. She had given me a purpose in life.

The funny thing about purpose is that you mix it with hate and it changes the very nature of your existence. You begin to operate ruthlessly and your mind and heart start working in tandem towards your goal.

I took out the same pack of cigarettes I bought the day Nandita left me.

I decided to pull out a cigarette every time I took a step towards destroying Nandita's ego.

I pulled out the first cigarette.

"Nineteen more to go," I silently reminded myself.

Lighting the first cigarette, I slowly closed my eyes.

Cigarette Number One

SCHOOL DAYS
HOW IT ALL BEGAN

I woke up to the sound of the worship bell. Dragging my head out of the blanket, I looked up with half-closed eyes. My mom always used to be my alarm clock. Seven a.m. sharp, and you'd find her sitting in front of the Gods and praying. It's such an experience to open your eyes to something as pure as that.

I was about to withdraw my head into the cozy warmth of my blanket when came the marching orders. "Get up, it's already seven, take a bath, and a proper one, no fooling around with a wet towel this time." I always tended to overhear instructions, orders, and suggestions, and nothing different happened to this one as well. After a few minutes, I heard another voice.

"Wake up," this time it was Dad and within the next forty minutes, I was ready for school. I was still struggling to fit my lunchbox in the schoolbag when I heard a knock at the door.

It had to be Bhagat. He used to knock at the door unusually, trying to create some weird music out of the entire process. My mother opened the door and there he was, a little round kid, wearing a school bag, looking at my mother with an innocent pair of eyes.

She loved Bhagat's cuteness as a kid. After customary cheek pulls and hugs from my mother, Bhagat and I would walk down to the school together.

I met Bhagat for the first time in L.K.G. (lower kindergarten). Things started as a formal conversation between us. I offered Bhagat my toy truck in exchange for his toy car and after a brief round of negotiations wherein we discussed the advantages and disadvantages of our toys, Bhagat finally agreed to my proposal. Thus, what started as a pure "barter system trade agreement" finally ended with us becoming friends.

Bhagat lived two blocks away from my house and was my first friend and partner in all the crimes we committed at school.

It was Monday. We were just back from the morning assembly.

"Open your books." Mrs. Bedi, our English language teacher, tapped the wooden scale on her desk to get our attention. Everyone pulled out their textbooks, neatly covered with brown paper, and like robots, opened to page number twelve, chapter number five. I checked my bag and realized that I had put in the English language textbook instead of the English literature textbook.

Damn, all the books look the same. Same cover, and same labels, in fact almost similar titles as well, English lang. or lit., Maths 1, Maths 2, Maths lab, Science 1, Science 2, etc. I did not even try reading the labels.

"Ma'am, I forgot to bring my book." I raised my hand.

"Share it with your partner." Mrs. Bedi was a lovely woman. She loved us, never shouted and I never saw her raise her hands on a kid.

Bhagat slid his textbook between both of us when suddenly Mrs. Sood, our class teacher, hurried a small girl into our class.

"Excuse me, Mrs. Bedi, we have a new admission." Our heads immediately turned towards the door. A new student always gets a lot of attention.

A little girl in tears stood at the entrance, desperately trying to free herself from Mrs. Sood's grip and get back to her mother, who stood just behind our class teacher. Even though her mother tried calming down the kid, she was in no mood to stop. It took around twenty minutes to control the little storm of emotions.

Finally, after much effort and assurances, she was made to sit between Bhagat and me. The teacher thought that making her sit between us would distract the little girl as we were the most talkative in class. Wrong move.

Her eyelashes were still wet. Wiping off teardrops from her round cheeks, she started fidgeting with her bag. Bhagat looked at me and I looked at the girl. As kids, you feel the pain in its purest form. Innocence and emotions drive your actions. Bhagat could not watch the little girl sobbing and decided to make her feel better. Wrong move.

Bhagat – "Guess you must be missing your mom?"

Girl – "SOB, SOB, and BURST."

Within minutes, the whole class was in the grip of a serious flow of emotions. I immediately turned my attention to my notebook as if I had no clue about what went wrong. Mrs. Bedi came running towards the girl and picked her up in her arms.

Mrs. Bedi kept looking at us suspiciously and we, in turn, kept staring at the blank pages of our notebooks.

"Did you guys say something to her?" Mrs. Bedi enquired, and we nodded in disagreement.

Mrs. Bedi finally calmed the girl down. She assured her that she was going to study with a group of human beings who do not eat people of their kind. As far as the case went with both of us, the teacher let us off with a warning because the girl was too busy crying.

The girl finally adjusted to us in a couple of days. Initially, Bhagat and I were too terrified to talk to her but as days went by, that fear disappeared.

Slowly, we became friends. In fact, she wasn't interested in talking to other girls and used to hang around with us throughout the day.

Right from her childhood days, Palak had a charm around her. She had those rare curls that kept dangling while she used to write, lips that were hardly visible between her puffy cheeks, and eyes so bright, yet so innocent. Overall, if there ever were a definition for the word cute, Palak would have been the most appropriate one.

I remember it was her birthday when she wore that white frock dress to school. That one picture of her never left my memory. Palak looked like a Barbie doll that day, only far cuter. Both her parents were working; in fact, the maid took care of Palak and gave her everything except the love she needed from her parents. We grew up sharing our childhood.

During these years, we three made new friends. Palak had Aanchal and Anisha and Bhagat had Neeraj as his friend. Initially, I didn't open up to Aanchal, Anisha, and Neeraj. I was more of a reserved guy who'd be committed only to his original set of friends, Bhagat and Palak.

Neeraj was a brilliant student. He was the most adored in class, liked by teachers, and loved by his parents; everything was great for him except for one thing. There isn't a word called "perfect life." Neeraj was not well off.

His father was a junior employee working in a factory. For him, life was not easy, and this very fact made him the person he was. Neeraj was an extremely responsible individual. He had a clear-cut face, eyes like that of an eagle (steady and always under his control), a skin tone fair enough to make him look like a foreigner and a mind that worked in perfect coordination with his heart.

Sentences underlined, Bhagat and I were no match for the guy. He knew how much effort his father had to put in to send him to school. Therefore, he realized the worth of everything he had, right from a pencil to a single page in his notebook.

For the five of us though, Neeraj's status did not matter. Class differences never touch you as a child. Everything remains the same for you and everyone is your friend. It hardly matters whether your friend is a rich lad or a poor guy because at that age your mind is free from all the bullshit that is later stuffed into your head.

On the other hand, Aanchal and Anisha were two different personalities. Aanchal was a statue. You could make her sit in a place for days. Except for roll calls and random questions, that teachers generally throw at students to test how attentive kids are in their class, I never heard teachers call out Aanchal's name. She was too busy staying quiet. The only time one could hear her voice was during breaks or after school.

Aanchal was beautiful. She had simplicity as a major part of her. Anisha, on the other hand, was a loud and bold girl right from her childhood days. She had slapped quite a few people in our class and had won several catfights. Looks wise Anisha was not far behind Aanchal and Palak, but attitude-wise she was way ahead of them.

***

Neeraj and I became friends over the Mathematics exam. My answer sheet lay blank in front of me and apart from my name and roll number, I had nothing substantial to write.

Twenty minutes into the exam, I had copied down a few questions just to avoid the embarrassment of submitting a blank sheet. Bhagat was busy poking his nose. I felt somewhat relaxed that at least I'd not be the only one who would fail.

Just then, Bhagat raised his hands, "Ma'am, SHEET."

It felt as if a bullet pierced right through my chest. If Bhagat was asking for an extra sheet, it meant that he found the question paper easy. This meant I was the only living asshole in that classroom full of students.

I kept looking at Bhagat. He, in turn, gave me a "sorry pal, can't help, you're screwed" sort of look.

"*If that guy scores and I fail, he'd make my life miserable. He would keep reminding me of this moment all my life.*"

The very thought of it made me cry. I not only had to pass but also had to score more than Bhagat.

There is an unspoken rule in friendship: if you and your friend are two of the dumbest living creatures on the face of this planet, aim to be the second dumbest.

Suddenly life had given me two challenges while I struggled to face one.

The only way I could win these two challenges was if God answered my exams.

I looked around, hoping someone would eventually take pity on me and let me copy down his/her answers. I know, that's optimism at its peak. The row next to me had no friendly faces. The girl sitting next to me would have given her exams in a bunker if she could have. She had covered her answer sheet well enough for even a fly to find it impossible to cheat.

I was still looking at her arms because that was all I could see when suddenly I saw a head bulge from the background. It was Neeraj. He was sitting in the row next to her. From that very moment, I knew God existed. The next forty minutes were like Xerox copying Neeraj's sheet.

He simply had to hold his answer sheet vertically so that I could see the answers sideways. I answered the last three to four questions on my own to avoid any doubts by the teacher at the time of checking.

It was then I realized that cheating is not a social evil after all; rather it is something that arises out of need. The results were out within a week and Bhagat had failed in Maths exam. People pass with flying marks but if there was one creature on this earth who had failed with flying colors, it was him.

I had managed fifty-two percent, fifty-one and a half marks more than Bhagat. If your calculations are not the worst, you already know how much Bhagat scored. The last three to four questions I had attempted had fetched me two marks; imagine what I would have scored without the use of unfair means.

Never did I realize that what started as friendship among a bunch of kids would someday have its twists and turns. Right throughout the school, the six of us created our world. But like everything beautiful, even this world fell apart. How? That is a different story.

THE REBOUND

Two months post the Nandita episode, I was still the same. All those commitments, goals, anger, everything was taken over by hopelessness. With each passing day, my mind and heart were beginning to convince me that obsessing over Nandita was useless. She was gone, happy and well settled, while I had ends to meet. Even though I wanted to change my circumstances, I couldn't figure out a way.

This stress of breaking the vicious cycle of the middle class kept me up most nights. Even though getting up on a cold, foggy, winter morning was the hardest thing to do, I couldn't stay in bed for long. Sleep was tough.

It was around four in the morning that day. As usual, I did not sleep the whole night, random thoughts about the impossible goal I had set for myself kept me awake. When I could not take it anymore, I decided to step out of my house.

The yellow streetlights illuminated the road, which was covered in a blanket of fog. It felt as if the night was slowly withdrawing as the romance of dawn lurked in the air. Early morning walks have their own charm. The silence, the subtle yet charged atmosphere, and the sky changing its color by the minute.

I stayed outside until sunrise and came back a different person that day. More calm, clear in my thoughts, and most importantly, at peace with my present.

Two weeks later, it became part of my routine and by the third week, I had begun running. Discipline and routine have their advantages. I felt less stressed, my anxiety levels went down drastically and I started thinking logically about everything rather than emotionally.

I began saying no to things I did not want to do like going out with office colleagues, night outs, parties, etc.

I started showing up on time for work. Less chitchat and concentrating on my job enabled me to finish my work well in advance. All those bank customers I had never met or known, now had my name in their contact list.

Most of the days, I was on the field, meeting customers and chasing my targets. For the next three months, I worked so hard that my targets were overachieved with a week still left in the quarter. This was something hard to digest, both for my branch manager as well as me.

I stayed in touch with Bhagat regularly and before I realized it, Nandita was a chapter in my past, which I had bookmarked. There would be days when I would go to bed and think about her for a while and then there would be days when she would not cross my mind even once.

Things at work started improving and I began performing consistently. I had accepted my reality and come to terms with the fact that I needed to continue working as a relationship manager until the time I did not get a good opportunity.

The truth about sales is that numbers build or destroy

the way you are perceived as an employee.

If you don't have the numbers, no matter how good a human being you might be, you will be kicked off. At the same time, if you have the numbers, no matter how big an asshole you are in real life, you would still be a hero for your team and boss.

It took me a while to understand this, but the moment I did, there was no looking back.

There were a few things I learned as a banker:

1) The guy who sells the greatest number of insurance policies is eventually the guy who sits on the Iron Throne (branch manager's seat).
2) Churning the client's portfolio – A client's portfolio consists of various combinations of mutual funds and other investments. These include bonds, debentures, debt funds, liquid funds, mutual funds, equity-linked saving schemes, etc., Mutual funds, liquid funds, fixed deposits, etc., can be redeemed easily. Every time a client invests/reinvests in a mutual fund, the relationship manager achieves a certain percentage of his investment target.
3) Every day is a race for survival. The branch manager would forget what you did the other day or if you had the highest sales numbers. The next day is a new effort and a new battle to win.

To win, it was important for me to survive. To survive it was important for me to be ruthless, and to be ruthless, it was important for me to be emotionless. I changed the way I used to pitch insurance policies to my clients. I rather pitched it as a 5-year-long mutual fund with the added benefit of insurance. Now, generally, the policy matures in ten years. However, the customer has an option of withdrawing after five years. Ideally, a unit-linked insurance plan starts giving some returns in the seventh year. No client wants to remain locked in an investment for ten years and keep paying annual premiums for that entire period. Thus, a lot of information regarding the charges associated with an insurance policy was purposely held back.

We further spiked up the annual returns by at least three or four percent to gain customers' interest. Soon, I started converting even fixed deposit clients to insurance clients. Next three months, I shattered a lot of records. From selling the most number of policies to selling policies with the highest premium in a year, every day I moved a step closer to happiness.

Colleagues started noticing and asking for advice, the branch manager started entrusting more responsibilities to me, and by the time we crossed the third quarter, I was the topmost relationship manager in India.

"Your account number XXXXXX461 has been credited with Rs. 2,33,000." The salary credit notification lit up my cell phone screen. After all the bullshit in a sales job, there is one thing that acts as a balm, your bonuses, and incentives.

One year of incentives and bonuses had been credited to my account along with my salary. I was sitting in a meeting when the text popped up. For a guy who had difficulty saving a hundred rupees at month's end, this was an amount beyond expectation.

"Excuse me, can I use the washroom?" I requested the client.

"Yes, please, it is left from the end of the lobby." The client was guided.

I walked inside the washroom and checked my bank balance again. For the next few seconds, I sat on the washroom floor and laughed my heart out.

Money, whether you like it or not, can change things very quickly for you.

I pulled out my second cigarette after the meeting.

Cigarette Number Two

ALWAYS KNOW THE ANSWER, ALWAYS

The mathematics period still had 20 minutes left. Bhagat was half asleep, courtesy: heavy lunch. Even my eyes had begun watering as well. I had yawned almost seven times in two minutes and it spread like an epidemic among the students sitting around me.

I hated Maths. The very name of the subject sent shivers down my spine.

"Yes you, the boy in specs, stand up," yelled the Maths teacher. His fat finger pointed at me, like a missile towards its target. I stood up and looked at him, petrified.

"Come to the board and expand this equation – (x-25) the whole square." He had a smirk on his face as if he knew I would not be able to answer it.

It was enough to wake me up. I looked around and saw those eyes. Everyone in the class thought I was screwed. Then there were assholes in my class who were jumping from their seats to answer the question and gain that elusive brownie point from the teacher.

However, there was one pair of eyes that hoped I would answer the question. I looked into Palak's eyes for the first time so deeply. It felt as if she was talking to me, I could almost hear her say, "Answer them, Abhay."

"(x+5) into (x-5)," I answered, keeping my eyes fixed on Palak as she smiled. That smile on her face is what defined love for me.

The teacher stood there in surprise for a moment looking at me and Palak at the same time.

"Ok, solve this." He wrote another equation on the board and asked me to write the stepwise solution. I had never answered a question correctly in mathematics class and yet here I was, walking down to the board with a smile on my face as I wrote the stepwise solution.

I always knew the answers, always. It was just that I never had my mind on my studies. For me, studies were not a priority and that is why I was a backbencher. However, a student is only a backbencher until the time he participates in class.

I turned my gaze towards the teacher, waiting for the next question.

"Go and sit." I could see the disappointment in my teacher's eyes. He just missed an afternoon entertainment slot.

Palak was still smiling. I failed to figure out how, but our eyes used to talk to each other. I would understand every emotion of Palak even without her saying a word. I was in love with Palak right from the time I had seen her as a kid.

Palak had never left my side. Her silent support always kept me going. From walking home together even though her parents sent a car to pick her up to sharing our lunch, we had an unsaid and undefined bond.

Now, there would always be people who would try

to give a name to something so pure. Apart from Neeraj, Bhagat, Aanchal, and Anisha, everyone thought we were a couple. Even the teachers would at times poke Palak for being friends with a student like me and every time Palak would just keep quiet and look at me.

I used to feel embarrassed about how Palak had to hear so much just to be friends with me. After all, she was a very good student, and everyone wanted her to mingle with the talented bunch.

There would not have been an Arjun without a Dronacharya. The Indian education system lacks those Dronacharyas. Everyone wants to place their bets on the best student. No one gives a damn about the weak ones.

Both I and Bhagat were poor students; in fact, Bhagat was worse but I had been trying hard for the sake of Palak.

The class got over fifteen minutes later. Everyone left the class except the six of us.

Palak walked up to me, that infectious smile fixed on her face. All I could do was just keep looking at her.

"You always know the answer, always," Palak whispered silently with a smile. I smiled back, looking straight into her eyes and deep within saying – "Thank you."

The rest of them watched a beautiful love story spreading its wings for the first time.

MEETING MY PAST

"Water or soda?" Bhagat asked as he poured whiskey into my glass. I had randomly decided to visit Bhagat over the weekend. The branch manager had readily granted me leave as I had overachieved my targets with five days still left in the month.

I had got my head, heart, and job back in place. Next on the card was to find happiness.

"You are thinking about her?" Bhagat asked, looking at me as I kept staring towards the sky.

"Who?" I pretended to not understand what he was saying.

"You know who," Bhagat replied with a smirk on his face.

"No, I don't think about her anymore. It's a chapter I have closed long back Bhagat." I picked up my drink.

"You can never close Palak's chapter Abhay, she is the story that defines you," Bhagat replied.

"Not anymore. Anyways, what is up with you? When are you planning to get married?" I changed the topic. Palak was one aspect of my life that I did not want to revisit now.

"Nothing much, just Dad's business. Planning to expand it now but it would take some time. You know how old men are". He chuckled, referring to his Dad, and ignoring my last question completely

"Where is everyone else these days? Have you been in touch with anyone?" I asked.

"Neeraj is in Mumbai, running his startup. Aanchal has moved to the US with her husband, Anisha is working in Chandigarh and Palak is in Jamshedpur, preparing for civil services." Bhagat deliberately mentioned Palak's name because he knew whose whereabouts mattered the most to me.

"So what do you do these days apart from just work? Listen to sad songs and get depressed about how pathetic your life is?" Bhagat chuckled as he poured another drink.

"Yeah, you can have all the fun you want brother. It is not you at the receiving end anyway. Have you ever realized how it feels to be rejected because you are not well off? Oh, how would you, son of a businessman." Bhagat's jab did not go down well with me.

"Moreover, you have Anisha, your childhood love since school. You know what, I do not give a rat's ass about what you think about me or my life." I did not just stop at this. Already a few drinks down, suppressing my anger and frustration for a long time, Bhagat's comment about my life blew the lid off my emotions.

While I knew perfectly well that whatever I was saying, or about to say, would pinch Bhagat, still, I could not control myself. Bhagat patiently stood there, holding both glasses of whiskey in his hand. Once I was done spewing venom, he quietly handed me one of the whiskey glasses with a smile on his face.

I shamelessly took the glass and gulped down half of it, coughing and spilling the remaining. It was beyond me to gulp an entire glass of whiskey without coughing or puking.

"You know Abhay, here is a fact check for you. Neeraj is richer than all of us. From a guy who took tuition to support his studies to now running a million-dollar company, he has proved that talent and time when properly used can do wonders for anyone's life. So, that thing about you not being well off does not fly mate." He paused and took a sip of his whiskey waiting for me to reply but I was already embarrassed enough to say another word, so I decided to listen instead.

"It was Anisha's birthday. I had been keeping busy with Dad's work in Chandigarh, so I hadn't been able to give Anisha the time she needed. Long-distance relationships suck anyway." Bhagat paused for a while, sipping some more whiskey.

"So, I decided to give her a surprise. Anisha was, at that time, working at an advertising company in Delhi. I planned to visit her there and celebrate her birthday together. I had planned out the entire day. I called her the night before leaving for Delhi.

"I tried to be cheerful and asked if she had any special plans for her big day. She responded with a distant tone, saying there was nothing planned, just work. I felt a hint of something off in her voice and tried to keep the conversation going, asking if she wasn't going out with friends. But she just sounded tired and uninterested.

"That was the first moment I realized that maybe

Anisha had already drifted too far from me. But like all people in love, I ignored the red flags and convinced myself that things would be fine.

"The next day, I left for Delhi and went straight to her office. When I arrived, I couldn't find her anywhere. I tried calling her, but she didn't answer. Feeling a bit uneasy, I approached the receptionist and asked where she was. The old security guard at the reception told me that Anisha was in the cafeteria, celebrating her birthday with her colleagues.

"I quickly made my way to the cafeteria, and when I got there, I saw Anisha surrounded by a group of people, all singing the 'Happy Birthday' song as she cut the cake. I stood quietly in a corner, watching her. She looked so happy as she cut the first piece of cake and turned to a guy standing behind her, feeding him the cake with a smile. The crowd erupted in cheers as the guy playfully smeared some cake on her face.

"Everything seemed fine until that same guy suddenly dropped to one knee and pulled out a ring. He proposed to her right there in front of everyone, including me. Anisha said yes, and within seconds, he lifted her into his arms while everyone around them cheered.

"I stood there, stunned and unable to process what was happening. The reality of the situation hit me hard, but all I could do was watch in silence as the woman I loved accepted another man's proposal."

"So you just kept standing there?" I asked as Bhagat stopped and looked towards the dark skies.

"No," he replied.

"I walked up to the group and handed over the gift to Anisha. It seemed as if she had seen a ghost. She had turned pale and covered her face with her hands in shock and embarrassment."

I said, "She loves minions and is a total movie buff. Congratulations man."

"The guy looked both surprised and confused, clearly unable to grasp what was happening. I introduced myself as an old-school friend and explained that Anisha was in shock. I knew I had to leave, so I called Anisha over and pulled her into a final embrace. I could see that her eyes were filled with tears of embarrassment as I looked directly into them and wished her well.

"I walked away. I heard it from a distance Anisha started to apologize and explain herself, but I was already too hurt to listen. I left, carrying the weight of the moment with me."

Bhagat hung his head in dejection.

There was an odd silence for a minute. Both of us kept sipping on our whiskey glasses.

"Bhagat." I finally broke the silence.

"Yes Abhay," Bhagat replied.

"Anisha liked minions?" I asked.

"I don't know. Most girls do," Bhagat replied.

"Oh." I looked at Bhagat as he filled another glass of whiskey and handed it over to me.

He avoided eye contact, trying to control his laugh but men will be men.

We kept drinking and talking late into the night before Bhagat dozed off on his chair.

I looked around, the calmness everywhere, the empty streets that I could see from his roof. It felt as if my soul had downloaded a long-forgotten version of me. Carefree, observant, more action, and less show of emotion while still being emotional. I missed my previous version, the stubborn, egoistic guy I was.

Maybe, just maybe, meeting Bhagat was where I reconnected with my past self, which I had abandoned. A past that held the key to the future.

I pulled out my third cigarette.

Cigarette Number Three

PAKSHI

The three of us (Bhagat, Neeraj, and me) stood outside the school, looking blankly at the closed gates. This is what happens when you get a new bike and instead of riding it straight down to the school, start taking victory laps around the society.

We had a fifty-mark test scheduled at nine-thirty a.m. I looked at my watch; it read 9:25 a.m., which meant we had 5 minutes max. We decided to jump over the gate, sometimes necessity is the mother of all crimes committed. Our bags crossed the school gates first and we followed soon after. Bhagat, as usual, had problems jumping over the gate; instead, he tore his pants while landing.

Now, being a student of the tenth standard, people expect you to become more mature as you take your first step towards that golden period we call TEENAGE. I along with Neeraj was already running towards our classroom while Bhagat still stood there, examining his torn pants. We shouted back at him – "Stop looking at those pants of yours and run, we are not going to make it." Bhagat clumsily picked up his bag and began running. We hardly had climbed the first few steps when we heard the bell ring.

This meant no more tests for the three of us, which instead meant missing an excellent opportunity to clear the final term exams. The calculation was simple. Whatever marks we scored in that fifty-mark test would be brought down to marks scored out of thirty.

The final term paper would carry only seventy marks, the rest thirty marks would come from this class test. I quit running even before I reached the classroom and Bhagat had quit long ago. Neeraj continued his run trying to avoid the inevitable doom that was now destined on our report cards, his footsteps echoing right across the silent lobby that leads to our classroom.

It was Mr. Bakshi's class and the test we were supposed to give happened to be Physics, a subject that always earned a beautiful red mark on my already marks-starved report card.

P.K. Bakshi, whom we nicknamed "Pakshi" (which means a BIRD in Hindi), was the most ruthless teacher I had ever come across. Pakshi would have even failed himself if he hadn't been punctual to school. We three stood at the class entrance, heads down.

"Wow, look who has just arrived?" said Pakshi. His face had lit up at the very sight of us; maybe he had been waiting for this moment all his life. "Mr. Abhay, I suppose you must be wearing a watch? Can you please tell me the time?" I looked at my watch, "9:40 a.m., Sir."

"Thank you, Mr. Abhay." Pakshi smiled.

"Mr. Bhagat, I see you have quite some courage to wear those torn pants to school. What are you trying to flash?" The class erupted into a huge roar of laughter. I felt bad for Bhagat. He was always a laughingstock among people. Bhagat hung his head in dejection. One more comment on Bhagat and he would have burst into tears.

"Neeraj, I never expected this from you. This is what happens when you roam around with useless fellows like them." Bakshi's beak-like nose shone as he said those words. He seemed to enjoy every bit of it.

"I am sorry Sir," Neeraj said in a visibly shaken voice.

"Get in Neeraj and you two leave right now." I knew Bakshi hated us but this was an injustice. Neeraj looked at us as if we were some pre-independence freedom fighters who were about to be hanged.

"Leave, I said." Bakshi shouted.

"Sir, but why not allow us?" asked Bhagat. After that question, I could imagine two nooses dangling right in front of our necks, and Bhagat moving towards one of them. What was worse was that I was about to follow him soon.

I gave it a thought, we anyways had screwed up our chances of appearing for the test, even if we did appear, Bakshi would decorate our answer sheets with various cross marks and comments, so why not go down fighting? I decided to join Bhagat.

"Yes sir, why are you not allowing us if you allowed Neeraj?" My words hit Bakshi like an arrow.

"What did you say? You dare to answer back to your teacher?" Bakshi started walking towards us, his anger giving more strength and speed to every step he took.

I was just getting ready to face his wrath when Bhagat started running. I did not expect Bhagat to run away, we always braved slaps together. This made Bakshi feel as if he was insulted by two upcoming hooligans who'd abused him publicly and were now giving him a slip.

Bakshi reached dangerously close to me, so I had no option other than to run as well.

"Wait you bastards; I am not letting you go easily." Bakshi broke into a run. He was faster than I thought. Imagine if a lion, tiger, mad dog, etc., were let loose after a person. That guy could overtake even Usain Bolt in a hundred meter sprint.

I was fast enough to overtake Bhagat, but Bakshi too was not far behind. I still remember I could hear Bhagat crying in a subdued voice even before Bakshi caught him, I guess he knew his end was near.

Suddenly I heard a loud thud behind me. For a moment, I had a bad feeling as if Bhagat's days were over. I looked behind to find Bhagat still running, but I could not see Bakshi. He lay flat on the floor among a few broken pots placed in the gallery.

My heart stopped for a moment. If Bakshi was hurt badly, it meant rustication from school for both of us and if he wasn't, it meant suspension, beating, and maybe a few bonus punishments as well, and if he was dead, it would mean we were born under a lucky star. I prayed for the last option.

We went back to find Bakshi still lying flat with no movement. This made us even more nervous, a dead teacher lying in front of you and that too while he was chasing you meant we were sure to accompany Bakshi to hell.

We were still looking at each other when Bakshi got up suddenly and grabbing each of our necks, he dived onto the floor. We landed on the floor with a loud thump; Bhagat's head hit a flowerpot placed near the gallery.

Bhagat let out a loud cry, loud enough to alert the principal and a few guards. Bakshi got up holding me by my neck. Bhagat, on the other hand, lay on the floor, WITHOUT ANY MOVEMENT. For a moment, I feared the worst as well. Bhagat's head had hit the pot hard enough. Freeing myself from Bakshi's grip, I knelt next to Bhagat. He winked back at me as I finally let out a sigh of relief. That bastard was acting.

I began shouting and started shaking Bhagat. He didn't move but I could see him smiling, I controlled mine anyhow. I looked up to find Bakshi standing, holding his head in panic. The principal and guards had reached the scene by that time.

"Ma'am, look ma'am, what has Bakshi sir done? Please do something, ma'am." I cried like grief-stricken women in villages.

I managed to create a scene and Bhagat did not budge the whole time. Bakshi knew he had screwed himself. Ten minutes after this incident, the whole school administration had gone into damage control mode. Bakshi already took a firing from the Principal and if Bhagat did not get up soon, he would lose his job as well.

Bhagat's dad was a government contractor. It was only a matter of time before the principal would have to inform Bhagat's parents about what Bakshi did to their son. After that, all I could imagine was a typical Hindi movie chase sequence in which Bakshi would be running on those wet, dark streets and Bhagat's dad would be after him wielding a revolver in his hand (and shooting a few bullets here and there as he chased Bakshi).

My whole class had reached the crime spot by then. Palak, Anisha, and Aanchal had already begun crying and shrieking. No one on this Earth can match the ability of women when it comes to creating a scene. This created even more panic among people. Bhagat still showed no signs of movement. He had dozed off lying on the floor.

The ambulance was at the school gate and I started to have a bad feeling about overdoing this. There was still some noise around when I heard a heavy voice interrupt, no one moved after that. I looked up to find a six feet seven inches huge figure, clad in a white kurta pajama. No, it was not Gandalf The Great from the Lord of the Rings, it was Bhagat's dad and someone was to witness his worst nightmares come alive. Guess I heard Bakshi squeak as Bhagat's father arrived.

Sardar Puran Singh had Bhagat as his only son apart from two sisters. His son meant a lot to him. Watching him lying senseless on the couch meant my dreams about Bakshi being chased were about to see daylight. He quickly reached for his son and broke down; it was the first time I saw a stone cry.

Bhagat was soon loaded into an ambulance and I accompanied him to the hospital. Bhagat's dad though remained behind to settle some scores. Bhagat was back home by evening. Even though his head was bandaged, he was fine.

We went back to school the next day and as we entered the class, there was a roar among students. We got a hero's welcome as if we were back from World War III – ALIVE.

Bakshi had to quit his job and the same evening, he landed in a hospital with multiple fractures. who brought him to the hospital said some car had hit him from behind, not hard to guess whose car that might have been.

From that day, Bhagat was an icon for everyone in our class.

"Due to rising popularity, I think I need to carry myself well, you know." Bhagat shared his thoughts with us while we were having our lunch together.

Neeraj looked at me with disgust. I was the one who had given Bhagat an idea for a style makeover.

"I think you should wear sunglasses to school, keep wearing those till you enter the classroom, in style." Neeraj further advised Bhagat. I imagined how Bhagat would look if he did that and immediately rushed outside suppressing my laugh.

"What happened to him?" Bhagat turned back to Neeraj in surprise.

"I'll just check." Neeraj rushed outside as well and we both laughed our lungs out before entering the classroom again.

The next day, Bhagat got himself a pair of aviators and stepped inside the classroom wearing them. A chewing gum in his mouth and a serious look on his face. He looked around before keeping down his bag. Then, he let the bag fall freely on his chair, still looking around. I looked outside the window, covering my face with a handkerchief while Neeraj put his head down and laughed his heart out.

This continued for a while until Anisha informed Bhagat that the girls had named him after a Hindi film villain.

Bhagat handed over his sunglasses to his father the next day.

HOW I MET RAJPUT

A week had passed since I returned from Chandigarh after my small reunion with Bhagat. Nandita on the other hand had started her restaurant. While it's also a normal human tendency to be jealous of someone's rise to success, watching her progress was the last thing I wanted.

I was desperately looking for opportunities when one fine day it walked right into my life. It was a Friday afternoon. I was going through a list of prospective clients I had to call up to get a meeting. The branch manager had given me a target of fifteen lakh rupees of life insurance, and I was still five lakhs short of my target.

Though other relationship managers were not even close to ten percent of their targets, it was a golden opportunity for me to beat myself and become the best relationship manager in India. I somehow had to crack a sale that day.

"Abhay, come here." The branch manager walked up to my desk and asked me to follow him to his cabin.

As I walked towards his cabin, my eyes fell upon the armed security guards. These were not normal security guards but NSG commandos. Outside my branch manager's cabin stood two more guards.

The rest of the employees inside the branch kept looking at me. The security officials frisked me and asked me to hand over my mobile phone, pen, and wallet to them.

I silently obeyed. As I entered the cabin, my eyes fell on a man sitting in a white kurta pajama. He must have been in his mid-forties and had a pleasant smile on his face. I could make out that it was a fake smile; bankers generally know when you are bluffing.

"Meet Mr. Ratan Rajput. He is the Minister of Rural Development. Sir wants to open bank accounts for his family members. Please ensure that he gets the best of services. Ratan sir, Abhay is our best guy," my branch manager said, pointing toward me as if I were his masterpiece.I would not lie but it felt satisfying to get appreciated, irrespective of whether he meant it or not.

"Hello sir, I have seen you on TV but you look even more handsome." Like a typical banker who had targets to meet, I began the process of patronizing my potential client who if approached the right way had all the possibilities of becoming my biggest client as well. To us bankers, clients like him are a gold mine.

"You were right; he indeed is your best sales guy." He laughed and extended his hands for a handshake.

"I will ask my secretary to keep the documents ready; you can come and collect them tomorrow from my residence." He pointed towards another man standing outside the cabin with a couple of files in his hand.

"Please allow me." I opened the cabin's door as Rajput walked towards the exit signaling his secretary to come to him.

"Abhay, this is Yadav, my officer. He takes care of all my work, as I am too busy with my stuff at the ministry. Yadav, ensure Mr. Abhay gets all the documents by tomorrow. I will keep seeing you, Abhay."

Yadav was a fat guy in his early forties who had a calm composure and a genuinely pleasant smile. Unlike other government officers I knew, Mr. Tejeshwar Yadav seemed by far the most decent of them.

As Minister Sahib walked towards his car with a red beacon, Yadav politely shook hands with me and left with a promise to meet me tomorrow morning. As they left, I could see my colleagues looking at me in sheer awe and surprise. They realized I had bagged a very big client. They also knew my reputation and track record, and that I would soon be getting out a lot of money from Rajput.

"Let's go out for a smoke." My branch manager tapped my shoulder as I was still recovering from the entire episode.

My branch manager bought two cigarettes.

"You see, that is how it feels to be a big man." My branch manager referred to Rajput's show of stature a few minutes back.

"You need to become a big man to handle a big man's money," he continued.

"Sure sir," I replied in a puzzled tone.

"Start thinking big Abhay, unless you don't let this mentality go that you are just another ordinary guy you will never become a big man.

"You don't need to own expensive shit to look big; your brain needs to think that you are big enough to handle people like them. Whatever happens, never get intimidated by someone's stature. Build your own and build it better." He slowly dropped the half-finished cigarette on the ground and stepped on it.

I nodded in agreement as he walked back to the branch. I stood there for some time. My manager was right.

After Nandita left, I began thinking about myself as just another guy who did not have the money nor the talent to make it big enough. Today was different. I rewinded the moments from my meeting with Rajput and that small taste of respect and appreciation from my colleagues because I was handling his account.

I wanted to taste this power that got such respect.

I pulled out my fourth cigarette.

Cigarette Number Four

PALAK

It's true; you never forget your first love.

The 10th standard boards were thirty days away and with each passing day, a sense of seriousness seemed to seep into every student.

Neeraj, Anisha, Palak, Aanchal, and even Bhagat had started taking things seriously. I was the only one who thought life and jokes weren't supposed to be taken seriously. All six of us, though in one class, now hardly had time for each other.

I wondered what an exam could do to a group of best friends; apart from my mom, there were other people in my group as well who used to lecture me regarding my studies. All six of us used to sit together for lunch at either Bhagat's, Palak's, or my house, and nowadays the only topic of discussion seemed to be – "How the hell do we cope with the syllabus?"

This somewhat used to piss me off; in fact, I never took part in the discussion. Soon I stopped joining them for lunch. I was wrong; after all, what do you expect students to discuss when exams are near? The problem with me was that I never got nervous about anything. Not even exams.

"What's your problem, Abhay? Why have you stopped

talking to us?" Bhagat shot the first question at me.

Anisha followed soon after "Or is it like you think you are too cool for us?" She always had poison on the tip of her tongue.

"At least share your problem with us; after all, we are your friends, right?" I always loved the way Aanchal spoke, though I hated the sarcasm in her tone that day.

I looked at Neeraj; I was expecting one from him as well.

I wasn't wrong. "Either you tell us, or we have ways to get it out from you." I felt like laughing. Ways of getting things out, imagine a dark warehouse, I am tied to an ice slab, a hundred-watt bulb hanging over my head and five of them beating me up.

Palak had remained silent all this while. I looked at her helplessly and she didn't take time to realize what was wrong with me.

"Let's leave him alone for a while, maybe it's something he needs to sort out on his own but anytime you need us, we are always there for you." She smiled.

Soon everybody left and I returned home feeling disgusted. Why couldn't I just sit down and study seriously? I was hungry, and all the sorrow and disappointment vanished at the sight of *Rajma Chawal* my mom cooked for lunch. I ate like a famished farmer.

The plan was to study for an hour after the heavy lunch. However, I decided to take a short nap for a couple of minutes before starting to study. My mom woke me up around about five in the evening. The five-minute nap had transformed into a full-fledged three-hour sleep.

I looked up to find Palak standing in front of me.

There are times when you feel everything around you is virtual and that one person you love becomes your reality. It would be magical if I could put words to feelings. She stood right in front of me in a yellow salwar kameez, her untied hair swaying in by the breeze as it playfully threw a couple of strands onto her beautiful face that she carefully tucked behind her ear.

The sunset added a romantic purple tinge to the skies.

"Can we go out for a walk?" Palak said in a soft voice.

I nodded as we walked towards a park nearby. I kept looking at Palak from the from the corner of my eye the whole time. "So, what's your problem?" Her eyes widened as she said those words. I instead kept staring at her.

Palak was close to Bhagat and me. She always found herself pampered by both of us and if anyone of us was in trouble, Palak was the first person who knew about it.

"Nothing." I tried acting calm and kept walking. She repeated the question once more and got the same reply from me.

We were still walking when Palak pulled me by my sleeve. I turned towards her to see a teardrop slide down her cheeks. Before I could react, a dozen more rolled out. Every drop that rolled out seemed to slap me right across my face.

I quickly reached for her eyes and wiping off her tears told her everything.

All my life I had been an average student, somehow managing to score marks that got me over the line. Both my teachers and parents had given up on me. I was nothing more than an invisible student in a school full of sharp and intelligent kids.

Result day and parent-teacher meetings used to be my dark days. My report card carried marks, which were only good enough to promote me to the next grade. Parent-teacher meetings on the other hand used to be nothing short of mental and emotional torture for both me and my parents.

Teachers used to rip me apart in the name of feedback and my parents used to walk out of these meetings, head hung in dejection cursing me back home.

All this thrashing and beating had only lowered my self-confidence and self-esteem. Had it not been for my group of friends who used to stick by me even when the world seemed against me, I would have quit long ago.

"It will be fine Abhay." She smiled reassuringly. My anger, dejection, and lack of interest in worldly affairs, everything seemed to vanish upon hearing those words.

We didn't move for a few seconds and I could sense she exactly knew how I felt about her.

"Everyone says you will fail this time, but I don't believe them. Irrespective of you failing or passing Abhay, you will still be special to me." She smiled reassuringly.

For the first time in my life, I saw hope in someone's eyes for me. I dropped Palak to the auto stand, all this while managing to tightly hold on to my emotions. Sometimes a small word of appreciation overpowers years of criticism.

For the next twenty-nine days, I went all out on studying. I had to do this for Palak. No television, no more going out and the only truth for me was the course books.

My parents were surprised by the sudden surge in the level of effort I was putting in for the board exams. With almost no sleep and very little appetite, I had shed weight and developed dark circles below my eyes. It was one of those phases in my life wherein I had pushed myself beyond madness.

Palak used to visit me sometimes just to check my progress and if I was alive. She tried numerous times to drag me out for an evening walk, but I wouldn't leave my study room.

Our boards began and continued for nearly a month. That month is the toughest for students. I have seen brilliant students crack under pressure in the examination hall. Be it, teachers or parents, everyone would expect ninety percent from a student with a good track record. The pressure and expectation levels are so high that it seems like they are going to war.

Board exams seem to be one such mega event, it is more like the Olympics for students where talented students are expected to fetch gold medals and nothing else. These elite students make it to great colleges while average students with seventy or eighty percent land up in average colleges.

Nevertheless, trust me it is this average lot that produces writers, actors, directors, sports personalities, etc. Backbenchers are gifted students who blossom late but when they do, they end up ruling the world.

The board exams finally got over after a month. After my last exam, I returned home all exhausted. It felt as if I had just returned from the biggest battle on Earth. I slept until late evening that day and finally started talking to my parents again.

I had cut myself off from everything and everyone during that one-month time. My mother was scared that I had gone mad as I did not respond or react to anything she said. It was a different feeling that evening. The world looked like a better place, but I had changed as a person altogether.

Sometimes you are not aware of the wonders you can do. You are ordinary only until the time you think you are.

I discovered one thing about myself during that phase. I could go beyond the point of sanity to achieve my goal at all costs.

We had a fifteen-day break before our class eleven sessions began. After the board exams, students are supposed to make an important choice, whether they would want to opt for humanities, commerce, or science.

The same evening Bhagat planned a get-together at his house for the six of us. Everyone reached the venue dressed up for the occasion apart from me. I reached his place in a pair of jeans, a plain white T-shirt, and flip-flops.

Bhagat initially gave me a puzzled look as to why I did not wear something awesome to the party but then he also realized fashion and dressing sense were my weakest points. Palak looked beautiful that day though. She saw me sitting in a corner and enjoying Bhagat mimicking our Physics teacher.

She pulled the chair and sat next to me. I had started looking at Palak very differently by then. She was no more a friend and I knew I loved her. It wasn't just her beautiful face but also that she believed in me.

"How did your exams go?" she asked and handed me a soft drink.

"Don't know." I did not want to give Palak or myself any false hopes.

"I saw you studying, Abhay and I've never seen you work so hard ever before. Why did you push yourself so hard?" Palak knew the answer but she wanted to hear it from me.

I wanted to tell her that she was my answer to her 'why'.

What if Palak thought of me as a very good friend? What if I am vocal about my feelings and she declines? I was in no mood to take risks or face rejection, so I decided to hold on to my emotions but still let her know that I tried because of her.

"Thank you for trusting me Palak," I replied.

"Thank you? Acting like a gentleman these days, aren't you?" She waited for me to say something more than thank you, but I was too scared at that moment.

"I'll always support you, no matter what." She looked straight into my eyes as she said those lines.

We left for our home around ten at night. I walked Palak up to her car. Her father had come to pick her up. Just before she sat inside the car, she turned back and hugged me. This was the first time I had touched Palak. I could hear her heartbeat. Both of us wanted the hug to last a little longer but I had to let her go.

"Goodnight Abhay, I am so proud of you." Palak kept looking at me as her father drove her away while I stood there replaying that moment in my mind when she hugged me.

A few days later, the results were announced. My mother had switched on the television to catch up on her daily afternoon soaps when she stopped on a news channel.

Breaking News – ICSE Class 10th and 12th results declared.

I was sleeping in the same room when I heard the news. Bhagat had already come down to my place by then. He looked nervous.

Suddenly there was anxiety all around. I did not have a computer at home back then and had to go down to the cybercafé to see our results. Bhagat tagged along with me. He did not dare to watch his results alone.

We had to wait for some time, as there was already a queue of students who were anxiously waiting for their results. Finally, after thirty minutes, we got a system. It is human nature to bother less about one's own life and peep into others.

As we logged onto the result website, I noticed other students staring at our screen to check our results as well.

"Bro, come stick to the screen, come," Bhagat interrupted one of the students who was trying to act smart.

Bhagat logged in first. He put in his roll number and pressed enter.

After a few seconds, the result screen appeared. Bhagat had scored seventy-seven percent. Way above his expectations. He somehow controlled his happiness and looked towards me in excitement.

I was next. With trembling fingers, I entered my roll number and waited for the results to flash on the screen.

The screen took some time to load before the result finally appeared. Eighty-four percent. My life changed as a student from then onwards. Bhagat looked at the screen in disbelief. It was my best grade since the time I started studying.

I covered my face trying to control my emotions, but the feeling was too overwhelming. I sobbed out of happiness. The first person that came to my mind was Palak. I wanted to rush to her and break the news.

We walked back to my home silently. Two guys who were termed failures by their teachers, parents, and kids at school had managed to rub it back in everyone's face.

The news of my success had reached my home before me. My father had called up my mom from his office and asked for my roll number. She held the line as he checked the results online.

I reached home to be greeted by a proud mother and jealous neighbors. I had scored better than most of the so-called talented students in my school.

"I need to see Palak," I said to Bhagat and asked if he could come along with me. He knew what this meant for me and shook his head in agreement with a sly smile on his face.

Palak somehow knew I would be coming down to meet her. She was standing on her balcony waiting for me. As soon as I stepped outside the auto, she shouted my name from her balcony.

"ABHAY, CONGRATULATIONS." She came running towards me and hugged me tightly. Palak herself had managed an eighty-six percent but she was far happier with my success.

"Palak, I need to tell you something." I had decided to let her know that I loved her.

"Dad is coming down to congratulate you, we'll talk tomorrow." She winked as she gave me another tight hug.

THE TASTE OF MONEY

I parked my car outside Rajput's bungalow. The golden nameplate read proudly, Ratan Pal Rajput, Minister of Rural Development.

The entry gate had Delhi Police barriers with armed men in elevated bunkers along the walls. After a thorough check and security personnel confirming my appointment with Mr. Yadav over the intercom, I walked in without my bag. My phone and bag were deposited at the gate itself.

I was led by the security guard inside Rajput's room. I had never seen a minister's house from the inside. Rajput sat on a sofa that looked like a throne while Yadav stood next to him.

"Hello Mr. Abhay, I was just about to leave. Nice to see you." Rajput was dressed in a white bandh gala suit. He looked absolutely like a king and his room's interiors further added to the royal feel.

"Good morning sir." I smiled confidently.

He handed me over the forms and patting my shoulders left the room trailed by his security guards.

"All documents complete?" Yadav ji interrupted.

"Ye.. yes Yadav." I got up to leave.

"The tea is almost ready. What's the hurry young

man?" Yadav Ji stopped me.

"So Rajput's family does not stay with him?" I asked curiously.

"His kids live abroad with their uncle. They will be visiting India next month. His wife had divorced him during his struggling days to marry another businessman. The bank accounts he is opening are for his kids so that he can keep aside some money for them. Things can change very quickly in politics Mr. Abhay, it's always good to prepare for uncertainty." Yadav Ji smiled as he sipped his cup of tea.

"If his kids are abroad then who signed these forms?" I inquired.

Yadav realized that he had spoken too much too soon.

"They flew to the US today morning." Yadav stammered as he said those lines and I immediately knew he was lying.

The signatures on the account opening form were fake. It did not take me time to figure out that the whole set of KYC documents along with the signatures was fake. I further cross-verified the documents to find out that the name of the father on their PAN cards mentioned 'Ratan' and not Ratan Pal Rajput.

I looked at Yadav Ji and directly asked him the question without mincing any words, "Sir, you are asking me to open a bank account with fake signatures and improper documentation. Tomorrow if there is an audit, I might end up losing my job as well. Why does Mr. Rajput want to open a fake bank account in the name of his kids? Also, if his kids are living abroad, why does he want the debit card, pin, and cheque book to be delivered to this residence?"

Yadav ji took a moment before replying, looking at me, as if deciding what to say or do next.

"Abhay, I am going to tell you something, how you react or what you do next is going to define your life from here onwards." Yadav ji looked straight at me, the pleasant smile on his face was now replaced by a serious and 'I mean business' sort of look.

I nodded in agreement; however, deep within me, I was already panicking, wondering why the hell did I get into this mess.

"This account will be used to park Rajput Ji's extra funds. Looking at you, I can very well make out you are smart enough to understand what extra funds mean. My question is, would you be willing to trust me and get these accounts opened? Your branch manager did not choose you for this work because you were the best, it was because you are the smartest and meanest." Yadav ji waited for my answer.

"No issues Yadav ji, I'll get these forms processed." I smiled and kept the forms in my bag.

"Thank you so much Abhay ji, you know how it is with these big people. They just want to get the work done at all costs. I will remember this as a favor." Yadav breathed a sigh of relief. The whole show he had put up worked.

"Relax sir, I got this. You will get a call from my branch operations team and they will ask you if Abhay was present when the forms were signed. Just say yes, I'll handle the rest." I wanted to leave Rajput's residence as soon as I could and picking up my bag, I started walking, in fact running, towards the exit.

"Stay back for lunch, Mr. Rajput just hired a new chef from Lucknow, and he cooks brilliant Mughlai food." Yadav wanted to return the favor somehow but that is what we salesmen are taught. Keep the customer interested in you. He does not just buy your product because it's good but because you are good as well.

"Thank you for asking Yadav ji, but I prefer non-veg with a drink. We'll sit someday and drinks would be on me." I laughed sending a subtle message to Yadav that I was not just about work.

"That is great Abhay Ji, look forward to it." Yadav smiled as he shook hands with all the strength he had.

Successful people generally are surrounded by parasites. They always have a group of loyal followers around them who would do anything to get their attention. What they do not have though are loyal friends.

Over the next couple of months, Yadav ji and I became good friends. He would use me for his smaller tasks like collecting cheques, delivering cash from the bank to his place, picking up girls and dropping them at Yadav's room, etc.

I almost became Yadav's assistant. At times, he would ask me how to convert all his black money to white, and being a banker, I had an idea about every goddamn way in which this could be done.

Yadav was too uneducated to handle all the wealth he had acquired working with Rajput. He at times would subtly share his fear about the amount of cash he handled on the minister's behalf.

Slowly, over some time, using my client network and approach within the bank, I brokered a few real estate deals for Mr. Yadav and did not charge even a single rupee in return. This included farmhouses he bought for hard cash, investing in shares and bonds through my client's accounts, pumping all the bribe money received by Rajput into stock markets, and earning handsome margins on it.

I was helping Yadav do everything illegal as per banking policies to earn money. Within a few months, Yadav's net worth was more than he could have ever imagined.

Slowly, Yadav started introducing me to Rajput as one of his loyalists. Within these few months, I became a regular figure at Rajput's house.

It was a Friday evening and I was back home after surviving a boring training session on bank compliance. The training session was to inform bankers about compliance and audit rules, basically what to do and what not to do. I was practically doing everything possible for Yadav and Rajput that the bank considered a breach of compliance/fraud.

I settled down for dinner when I got a call from Rajput. I picked up the phone checking the time twice. It was almost eleven-thirty p.m., why would a cabinet minister call me up so late?

"Hello, good evening sir, how are you doing? I said in a nice, flat formal tone, keeping my anxiety well within control.

"Hey Abhay, can you come down to my place now?" Rajput got straight to the point.

"Sure, hope all fine?" My throat had gone dry. Why

was he calling me to his place?

"Yes, just come down if you can." He passed the phone to Yadav ji.

"It's sahib's birthday sir. We were expecting you today. I had called you in the morning and had dropped a text inviting you."

"Yes Yadav Ji, I am sorry, was in training. I will be there in the next half an hour." I hung up the phone with a smile on my face.

A cabinet minister inviting you personally on his birthday meant two things, either you are one of his favorites or he wants to get some work done through you.

I reached Rajput's residence at around midnight. All the guests had left by then. Yadav ji greeted me with open arms at the main gate. He had just seen off the last drunk guest.

"That guy looked sloshed. Must have been a wild party. I am sorry I am not carrying any gifts. All this was so sudden that I did not get time to pick up something for Minister Saab." I felt awkward meeting Rajput empty-handed on his birthday.

"Please relax, as such he is not fond of gifts. What can you gift a man who already has everything?" Yadav raised his hands in the air as if speaking about the almighty himself.

I followed Yadav ji to Rajput's drawing room.

"You made it finally." Rajput hugged me as I approached him.

I was taken aback by the sudden display of emotions from Rajput. He was known to be a man who always kept very tight control over his emotions. I then realized that he was drunk as well.

"Happy birthday sir." I greeted Rajput as courteously as possible. There are times when you are so overwhelmed and thankful for a gesture made by someone that respect automatically comes from within that person.

"Give this man a drink Yadav. He is still sober." Rajput and Yadav broke into laughter as Yadav poured me a drink.

We drank and talked about so many things that Rajput would have never dared to speak in front of a journalist or reporter. He shared stories about how Yadav ended up running naked on the streets of Amsterdam after smoking a pot.

All three of us laughed and shared our life experiences and it never seemed to me that I was just a banker who used to handle their finances, broker their deals, and recommend people who could convert their black money to white free of cost.

"Abhay, I don't know how, but you have been one of my most trustworthy bankers. Others charge me or take favors for anything they do for me. You on the other hand never demanded a single rupee from me. I have something to give to you." Rajput got up and walked up to his bedroom.

"I think he needs to sleep now; I will leave," I said to Yadav. A drunk politician is always a red flag. Knowing Rajput's history, I wondered what did he have to give me.

"You dare not move that ass of yours. If sahib said sit, then you sit." Yadav refilled my glass to the brim with whiskey. Rajput returned a couple of minutes later with another bottle of whiskey and a bag,

"I am not drinking anymore of that whiskey." I raised my hands in surrender.

"Why are you acting like a 'chutiya'? You are drinking with a lion, don't act like a sheep." Rajput gulped down his peg and signaled me to finish my glass with a bottom-up.

"Cheers," Yadav gulped down his half-empty glass while I was still holding my almost full glass. I gulped down the whole glass of whiskey in one go and it took me almost a minute to control my urge to puke.

"I AM SO PROUD OF YOU. Look at this Yadav fucker. He is two glasses behind us. Give me your glass." Mr. Rajput shoved two pegs of whiskey down Yadav ji's throat.

"Here, please take it." Rajput pushed the bag he brought from his bedroom towards me.

"What is this?" I unzipped the bag to find a fresh bundle of five hundred-rupee notes.

"Please take this with you." Rajput reached for the bottle again.

"I'll get this deposited tomorrow, sir. As you can see, I think I will be going late to the office. Might be able to deposit all this money by the second half." I presumed Rajput wanted me to deposit this money into the bank.

"It is for you Abhay ji. Please accept as a token of appreciation from Minister Sahib," Yadav said with a smile.

I had never seen so much money in front of me in my entire life. The bag had cash worth twenty lakhs lying right in front of me and I could not understand if this was a joke or reality. I was frozen out of shock for a moment.

"I don't expect loyalty from you Abhay, but I know you are a good man who values relationships and friendship. From now on, you are my friend." Rajput put his hand on my shoulder and looked straight through my soul.

I could feel a hardened soul within him. Rajput's journey had not been easy. His wife had separated from him years ago post a rumored scandal. She also took the kids along leaving Rajput with no family.

He had to counter fierce opposition both from within and outside his party. It took some blood, sweat, and money for Rajput to get to that position of cabinet minister.

"But you have so many people who would do anything at your command, why are you trusting me instead? What use will I be to you?" I was drunk and wasn't in a state to sugar-quote my words.

"You will know when the time comes. I have never been wrong about people." Rajput lifted his glass and raised a toast. I joined him as we both gulped down the whiskey.

Soon Rajput dozed off on his couch while Yadav crashed behind him on the expensive rug minister sahib had bought from Russia.

I, on the other hand had become restless. Twenty lakh was a lot of money and so much money generally never comes without a cost. Either Rajput was too drunk, or he had some ideas in his mind for me.

I dozed off on the couch shortly and woke up late the next morning. I checked my phone to find forty missed calls. Half of them were from home.

Rajput woke up shortly and looked around.

"What the hell happened here last night?" He looked around his drawing room to find empty whiskey bottles all around.

"Sir, I guess we had a bit too much last night," I replied.

"Where is Yadav?" He looked around to find him lying on the carpet.

It took us a good three hours to get back to normal. Yadav was dehydrated and had been drinking water and juices like a camel all morning whereas both Rajput and I were still hungover from last night's carnage.

"I will have to leave sir. It was an absolute honor for me. I am going to remember this for a long time." I took leave from Rajput and started walking towards the exit, leaving the bag full of cash behind.

"Abhay, you forgot something." Rajput shouted from behind, pointing towards the bag.

"Sir, thank you so much but I did not do any of this because I expected money. I am just happy to have been of some use to you." I smiled innocently. Heck, I needed the money more than ever but at times, you need to put a higher price tag on yourself.

"You think I took this decision because I was drunk? This is your commission for all the deals you brokered on my behalf and helped me on other fronts as well. Also, never say no to me again. Understood?" Rajput looked straight at me.

I nodded sheepishly and took the bag. Rajput knew that I was the perfect guy to launder all his black money.

The income tax authorities would never even suspect a salaried guy because all my returns and taxes were in place.

Moreover, I had won his trust slowly; brokering deals, ensuring the cash reached him through defined channels, and not asking for anything in return. Trust is an important factor in the dark world of corruption.

You need honest people to carry on your legacy of corruption and I was exactly that guy to Rajput. Twenty lakhs were peanuts for Rajput but by giving this money to me, Rajput ensured that I remained loyal to him.

I left the place around the afternoon with a bag full of money and a heart that was pumping excitement rather than blood. My mother would have freaked out if she had seen so much money. She would have thought I earned all this money through the wrong means, which I did.

To avoid all the fuss, I silently stuffed the note bundles in my laptop bag, jacket pockets, jeans, and everywhere I could before entering my home.

Later that evening, I locked away all the cash in my wardrobe's locker and kept the keys with me.

It took me a while to come to terms with the fact that my life had changed. I was no more a struggler; instead, that door of opportunity I had always been knocking upon had just slightly opened for me.

I took out the cigarette packet and pulled out my fifth cigarette.

Cigarette Number Five

NO LOVE LOST, NO LOVE FOUND

"Why do you keep looking at me all the time in class? Am I your blackboard?" Palak playfully hit me with her notebook.

"It's because answers to all my questions are written on your face?" I took out a pen to reach for her face.

"I'll kill you Abhay if that pen of yours touches my face." She hit my hand with her notebook.

Palak and I had opted for commerce so that we could study in the same section. My bond with Palak was getting stronger by the day and it was just a matter of time before I would give up on my inner voice and tell Palak about my feelings for her.

We entered the classroom for the business studies lecture. I was in no mood to study after lunch and Palak almost dragged me to the classroom. My grades had improved since my board exams. I scored ninety percent in the first term at the school and it was all because of Palak.

I could not afford to let her down or feel she was friends with a loser, though it meant putting in a lot of effort, I'd do anything to make her feel proud about walking next to me.

I occupied the last bench with Bhagat while Palak, Aanchal, and Anisha used to always be frontbenchers. Neeraj, on the other hand, had joined the science section because his Dad wanted him to become an engineer.

"Hey, tomorrow is the school's annual day. Palak is performing along with Aanchal." Bhagat informed me. He was my CIA, he always had all the crucial and critical intelligence about every girl in school.

"What about Anisha?" I asked.

"She sprained her ankle," Bhagat replied.

"Are you sure? I saw her playing badminton during lunch."

"Yes, exactly when she sprained her ankle." Bhagat just would not give up.

"Aww, that's cute, protecting your darling." I playfully pinched Bhagat's cheek.

"I guess you need to protect yours." Bhagat pointed towards a student sitting next to Palak.

Rohit Jain is one of the most cunning students in the history of mankind. There was a time when Rohit Jain and the gang would make fun of backbenchers like me and Bhagat. Neeraj however always stood first in class; therefore, no one messed with him. Neeraj was to students what Sachin Tendulkar is to cricket.

I had toppled him from his patented second rank the last term. He went complaining to the principal about me using unfair means during exams after which both Rohit and I had to reappear for mathematics exams.

I managed to score three marks more than Rohit and eventually Rohit was asked to apologize to me in person.

After that, Bhagat and I would look for reasons to pick a fight with him.

Our hard work eventually paid off and I got into a full-fledged brawl with Rohit after school. We both threw punches at each other and I managed to connect a few better than Rohit. I won the fight eventually as he ran away halfway into the fight.

Rohit somehow managed to slip through my vigil that day and sat next to Palak for one lecture. He knew I liked Palak and was insecure about her. My eyes were fixed on both as they giggled, whispered into each other's ears, and scribbled on each other's notebooks, and every time Rohit did something to make Palak smile or laugh, it felt as if someone had shot a burning arrow through my heart.

Bhagat watched in anger as well, we both could have taken anything but a defeat from Rohit. As the lecture was over, the class broke for lunch. Palak and Rohit walked out together while I stood there waiting for Palak to look at me once. It seemed as if she had forgotten about my existence.

I wanted to stop Palak and fight with her for even talking to Rohit, that too when she knew everything that happened between both of us. But who was I to Palak? Just a friend like many others. We both as such never spoke about how we felt for each other and all we shared was an unspoken bond of friendship.

"We need to beat this guy one more time."" Bhagat put his hand reassuringly on my shoulder but I was in no mood to calm down.

I walked up to Palak's desk and turned to the last page

of her notebook. The page was filled with lots of drawings, signatures, a cartoon of me and Bhagat, flowers, etc., and then my eyes fell upon a few lines written towards the bottom of the page.

There were a few lines scribbled by both Palak and Rohit.

Rohit – "Palak, can we be friends?"

Palak – "No."

Rohit – "What is wrong with being friends?"

Palak – "I have friends."

Rohit – "One chance, please ☹"

Palak – "Ok, but you cannot tell this to Abhay."

Rohit – "God promise, I won't."

I quietly closed the notebook and turned to leave. Palak was standing right behind me all this while.

We did not say a word to each other. I quietly walked out of the classroom. As a teenager, emotions are what drive your decision-making. You would want to achieve everything in the world, but handling failure or disappointments is not your strongest point.

Not being expressive has its advantages and disadvantages. I never expressed what I felt about Palak, took it for granted that she knew. I was wrong. Today, I was staring at the biggest disappointment I ever faced; still, I did not express my anger or disappointment.

Things didn't remain the same anymore. I distanced myself from Palak after that. I avoided any get-togethers, parties, or events where Palak was present.

Slowly, we drifted apart and just like that, my love story with Palak was over even before it began.

THE DARK SIDE

My life had taken a complete U-turn since the day I took over as Rajput's relationship manager. His account was by far the biggest portfolio the bank had and I had become more of Rajput's gang member rather than his banker.

Rajput meanwhile had introduced me to many of his fellow politicians and all of them had not only opened bank accounts in the name of their relatives in my branch but also left it to me to channel their money into the banking system without coming into the radar of income tax or other authorities.

I started minting money with every transaction and favor I did for any politician. For one year straight, I went all out laundering money for some of the biggest politicians in Delhi. During this entire period, I maintained a low and simple profile. I ensured sticking to the approach of not asking for any additional favors from ministers and at times paying from my pocket to get things done.

One fine Sunday, I finally decided to take a break. I decided to take stock of all the money I had been blindly stashing in my locker without counting.

My mother had gone to visit one of her friends that afternoon. This was the best time to account for all the sins I had been committing for a while now. I opened the wooden cupboard and for the first few minutes kept looking at the view. I had never seen this much money in my entire life and all in hard cash.

The cupboard was stashed from top to bottom with bundles of notes. I took out the note-counting machine I had borrowed from one of Yadav Ji's office assistants. Throwing all the bundles on the bed, I started counting them one by one. It took me almost an hour to count all the money I had.

When I finally looked at the number, it was a staggering one crore and fifteen lakh rupees. I fell back on the couch in sheer shock. This was way too much money beyond my expectations or needs. The feeling of realizing that you are rich is priceless.

My family had no clue that their son had earned so much money through illegal means. Keeping so much cash in my house was risky. It was only a matter of time before my mother would find out.

One of the best ways of converting cash to white money is real estate and gold. I took a month's leave from work citing personal reasons. The branch manager could not have denied me the same, after all, I was his top guy.

Over the next few weeks, I traveled to various parts of India, namely Uttar Pradesh, Haryana, Kerala, and Tamil Nadu, and bought lands from farmers at dirt-cheap prices. A few weeks before I went on leave, Rajput had supplied me with names of all those locations from where a proposed National Highway was supposed to pass.

He wanted me to allocate a certain part of his cash

portfolio to the National Highway project. The budget allocation and highway project approval from the central government was still a few months away.

The deal was that I would be buying land from farmers at dirt-cheap prices, and putting Rajput's cash to use. The farmers as such did not know that one day their land would be almost a hundred times its current value.

Once the National Highway project was approved, the government would then have to buy or compensate all those landowners whose lands fell on the proposed highway. While allocating money on Rajput's behalf, I came across a piece of land bang opposite the site that was proposed for the airport.

All these months of experience in buying land had given me enough idea to realize that this piece of land would soon become a gold mine. I contacted a farmer who happily sold me his twenty-acre land stretch for Rs. one crore cash. None of the properties bought were directly in my or Rajput's name.

We used a lot of fake IDs of individuals and companies to buy land. Opening bank accounts against these IDs was easy as I was still working for the bank. Two months before the project was announced, Rajput and I had owned lands in every part of India through which the National Highway would pass.

Corruption of such a huge scale cannot be pulled off unless higher-ups are involved but the rest of the backend work was taken care of by Rajput.

A month later, I rejoined the bank. Post submitting all the fake health certificates and test reports, I went back to doing what I did best, laundering more money.

To my friends at the bank though, I was a normal guy who was earning a normal salary, roaming around on a bike, and trying to save enough money to buy an iPhone. What they did not know was that I had enough cash to buy out their three generations.

It was a Friday evening and I was engrossed in preparing my daily sales report. Suddenly a young man walked into our branch. Next to him stood his wife whose face seemed very familiar.

It was Nandita. She looked stunning. It was almost a year since I saw her. She looked at me with the same pride that I saw in her eyes when she ended our relationship. The entire branch had by then gathered to welcome her. She introduced everyone to her husband who was the son of a business tycoon.

Nandita's husband was the owner of the second-biggest steel plant in India after the Tatas. The guy had also diversified his business into renewable energy and power. I thought I had achieved my goal of becoming richer than Nandita but unknowingly that day she had set a new benchmark, which was way higher than I had imagined.

I silently started walking outside the branch when she called out my name.

"Abhay." This time I did not turn.

I ignored her and walked out of the branch as if I never heard her voice.

From what I knew about Nandita, insults did not go down well with her. I received a call a few minutes later from one of my branch colleagues.

"Bro, you need to move your bike a bit, Nandita's car is stuck in parking." It was my branch manager.

As I reached the parking lot, I could see Nandita seated in a luxurious white BMW. Her husband though seemed to be a gentleman and smiled at me as I moved my bike, making way for him to reverse his car.

"Sorry for the trouble brother." Her husband raised his hand in apology.

"You don't need to apologize to him, Naman. He is lucky to have even seen such an expensive car." Nandita waved at the parking lot guy with a five hundred rupee note in her hand.

Naman looked at Nandita in surprise. He could not believe his wife could be so ruthless. I kept looking at Nandita as she handed over the note to the parking guy.

"Bhaiya, hand over the change to this guy." She directed him to me. "Abhay, you can keep the change. Let's go, Naman."

The white BMW sped past me as the parking guy extended the remaining change. I asked him to keep it. While walking back to the branch, I had a smile on my face; I knew the next round of battle with Nandita was going to be far more ruthless.

I went back to my desk, still replaying the look that Nandita gave me as I removed my bike from behind her car.

"How could I be so wrong about a person?" I said to myself.

I was still thinking about whatever had just happened when I received a friend request notification.

“Shefali wants to connect with you.” Read the notification. For a few minutes, I could not believe what I was seeing.

“So you found me.” I smiled.

Walking out of the branch, I pulled out my sixth cigarette.

Cigarette Number Six

SHEFALI

It was the sports day trials. Bhagat and I as usual were worst in pretty much every sport apart from cricket. The school cricket team again had all-rounders who were good in studies, good in sports, and good at pushing away students like us who were looking for an opportunity to shine among the stars.

Cricket wasn't part of the sports day meet. It was more of a marchpast, track and field events, and aerobics. I'd like to take this opportunity to especially mention aerobics.

As per Wikipedia – "Aerobics is a form of physical exercise that combines rhythmic aerobic exercise with stretching and strength training routines to improve all elements of fitness."

Myth, ladies and gentlemen, the above definition is nothing but a myth. If someone would have asked me the definition of aerobics during my school days, I would have defined it as follows:

"A form of dance that is designed to humiliate people who suck at dancing. It is an art which remains elusive to most of the male community on this planet and even the elitist alpha male can never achieve the grace and finesse of a female while performing this art."

Aerobics was despised by all the boys in school but the only reason all of them turned to this embarrassing event was because of Shefali. She was every guy's dream apart from obvious students like us who'd simply look at her and feel happy about her being aware of our existence.

Heads turned when she walked past a classroom, library, music hall, water cooler, school entry, exit gates, groups of guys and girls, and a lot many places that I'd not be able to list down here.

Shefali was a personal favorite of our sports teacher. Our sports teacher, Mrs. Himanshi, was unwelcome news for underachievers. Her comments or rather insults directed towards us stung more than our inability to become better sportsmen.

Shefali was the one who mastered this art like the monks of the thirty-sixth chamber. She was so gracious in her moves that the sports teacher had assigned her the responsibility of teaching aerobics to the entire school.

The preparations for aerobics used to start a month before sports day. The venue for sports day was the iconic Telco Colony stadium. An open-for-all, Colosseum sort of structure where our embarrassing aerobics skills were displayed to the rest of the world.

The initial preparations used to take place at our school grounds where Shefali would perform the steps in front of the entire school on an elevated cement stage. The entire school would then copy her steps.

I think it was more of a cleverly thought-out plan to segregate the worst students from the remaining. I oscillated between bad to OK but Bhagat and Neeraj were benchmarks for the worst.

Aerobics was the only event where losers like us could fit in. Also, Himanshi needed us more to fill up empty spaces towards the back rows.

It was a Friday afternoon and I was somehow dragging myself through the Economics lecture when Shefali walked into my class. The teacher stopped the lecture while the rest of the class turned toward Shefali.

Shefali stood right next to me, close to the last bench near the entrance. I preferred sitting there as it was easy to just get up and leave without attracting much attention in case it came down to choosing survival over attending the entire lecture.

I was busy writing poetry on the last page of my notebook and did not bother lifting my head to listen to what Shefali had to say.

"Good afternoon ma'am. Himanshi ma'am has arranged for a practice session at three p.m. today. She has requested for the class to be dismissed early today so that the practice session can begin on time." Shefali delivered Himashi Ma'am's message as her ambassador.

Now, there are two types of teachers in this world:

- Ones who prefer to finish their course well in advance and prepare students for exams via mock tests.
- And Himanshi, who would interfere in the perfectly laid out calendars of other teachers like a boss because it's sports day, probably the highest point of her career every year.

"Couple of minutes, let me wrap up the last point,

and then you can lead the class to the playground." The Economics teacher was in no mood to go down easily.

Shefali obeyed the orders and took the seat next to me, waiting for the class to get over. While almost all the guys had become conscious of Shefali's presence in class, I kept adding lines to my poetry, penning down every emotion I had shared with Palak. So engrossed was I that I completely forgot about Shefali sitting next to me.

Shefali on the other hand had her eyes fixed on my poetry and without asking pulled my notebook towards her to continue reading further. I instead pulled back the notebook, closed it, and returned it to my bag.

I kept looking at the blackboard while Shefali kept looking at me in sheer shock. She wasn't used to such treatment. I hardly cared about how she felt anyway, for me the upcoming aerobics session after lunch was a bigger disappointment.

"You write well. You know, I have a diary where I pen down my random thoughts. Can I read your poetry someday?" Shefali asked in a soft tone.

"That is if I survive this aerobics session," I replied looking at her pretty face. I'd never observed Shefali from such a close distance before. It was only when I carefully looked at her that I realized why people were so crazy about her.

Shefali's face was a rare combination of cuteness and beauty. Her eyes were deep, and those brown pupils further added to the aura surrounding her. Her lips were a perfect shade of pink, a subtly curved neckline and those curls tucked behind her ears made her look more like a princess destined to become a queen someday.

It had been a while since any sort of emotion close to even liking someone had crossed my heart. I was aware there was a league of fine guys waiting and craving for her attention and I had no intentions of stepping into their territory. Also, I did not expect Shefali to be friends with me. I turned my attention towards the blackboard.

"Listen, how about you and me…" just before she could complete her sentence, the lecture got over and everyone in the class stood up to leave for the ground. The only two people who remained seated were us.

I was aware that most of the guys in class would be having their eyes on us. Any conversation between both of us, exchange of smiles, etc., would have attracted unnecessary attention and gossip.

Even though I was among the toppers in my class now, the fact remained that no one from the elite league of students was ready to accept me as one of them. To them, I was still a fluke, subject to their usual taunts and comments. Talking to icons like Shefali was a kind of luxury that students like us could not afford.

I got up from my seat as well, waiting for the Economics teacher to walk out of the class.

Shefali stood up seconds later and graciously walked out of the class. The rest of the class followed her like rats behind the Pied Piper. Bhagat walked up to me with a broad smile on his face. For him, it was a victory of sorts that his best friend managed to sit next to a celebrity.

We both dragged ourselves to the ground and silently took our places at the back of the line. Bhagat joined the line next to mine. Neeraj stood in front of Bhagat. We were patiently waiting for Shefali to display her superior aerobics skills when suddenly Himanshi took charge of the mic.

"Pom-poms are lying in the box in front of each line. Pick one and pass it to the person behind you. Going forward we will be using these as props."

There are times in your life when you simply go numb. All the logic about life knocking you down seven times and you getting up eight times goes for a toss. You begin questioning your existence on this planet and slowly drift into the abyss. Performing in front of parents, teachers, and random spectators with pom-poms was something I could not imagine in my wildest dreams. It still sends shivers down my spine.

That very moment I decided that whatever happened, I would not inform my parents about the sports day. I was still trying to come to terms with the announcement when the guy in front of me handed me a set of pom-poms. Stylish, multicolored objects that we were supposed to wave as we performed all the steps.

I looked at Bhagat and Neeraj and realized that I was not the only one struggling, there were other human beings as well. Himanshi ensured that she added to the insult by consistently passing comments on all underperformers like us. I looked at Bhagat, Neeraj, and the guy in front of me and realized the word 'worst' had multiple definitions.

We all kept giggling, laughing, and making fun of each other during the entire practice. This continued for a few more days and finally, sports day arrived.

Himanshi had by then ensured that our sense of pride and embarrassment was all ripped apart. There was no sense of self-respect left in us. We had blunt expressions while doing those steps with pom-poms in our hands, and watching male teachers look at us and laugh their asses off.

I remember a special rehearsal was arranged for schoolteachers just before the sports day. The concrete stage was high enough to give them a perfect view and they exactly knew where to look for entertainment and fun.

The sports day finally arrived and after the marchpast and embarrassing aerobics event, all students returned to the spectator stands from where they would cheer for their respective houses.

We had four houses in school, Ashoka (Yellow House), Nehru (Blue House), Akbar (Red House), and Tagore (Green House).

Shefali belonged to the Nehru House while I was in Ashoka House. Ideally, I did not even deserve a house because I was below the poverty line in athletics but then some houses had to absorb losers like us. Tagore House was magnanimous enough to accept Bhagat and Neeraj.

The track and field events were about to begin in a few minutes, and I was sitting at the back of the stand looking for an opportunity to slip away from the event unnoticed.

I was busy chatting with one of the students sitting next to me in the stands when suddenly Himanshi walked up to our stand and shouted my name.

"Oye Abhay, come down immediately," she ordered.

The otherwise noisy stand fell silent suddenly. I walked

downstairs replaying the sequence of events since morning and wondering what I had done to be summoned by Himanshi on the most important day of her career as a sports teacher.

I stood in front of Himanshi with trembling legs expecting a slap anytime soon in front of the entire school. Even though there was no reason for her to slap me, I always had this impression about her that she punished students randomly.

However, it turned the other way around. Three of the sprinters from the Ashoka House had met with an accident while they had gone outside the stadium to buy snacks for themselves. During the trials, however, I stood fifth out of the eight people who ran, and due to an acute shortage of sprinters, I was called upon to fill in for one of the sprinters.

I suppressed my disappointment as Himanshi broke the news that I was supposed to run as a replacement in the 400-meter event. As if the day already had been not embarrassing enough that God chose me to further crush the last bit of self-respect I had.

Coming last in a 400-meter race was something that would not help my already negative morals towards sports. However, I had to obey Himanshi because she would slap her way into an agreement if she wanted to.

I was walking towards the starting line wearing spikes that I borrowed from one of the injured sprinters. I'd never run in spike shoes and there is a certain technique required for the same. I was far away from discovering that technique and successfully applying it in a race that might be my first and last chance to participate in a track event throughout my entire school life.

My mind was running in a thousand directions wondering what I was supposed to do to avoid mass embarrassment. I was sure I would become a laughingstock when all the sprinters would reach the finishing line while I would still be struggling to make it to the finishing line.

"Best of luck and stop thinking about losing. Just run."

I looked up to find Shefali standing next to the track. She was supposed to hold the ribbon and judge who reached the finishing line first.

"Thank you, but even a blind man wouldn't place his bets on me." I shrugged my shoulders and continued walking towards the starting line.

Palak was house captain for Tagore House and part of the organizing committee that acted as support staff to Himanshi during sports day. For the first time in seven months, we both looked at each other. Palak and I would never talk to each other but still, she would end up saying so much through her eyes and I would end up understanding everything she wanted to convey.

I saw hope in her eyes that day. The excitement and happiness of seeing me on the track. For her, I was already a winner. Rohit was standing next to her wondering how did I make it to the track events when he could not.

Palak's smile could change just anything for me. The whole perspective about a certain task, situation, moment, and everything would suddenly start looking positive. Nothing in my life could ever replace Palak.

I decided to give my everything to this one race. I

could hear losers like me cheer from the stands as I was wearing those borrowed spiked shoes. I ran a few yards to gauge if spikes were even helping me and then decided to run in my normal sneakers. Himanshi did not care much about what shoes I was wearing if I was filling up space.

It was all fine and exciting until the commentator started her commentary. She went about introducing sprinters one by one. Finally, he paused before my name.

"Ladies and gentlemen, in lane 4 is Pandey Ji. As you would have figured out from the name itself, Pandey Ji goes to the mandir every morning before coming to school. His prayers have paid off we guess. Pandey Ji has plans to run backward and win the race." The commentator was no other than Himanshi.

It turned out that I wasn't called onto the track to compete but became a laughingstock and source of entertainment for other people. My parents were sitting with other parents that day. Everyone was laughing at their son and them. My eyes swelled up as I tried faking a sportive smile. I wanted to walk away but that would have meant more embarrassment. No matter what you do or achieve, the tag of a backbencher or a poor student will never leave you if you have bad teachers and mentors.

What would you do if everything was at stake? Your self-respect, your parent's self-respect, Palak who stood there at the finishing line silently praying for you to win and proving a teacher wrong who had given up on you even before you started?

Everyone took their positions at the starting line and the noise volume in the stands reached the maximum level. It wasn't just a race, it defined life for me that day.

Himanshi blew the whistle and the first few strides I took were pure adrenalin running through my veins. I had seen other 400-meter races in the past and what I realized was that other sprinters generally started slow to conserve energy for the final 100 meters to the finishing line.

Well, my entire focus was on Himanshi's jibe at me. Channeling your anger and aggression in the right direction can do wonders at times. You might not be a natural at a lot of things but your desperation at times makes you do the impossible.

As soon as the race began, I broke into a sprint. My speed remained constant all through the first three hundred meters and I further picked up my pace as I approached the finishing line. The rest of the sprinters underestimated me because I was a nobody.

By the time they picked up, I was only a few meters away from the finishing line and the last ten meters were down to stiff competition with the champion athlete of our school. I lost by a fraction of a second to the guy but stood second in the overall race.

I crashed onto the grass after crossing the finishing line, closing my eyes, looking up towards the blue skies, gasping for air. I could hear the loud cheer from the stands and a louder heartbeat. Everyone from teachers to remaining students was stunned by my performance. I quietly got up and limped my way to the finishing line where other sprinters had gathered.

Respect – is earned. You are only a loser till the point you do not prove the world wrong.

Palak was the first one to walk up to me. The happiness in her eyes and those wet drops on her eyelashes spoke so much more than could be described in words. She knew what it meant to me. The force, the connection, that lost love, everything was there, in one single moment.

I wanted to hug her and cry my heart out, shout at her for choosing Rohit over me but all I did was smile and walk away; after all, she was one of those pages from the past I could neither turn nor burn.

Himanshi took some time to believe that her best athletes had lost out to a loser like me. The commentary booth was silent for the past few minutes. Himanshi sat there, shocked. She, however, showed me a thumbs up as I walked towards the first aid section of the playground. I had grazed my knees and arms while crashing on the track.

"What was that?" Shefali asked as she gently pressed a cotton ball soaked in antiseptic liquid on my grazed palm.

"That was a fluke," I smiled.

"Friends?" Shefali extended her hands offering a handshake.

"I know my place Shefali, your world is different. I won't fit in there." I smiled and walked away.

My brain was still replaying the moment when Palak looked at me.

Shefali stood there, putting the blood-soaked cotton ball to her pocket instead of throwing it away in the dustbin next to her.

DAVID VS. GOLIATH

Irrespective of being a top performer at the bank, the life of a relationship manager is far away from being peaceful. The branch manager will always find some way or the other to ensure that the sales team is always under pressure.

Financial year closing is like a test of fire for bankers. Auditors, cluster branch managers, regional heads, zonal heads, and the entire top management suddenly spring to life.

Adding to all this hustle are the annual ratings and appraisals of bank employees. This is the only time you would see an otherwise thick-skinned relationship manager on his/her toes. Customers who never picked up their relationship manager's calls now start calling and asking for annual statements. In a nutshell, otherwise considered bloodsucker bank employees become the most important people on this planet.

I used to handle around one hundred fifty high-net-worth clients on behalf of the bank. Post taking over Rajput's portfolio, I seldom met or called any of the other clients throughout the year. I used to complete my revenue targets by churning or investing Rajput's excess money in various investment plans. Apart from this, I was also handling a portfolio of other politicians as well who had opened accounts with my branch basis reference of Rajput.

Most of the other relationship managers used to either hate me or look up to me as their icon or savior because I completed a majority of the branch's investment target single-handedly and that enabled them to escape the wrath of our branch manager.

When you work for a bank, the rule is simple. You need to save your branch manager's ass if you want to lead a peaceful life as a banker. The moment the higher-ups screw a branch manager over a weekly con-call for numbers, he would ensure no relationship manager is spared from his wrath.

I did not need a job anymore but the reason I was still working for the bank was that it kept me connected to Rajput and his powerful circle. The only reason someone powerful would entertain you is that there is some benefit he derives from the relationship.

I had no intentions of working or performing during the second half of the month, so I decided to take a step back and enjoy all the hustle around me. I was busy preparing my daily sales report, which as usual showed a consecutive fifth 'NIL' in each product column.

My banking head was a sly guy, ready to blame his non-performance on relationship managers.

There is a harsh truth about banks, which we as relationship managers realize after joining the bank. The traditional concept of banking no longer exists.

Banks are no more establishments that act as custodians of wealth for customers. They have become sales agencies.

A relationship manager is a glorified sales agent who is trained to lie to a customer and get him to invest in a life insurance product or some mutual fund that would fetch him negative or positive returns depending upon luck.

What is worse is the fact that private banks don't give a heck about how an employee is treated in the organization. All that matters is numbers. If your sales figures are good, you're through; otherwise, your branch manager who himself had been through the same dirt will shower you with both personal and professional slang.

Slowly, as a human being, you become so good and adept at lying day in and out to your customers that these traits get into your blood. You become insensitive, professional, hard-hearted, and finally, a corporate zombie who is then promoted to a branch manager.

Relationship managers are hens that need to lay golden eggs, every day. No matter what, every day we need to get sales for the bank. We also need to smile and talk to every customer; the size of a smile varies according to the bank balance a customer holds.

We were like a multipurpose sales agent for the bank, wherein the bank does not have to incur the additional cost of hiring mutual funds agents, insurance agents, credit card sales agents, current account and savings account sales agents, etc.

In addition to this, we also need to service our clients and entertain their demands, for example, traveling twenty kilometers across the city to hand over a fixed deposit form. They would call you to their house, portraying that they are interested in investing in an insurance plan with an annual premium of lakhs, and on reaching, they would ask you to book a fixed deposit instead. All you can do then is smile and leave, cursing yourself for becoming a fool.

The bank also hands you over a phone that keeps on ringing all the time, most of the time, even after office hours.

I sometimes wonder why they call us relationship managers. After all, whom are we building relationships with? Customers look at us as dacoits, fearing we would snatch away their money. Even before we speak, they already know we are going to sell a life insurance policy.

"This is not going to work Abhay, you are supposed to lead by example here and no sales for five days is not acceptable." My boss started the conversation with his patent line

"Sir, I am trying my best, there are a few cases in the pipeline," I replied in patent lifesaving lines.

"Abhay, the branch is still short of achieving its targets and you are our star performer. There are so many remarkable things in the pipeline for you as well. Hope you convert yours so that I can convert mine for you." The branch manager subtly put across his point that my appraisal was on the line.

The branch manager then turned his attention to other unlucky relationship managers in the team. While he unleashed his fury on them like a dragon breathing fire. I kept myself occupied by looking at paperweights, and plants placed in the conference room and occasionally staring at a female NRI relationship manager present in the meeting.

The storm finally passed away after fifteen minutes and all the relationship managers hurried back to their desks. I picked up my bag and left the branch, fixing up a few fake calls and client meetings. Sitting on my desk would rather make me a soft target for my boss.

I waved at an autorickshaw.

"PVR Vasant Kunj," I said.

"Hundred and forty rupees," the autorickshaw driver said.

I hopped into the rickshaw, took out my phone, and started stalking other people on Facebook. The plan was simple, watch a movie and waste time until six in the evening. Then report back to the branch with a sad face and a disappointed look.

I had already achieved my share of targets, so did not care whether my branch achieved its targets or not. There was a time though when I'd go out of my way to fill in for other people's targets, but not now. Nandita had changed me as a human being. I bothered less about human emotions and would not even care if tomorrow my colleagues were lined up against the wall and shot.

I reached the location just in time to catch an afternoon show. Buying myself a large popcorn, I purposely took a seat in the last row of the movie hall. That is where all the action happens.

There were couples around me who then shifted their seats because I was checking out the girl while the guy was losing a precious opportunity to make out. It's a strange feeling, to see other couples and watch the guy do silly, stupid things to please his girlfriend. Feed her popcorn, pamper her, and concentrate on her more than the movie because he needs to have sex with her.

For people who are just out of a breakup, it's like already knowing how the love story ends.

Finally, I decided to shift my focus back to the screen allowing these couples a few precious minutes to make out. Suddenly my phone began to vibrate, my branch manager was calling me for obvious reasons, asking for the status report.

I disconnected his call and sent him a text – *'In a meeting'*.

Within a couple of seconds, I received back a text, *'With whom?'*

Now, you might be a legend at faking business meetings and calls but what you also got to remember is that your branch manager has trodden those paths much before you started walking.

An answer to that question would have meant more questions, like "send me a picture, send me your location, I am calling the client to check," etc., etc.

I'd seen a few relationship managers get busted during these sudden raids by the branch manager, but every species evolves to survive. The relationship managers then came up with hacks like recording the noise in a busy street with people shouting, cars honking, buses running, etc.

They might be sleeping at home or sitting in a café and chilling but as soon as the branch manager calls, they simply open their laptops and play the sound. The branch manager will not doubt them because they are on the field.

I chose not to reply to my branch manager and within a few seconds, I received a couple more question marks. No reply from my end, again.

Within the next few minutes, my phone began to ring continuously. The raid had begun, and I was more than prepared to mess with my manager.

I switched off my phone after his third straight call and continued watching the movie. The movie got over around five in the evening. I switched on my cellphone to find around thirty missed call alerts. It was evident, that I had taken on my branch manager (an iconic figure at the bank) head-on and the evening huddle was going to be more action-packed than ever.

There was an insurance policy of fifty thousand that I had picked up from one of the clients a few weeks back and had kept as a contingency backup. A fifty thousand insurance policy according to a senior relationship manager is negligible but lifesaving in these situations.

I could have walked into the branch and shut my branch manager with the insurance policy but for some reason decided to take him on. There are two ways you can rule, either replace the king or create your kingdom. It was time I took the throne.

The first thing I did was call up the client I had picked up fifty thousand worth of investment from and ask him if he was available for a meeting today. He said it would be possible for him to meet tomorrow only.

"Sir, my branch manager has asked me to meet you and understand if you had more plans of investing with us?" I started setting up my client to deny me a meeting.

"No, I have already invested and do not have any additional corpus with me currently," he replied immediately.

"I understand that sir, but you know how bosses are. In case he calls, possible for you to say that I had come to meet you and that you need some time to think and get back to us?" I moved in for the kill.

"Yes, sure, don't worry. I'll tell him you had come to meet me," he chuckled.

I disconnected the call with a huge smile on my face. Phase one of my plan had been perfectly executed.

The next phase was taking on my branch manager head-on in front of everyone at the branch. This would have only made me popular among the oppressed lot. After all, rebels, irrespective of whatever fate they met with, went down like heroes in history books.

I reached the branch around six thirty in the evening. All the managers had come back from the field empty-handed by then. My branch manager had already called the regional head and cluster branch manager at the branch, ensuring a special execution was planned for me.

He was still threatening to fire the other managers when I strolled into the branch casually. The cashier looked at me nervously. I could see the worry in her eyes for me. I used to flirt with her just enough to keep up the spice in my life. She smiled and pointed towards the branch manager's cabin.

The branch manager by then walked out of his cabin, fuming, red-faced, and had it not been for the CCTV cameras installed in the branch, he would have knocked me down then and there. On the other hand, I kept smiling shamelessly, arrogance dripping from every inch of my face.

"Show me your phone," my branch manager shouted at the top of his voice.

"Why?" I replied in a calm tone.

"Look at this guy's audacity." My branch manager looked towards the regional head and cluster branch manager in complete disbelief.

"Abhay, why didn't you pick up Brijesh's call?" My regional head stepped in defense of my branch manager.

"I texted him back that I was in a meeting. What else do you expect me to do in front of a client? Moreover, he frantically kept calling me." I drew out my sword as well.

"And so, you decided to switch off your phone? Who the hell do you think you are?" My branch manager stepped a bit closer to me, well within range to land a perfect slap on my face.

The entire branch watched in silence. They were experiencing a David vs. Goliath battle.

"Do you have something to prove your claim that I switched off my phone or ran out of battery?" Also, can you stop poking your angry nose into my face?" I replied keeping a calm but confident tone.

"Let's talk inside." My cluster branch manager stepped in.

"Fire him, I want this insect out of my branch right now." My branch manager was in no mood to back off from my public execution.

"Hey, listen, I am done with your threats." I pulled out

the insurance policy from the bag and placed it on the table.

Next, before my branch manager or any of the other heads could understand, I dialed the customer's number and put him on the loudspeaker.

"Hello sir, my branch manager wanted to know if I had come to meet you today or not. Could you kindly confirm the same?" I held the phone closer to the managers so that they could hear the customer's reply.

"Yes, he had come. Anything else? I am a bit tied up," he replied.

"Thank you, sir, just a confirmation call." My Cluster Branch Head interrupted even before I could say something and disconnected the call immediately.

"Brijesh, he was in a meeting." The regional business head was visibly pissed off at my branch manager for making a scene out of nothing.

"So, this is what I get after overachieving my targets month on month. While none of the other managers can achieve their targets, I am still trying my best to get you numbers." I could now see victory in sight.

"No need to overreact Abhay. This was a judgment error on my part." My branch manager realized that he just lost the round and switched on damage control mode. I on the other hand knew this was the perfect time to land the knockout punch.

"I am putting down my papers. Thank you, sir." I picked up my laptop bag and left the branch.

My branch manager just lost three precious things all at once: a top performer at the bank, his face in front of his seniors, and the respect of the staff reporting to him.

"Abhay, I understand your position, let's discuss this separately." The regional head knew letting me go wasn't an option currently because one of his best-performing branches would suddenly fall in terms of performance and I was a tenured employee whom any bank would not want to lose. The best part was, that I exactly knew my worth, so more than anything it was a calculated risk I took.

I was pulled into a room separately where the Regional Branch Head and Cluster Branch Head tried convincing me to stay back and withdraw my resignation letter. They threw a few baits such as promotion in the upcoming cycle, etc.

I wasn't a fool to have believed them but then during those forty-five minutes of discussion, I was able to establish a great rapport with both my Cluster Branch Head and Regional Branch Head. I withdrew my resignation and made it appear like I had done it out of respect for both gentlemen.

Over the next few weeks, I enjoyed absolute respect from all the relationship managers. Now almost every relationship manager had started answering back to my branch manager and slowly he lost almost all the control he had over his reportees.

Meanwhile, I had met Rajput and casually narrated to him the entire episode one night over drinks. What I carefully did was plant an idea in Rajput's mind that if I could be so useful to him as a normal bank employee, imagine what I'd do for him once I became a branch manager.

I am not sure whether it was Rajput's plan or something

genuinely happened but the next day, a female customer called our branch manager for a meeting at her place.

The same evening Vice President-Human Resources got a mail from the very same female client who accused the branch manager of sexual harassment. The bank has a very strict policy against such cases and the branch manager was terminated with immediate effect.

I wasn't aware of any of these developments overnight and reported to the branch the next day as usual. To my surprise, there was already a meeting going on since early morning at the branch attended by the zonal, regional, and cluster branch managers.

I was walking towards my seat wondering why everyone was so serious when suddenly my cluster branch head called me inside.

"Abhay, there was an unfortunate development last night because of which we had to let Brijesh go." Atul, our Cluster Branch Head broke the news.

"Listen, would you be willing to take charge of this branch Abhay? I've heard a lot of wonderful things about you and feel it's time you stepped into a bigger role." The zonal head cut Atul in between.

"Sure sir, I am up for any responsibility I am given but what exactly happened?" I was curious to understand the fate that Brijesh met.

I was briefed on what exactly happened in the past twenty-four hours and was assigned the task of damage control and winning back the customer.

The news of my promotion to branch manager was announced the same day. It's strange how human behavior changes towards people based on their circumstances. The managers who used to stand and smoke with me, abusing and bitching about Brijesh, were now shaking hands with me and celebrating as if they had been promoted. However, I knew there would be so much gossip behind my back. Well, who cares?

Power gets you two things, respect as well as criticism. I knew deep down that the news of my promotion to branch manager and preferring me over other tenured relationship managers working in the same branch would not go down well with most of the employees, but then I was prepared to take on anyone who would come between me and my goal. Emotions and empathy had left my soul a long time ago.

The zonal head left along with the cluster head soon. There was still a lot of damage control they had to do at the senior level. After all, everything happened under their watch.

I stepped inside the branch manager's cabin. The whole branch watched as I stood in front of the chair. I picked up the nameplate on the desk, it read Brijesh Patel – Branch Manager.

I walked out of the branch with the nameplate in my hand while everyone was still looking at me.

Tossing the nameplate into the dustbin outside the branch, I pulled out my seventh cigarette.

Cigarette Number Seven

FACING YOUR FEAR

They say weakness is only a strength waiting to be explored. Even though my grades kept improving, mathematics never let me breathe. There would be panic attacks every time I sat for a math test.

Even with all the mugging and practice, I never scored more than sixty percent in the subject. On a bad day, I would further slip down to fifty percent.

What the rest of the class found easy would take me hours to solve, just because I could not understand the logic behind solving problems. The Mathematics teacher's expectations of me kept on increasing each time. From five percent to sixty percent was a decent effort but who remembers a mediocre one?

I knew a day would come when all temporary solutions and hacks I kept using to pass would fail. You cannot survive a math exam just by mugging.

Finally, it happened. In one of the tests, the teacher gave questions from a book different from our coursebooks. After an hour of struggle, I was able to solve just two questions out of thirty. I was embarrassed to submit my answer sheet but the teacher had already snatched the same from my hands.

I had come a long way from being a bad student to an above-average student. This one test would again knock me down to the point from where I started.

No one generally understands the struggle weak students go through to make a place for themselves in a crowd of brilliant minds. The education system in our country is so flawed that every other talent of a student is generally buried under the burden of marks he needs to score in exams.

I ended up scoring a zero on that exam. When you break someone's expectation, there are two types of reactions you can expect. Either the person would just give up on you and never again place his bets on you or he would insult, abuse, or come back hard at you till the time he has vented his entire anger.

I witnessed the second option that day. My test answer sheet was pinned on the class noticeboard. Other students had scored less but I was the one who took a fall for everyone else. Instead of helping me or understanding my problem, my teacher decided to rip me apart in front of the entire class. After months of hard work, I was again standing in a familiar situation.

Students were laughing at me, and there were a few who had written 'Well done Pandey Ji' on the answer sheet pinned on the board and all this happened under the watch of my teacher who was supposed to teach the subject.

Everyone has those moments in life when you discover how strong you are. I took insults each day with a straight face. My friends tried their best to keep me away from all those insults but what is directed at you will hit you.

This kept happening for a while. My confidence in the subject had eroded to the extent that my other subjects started taking a hit. Teachers once again had their labels out for me: useless, brainless, cow dung in the head were the ones awarded regularly. I had begun accepting these titles comfortably when one fine day Dad came across my grades.

Like every other parent, he could have reacted or beaten the hell out of me but no one knows his son better than the father.

"So, what went wrong?" he asked me one evening when Maa was not around.

"Nothing, I am trying hard. Grades will improve," I replied, scared that any other reply would fetch me the similar reactions that I got from my teachers.

"I am not asking about your grades. I am asking what is wrong. It is fine, a few bad tests do not define you as a person." Dad finally spoke a different language from the rest of the world.

As a teenager who was learning to handle so many emotions and failures, his words were like oxygen. I let my heart out and explained to him that I could not focus on my studies anymore. He listened to me carefully without interrupting. When I was done speaking, he smiled and got up from his chair.

"Come with me." Dad kick-started the scooter and signaled me to sit.

A few minutes later, I was looking at a door that had a sticker on it.

"Boxing classes?" I asked my father.

"Think of the punching bag as mathematics and beat the shit out of it each day you train." Dad looked at me.

I was not sure if his idea would work but then it was a change from the normal routine. Boxing classes came with a set of instructions.

No punching anyone unless there was a direct threat to life. No picking up fights in school and all the aggression was to be left at boxing classes only.

He only wanted me to channel my aggression and learn about discipline.

I began training and a month later, apart from my improved punching skills, I was a calmer person than before. Slowly it helped me concentrate and focus more on my studies. I made additional efforts to understand mathematics. I asked for help from my friends and Neeraj would invest an additional hour teaching me chapters after school.

Asking for help is not bad. Everyone needs it at some point in his or her life. No one is a born hero.

It was a Monday morning. The math teacher walked into the class with printed question papers. It was a surprise test. He distributed the questions and while every student was given two sheets to write answers upon, I was handed over just one sheet.

I smiled, "It's good to start as an underdog," I recalled my boxing coach's words.

An hour later, I had taken two more extra sheets while other students were not able to finish even one sheet. The teacher came back with corrected answer sheets the next day. The entire class had failed the test apart from me. I had managed to score eighty percent.

"Abhay, what did you eat for breakfast yesterday?" My math teacher chuckled as he handed me over my answer sheet.

"Everyone's insult, sir," I replied with a smile.

My teacher's face suddenly had an apologetic smile. Walking up to the same board where my previous answer sheet was pinned, I put my answer sheet next to it.

THE BANKER POLITICIAN

"You like the one in white?" I asked Maa as she stood smiling in front of a brand-new sedan. I could see the happiness on her face as she nodded in agreement.

My father meanwhile enjoyed the hospitality of showroom employees. The manager ensured he felt like a king. My father had struggled all his life to give us a proper education and, in the process, sacrificed a lot of his dreams.

I could see the pride and satisfaction in his eyes and that was exactly the moment I felt as if I had achieved everything in life. The on-road price of cars was close to thirteen lakhs for the top-end model.

Even though I could have paid in cash, I decided to opt for an EMI option. I had stashed a lot of cash in different bank lockers, investments in shares, bonds, real estate, gold, etc. It made things look more real plus my parents would not doubt anything.

My father was still bargaining with the showroom dealer for free accessories when I got a call from Mr. Yadav. He informed me that the proposed highway project was finally approved, and the government had begun the process of compensating farmers whose land fell directly on the highway. With Rajput's blessings and extensive traveling with Yadav, I had close to thirty-five properties across India that lay directly on the proposed highway.

Going by the calculations, the amount of compensation that I was supposed to receive from the government was upwards of fifty crores. Half of this amount was supposed to go to Rajput. I decided to give an additional five crores to previous owners of these properties so that they do not feel cheated or open their mouths in front of anyone else.

However, there were around seven farmers who started blackmailing and threatening me about going on a strike and informing the media about the scam.

I informed Yadav Ji about the situation and soon these farmers and property owners had either committed suicides, died due to drinking country-made liquor, or mysteriously disappeared. Politics is a dark and murky world. I couldn't sleep for days wondering how the families of these farmers would survive. One night, I spoke to Yadav about my guilt trip.

Yadav patiently heard me speak. When I was done, he casually asked me to join him for an evening walk.

"Listen Abhay, either you can be morally correct or be rich. If we had not acted, these farmers would have taken all of us down. Imagine your mother visiting you in jail." He paused and looked at me.

"Abhay, people do not give a hell if the world is on fire. All they care about is that their own house is not on fire. Never mention something like this in front of Rajput Ji. Moral codes don't save people from dying." He smiled and placed his hands on my shoulder. His eyes said it all. Behind that smile was a man who was about to decide if I was a threat to him or not.

"Thank you, Yadav Ji, you do not need to explain further." I discarded the last ounce of morality or honesty within me.

"Good boy, you were telling me about the car you bought." Yadav Ji quickly changed the topic.

Life was continuing as usual when one fine day came the big announcement. The dates for state elections were announced and Rajput was asked to lead the campaign for his party. A strong lobby of loyalists was already projecting Rajput's name as the chief ministerial candidate.

Elections are the moment of truth for any politician. No matter how powerful you might be as an MLA, MP, CM, or PM, in the end, it's the people who decide your fate. It's a litmus test where people approve or disapprove of the work done by a government.

Rajput was a cabinet minister in the central government so he could not contest the state elections. However, the overall planning and execution of the entire election campaign rested with Rajput.

A month before the campaign, Rajput called me up and asked me to join the campaign. There was a lot of money moving in and out of the system and he could not have trusted anyone other than me to manage the overall campaign's finances.

I took a medical leave from the office for a month and submerged myself in Rajput's campaign. During this period, I also got introduced to some very high and prominent politicians from the central government. My network and reach further expanded.

During the campaign, I did a lot of background work for other ministers as well. I managed everything for a very elite group of ministers. My work was so clean that even enforcement agencies could never find a lead to build up a case against my clients.

Rallies, hoardings, party meetings, gifts to media houses, bribing girls to put allegations of rape and harassment against ministers from opposition parties, I had stepped into the darkest side of politics. This slugfest between political parties to grab power knew no limits.

I worked round the clock with Rajput and Yadav Ji and would not come back home for days, living my life out of a suitcase.

The exit polls showed Rajput's party as the favorites and Rajput looked poised to win the elections for his party. He had already started pushing his loyal base of supporters within the party to create noise around his name as Chief Minister of the state.

Rajput was in charge of a ministry that did not enjoy power like railways, finance, defense, etc. Becoming Chief Minister of India's capital would directly put him in the spotlight.

I returned to the office after the elections and it took me some time to get my concentration back to work. I had never tasted so much power and money. The newly discovered lobbyist title and working directly with some of the most powerful people in India further made me invincible.

I realized that there was a stark difference between what we saw on television and in newspapers as common citizens. Politics was a different world altogether. Everyone who succeeded in politics learned it the hard way.

The fact is that there are very few politicians who remain untouched by corruption. None of the political parties care about people. The taste of power is so addictive that no matter how honest or hardworking an individual is, there will always be people who know the price of his/her integrity.

I did not care about the nation, its people, or the system. The only thing that was going on in my mind was how to become part of this league. I had seen the most experienced politicians get toppled from their positions and I had also seen a nobody become a prominent figure in politics.

I wanted to taste this power now. I was waiting for that one window of opportunity that would change my world forever. And one day, when I was least expecting it, it came knocking at my door.

Election results were about to be declared the next morning. Rajput could not hide his anxiety and had been restless for over a week now. I was waiting for the guard to pull down the bank branch's shutter and hand me over the keys when my phone rang. It was Rajput.

"Hello," I answered the call.

"Come over to my place and get two bottles of Old Monk on your way. Yadav forgot to refill my stocks."

"Ok, on my way," I replied.

I reached Rajput's place in the the evening. Over the past three years, Rajput, Yadav, and I had grown in terms of power, reputation, network, and wealth, but the most important growth was the bond between the three of us. To them I was family and to me, they were the key to all my dreams.

We drank until three in the morning and talked about everything, from the cleavage of the new female party worker that Yadav used to observe to Rajput abusing the leader of the opposition party and swearing to shoot him in the ass.

I passed out early morning. As I opened my eyes, I saw a tense Yadav and Rajput sitting in shorts in front of the television. Their faces looked grim and tense.

The counting had begun, and the opposition party was initially leading in most of the seats. Soon other party workers flocked to Rajput's residence. However, by afternoon, the tables had turned, and Rajput's party was leading. The opposition though was not far behind.

One thing was evident, it was a split mandate by people and no party was going to get a clear majority. By evening, this mandate was reinforced. Rajput's party emerged as the largest party but was still four seats away from the majority. All four candidates were independent and had not contested elections under any party symbol.

As soon as the results were declared, it was clear that Rajput's party would get the first preference to form the government because they had more seats as compared to the opposition party. However, the biggest challenge now was for Rajput to ensure that these four independent MLAs supported him and not the opposition party.

It was evident that the four independents would extend their support to the party that offered them the maximum money. I returned home to catch some sleep. These were dealings of the highest level and there was no role I could have played in the same.

It was around three in the morning when my doorbell rang. My mother opened the door to find Yadav standing. My mother knew about my association with Yadav and Rajput. She had seen them on news channels, and I had selectively educated her about my involvement in Rajput's affairs. According to her, Rajput trusted her son with his accounts and investments, frequently meeting me to discuss how he could grow his wealth through strategic investments based on my advice.

Well, with Yadav standing in the middle of the night at my doorstep with security personnel behind him and red beacon ambassador cars just below my apartment, that logic of me being just an advisor to Rajput had already gone for a toss.

"Namaste mata ji, I am very sorry but where is Abhay? Have been trying to reach him but have not been able to get through."

"In his room." Nervousness was visible on my mother's face.

"Can you please wake him up? Sahib wants to meet him urgently." Yadav tried putting up a fake smile.

"Ok, but what is the matter? Is everything fine? What did my son do?" My mother barraged Yadav with questions.

"No, no, Mataji, your son is like a son to us as well. Sahib considers him a part of his family. We need his help urgently. Please wake him up." Yadav pleaded.

My mother woke me up and informed me about Yadav waiting for me. My sleep vanished immediately and I rushed towards the drawing room.

"Is everything fine?" I asked Yadav.

"No, dress up. We need to leave immediately. I'll explain to you on the way," he said.

By this time, almost the entire society was up. Everyone now knew about my political connection and everything that remained hidden from the eyes of the world was now in the open. I had voluntarily kept a low profile so that things remained normal around me.

Not anymore though. The moment I stepped out with Yadav, walking towards the red beacon ambassador car, I noticed people looking at me in complete awe.

"What is going on?" I asked Yadav as the motorcade sped past the society guards who were now saluting me more out of fear than respect. I wondered about the amount of power a red beacon on a car carries.

"We were able to convince three out of the four independents to join us but the fourth independent, Ganapati Dinanath, is a retired army veteran. We offered him money, but he threatened to go to the media and expose us. This asshole is an honest, old man who believes that our party is nothing but a bunch of thieves. Can you believe that?" Yadav reacted as if he was deeply hurt by Ganapati calling him a thief. On the other hand, deep within I knew Ganapati was right. I was more surprised as to why was Yadav hurt after all.

"So, what am I supposed to do here?" I asked Yadav.

"Convince him to join us, win his trust, and show him

that we are an honest party." A familiar voice in the front seat next to the driver spoke.

"Rajput sir! I am so sorry I did not notice you were here." I was taken aback.

"Abhay, there are a few people who do not put their moral values up for sale. I cannot trust anyone to do this but you. Help me form the government and I assure you, this favor will be returned in kind." Mr. Rajput looked at me with a smile on his face, the one which said I wanted the work to be done at any cost.

"Where are we going by the way?" I asked.

"Taj, Chanakyapuri. You will be staying with us for the next three days, away from all the media gaze. We have only seventy-two hours to convince this guy or we lose the opportunity of forming the government. I am placing my trust in you." Rajput regained his calm composure.

I read about Ganapati before meeting him. It was more like preparing before an important sales meeting. I had to first understand more about the person I was meeting. His background, his beliefs, his value system, and most importantly any weak or vulnerable spots.

Ganapati was an ex-army officer who had won gallantry awards in the 1962, '65, and '71 wars. An honest person who wanted to fight this corrupt system and set an example of good governance. An intimidating personality with pride, who would only bend a knee in front of the National Flag and no one else. A well-informed mind and eyes that could pierce right through one's soul.

The fact is that you cannot approach such people with the intention of shoving your thoughts, suggestions, ideas, offers, etc., down their throats. They would spit it back on your face and then all doors are closed for you. To sell them something, you need to win their trust and deliver every time.

Ganapati used to go on morning walks regularly with his dog. This was the best time to talk to him. However, after he won the elections, it wasn't easy to reach him. He had strictly instructed the society guards not to allow anyone including media personnel to enter the society until the next few weeks. Anyone who wanted to enter the society had to first mention the name of the person they were visiting. The guards would then call up the society resident and confirm the visitor's credentials.

However, for Mr. Ganapati, there were around five to seven police personnel allotted for his safety. The fact was all seven personnel were part of Rajput's security detail and had been stationed to keep a vigil on Ganapati. They knew me personally and to them, I was of the same stature as Yadav.

I walked up to the society gate only to be greeted by the police officials. The private security guards of the society obviously couldn't have doubted my credentials if the police themselves allowed me in. The thing about human behavior is that it easily gets influenced by what other people are doing.

The society security guards did not recognize me but still, they lined up to salute me as they thought I'd be someone very senior in either the police department or someone influential. I nodded and kept walking. Respect, no matter how you get it, makes you feel good about yourself.

It was around five in the morning and the thick white fog spread like a blanket. Winters have their charm. The society in which Ganapati lived looked mesmerizingly beautiful. The yellow streetlights seemed to splash golden color across the broad and silent society roads.

Winter was at its peak and how I wished to be in my bed, buried in a blanket, enjoying the cozy warmth of my home! Instead, here I sat on a desolate bench in the park, waiting for Ganapati to arrive.

I would have waited for around fifteen minutes when I spotted Ganapati enter the park with his dog. That animal looked more like a lion rather than a dog. Initially, I began having second thoughts about this whole thing. What if the conversation did not go as planned and he let his dog loose on me? Being bitten by a ferocious German Shepherd on a fine winter morning wasn't a great feeling.

The park had a circular road. I began jogging in the opposite direction so that I could directly come face-to-face with Ganapati. I approached Ganapati and crossed him just to make things look normal.

"Mr. Ganapati?" I suddenly stopped and called out his name.

He stopped and looked behind. His dog had already switched on the alert mode.

"Yes," he replied, a bit puzzled by the sudden interruption to his morning walk.

"Congratulations sir. We are proud of you as citizens. I voted for you sir." I extended my hands to congratulate him.

"Thank you so much, young man." Ganapati shook

hands with me. I was surprised by the strong grip he had for a sixty-year-old man.

"Sir, I am a huge fan of men who served in forces. Mind if I join you on a walk for a few minutes? Would be so awesome to draw inspiration from people like you. As such, now that you are an elected member, I am sure it will be difficult to meet you in person." I chuckled innocently.

"Yes, sure. Join us." He sportingly pointed towards his dog who had now begun wagging his tail.

"What's his name?" I lightly rubbed the dog's forehead. Ask a man about his pet and he will go on till eternity.

"That's Tyson. Got him from one of my friends. He was the weakest of all the pups his mother gave birth to. Initially, everyone thought he would not survive but I decided to bring him home. Look at him now." Ganapati gleamed with pride.

"Sure, looks like he has gone through rigorous military training." I had done my research.

"Yes, had him sent to Kashmir as a sniffer dog for counter-insurgency ops. He got injured in an IED blast, so the army had to release him." Ganapati lovingly patted the dog.

I suddenly felt a huge amount of respect for this animal whom I hated a few minutes back. This dog was a hero and no matter whom you meet in your life, no one can ever match the selfless love of a dog.

"This is so inspiring. Proud you must be," I smiled, this time genuinely.

"Yes, I am." We both kept looking at the dog for a moment before I made the next move.

"So, how does it feel sir? You must have development plans; how do you think youngsters like us can contribute?" I began the probing exercise, asking only those questions that got the client interested in a conversation with me.

"I feel thankful to everyone who has supported me. Honestly, I never thought I would ever fight an election in life, let alone, win. I am still not over the feeling, to be honest." He laughed. Our pace of walking had slowed down.

I ensured that the policemen did not allow anyone from the society to enter the park until we both were walking. The justification they gave to society members for the same was that they had received a tip about a threat to Mr. Ganapati's life for the next twenty-four hours.

"And development?" I made the move.

"I have a lot of ideas in my mind but not sure how will I be able to move things with this corrupt system in place," he said.

"Yes, I agree. Corruption runs deep in politics and that is why we need people like you to clean this up," I smiled.

"Hope so, but it's not going to be an easy fight." He shrugged.

"Yes, it's difficult for one person to effect a change. Ideally, one has to become part of a system to change it in the very first place. I mean if tomorrow you become a minister or someone influential in the state government, imagine how many lives you can change. You would have the power to make decisions, affect swift changes, and most importantly work on the development agenda." I delivered the first punch.

Ganapati stayed silent for a few minutes before

throwing in his first rebuttal.

"But all the parties are corrupt and I'll never want to be part of such a corrupt system."

"Sir, I think people like you are our last hope. What I feel is that you cannot fight such a huge system from the outside. It's important to dismantle this age-old corrupt system and establish a new one. You will be a role model for people like us, but everyone will ask you five years later about your achievements. Your answer cannot be I was busy fighting the system so could not deliver. That would be letting people down."

"I am sorry, did not get your name, young man," Ganapati said.

"I am Abhay, a branch manager working with a private bank, sir." I introduced myself.

"Interesting thoughts young man." He smiled.

"I'll take your leave sir, got an office to attend. Wishing you all the best for the future sir." I began leaving.

"Join me for tea someday if you can. Would be great to catch up with you again." Ganapati smiled as we shook hands.

"Sure, I am honored that you asked." I smiled and shook hands. One thing was clear, I had got Ganapati thinking.

I returned to the hotel later that morning. I was surprised to find Rajput and Yadav waiting for me there.

"He did not agree. Right?" Even though Yadav sounded pessimistic I could see hope in his eyes.

"Call him around afternoon and whatever you do, please don't offer him any money." I handed out a clear set of instructions to Yadav. Ganapati was contacted soon, and he agreed to meet around the evening. Yadav delivered a perfect pitch that evening to Ganapati. Also, Ganapati was offered a ministry in state government which further made him feel important and responsible at the same time. He finally cracked and agreed to extend his support to Rajput's party.

Within the next twenty-four hours, Rajput resigned from his cabinet position and was elected as a chief ministerial candidate from his party.

In another week's time, Rajput was sworn in as the Chief Minister of the state. I was back home watching news channels cover the sudden rise of Rajput to power and was wondering if he would even remember the huge favor I did for him when my phone rang. It was Rajput.

"Congratulations sir, I was just watching your interview on a news channel." I began.

"Abhay, you remember I promised you something? Your life son is about to change. I have seen people doing a favor and running after me seeking something in return. You are a selfless asshole and I am so proud of you. Come over to my place, we need to celebrate this together." Rajput sounded visibly excited and happy. I had won over Rajput's trust completely and now that he was the Chief Minister of a state that also was the capital of India, he had become larger than life.

I reached the Chief Minister's residence around evening and all three of us drank like fish.

"Abhay, I need you to now resign from your job." Rajput looked at me, drunk, but very much in his senses.

"Sir, I am happy managing your accounts. Why do you want me to quit?" I knew something big was coming up for me, just that I did not want it to show up on my face.

"I've spoken to the high command. Elections are supposed to be held in Haryana six months later. I want you to now enter politics and contest elections." He put his hands on my shoulder and continued.

"Real estate in Haryana is like a gold mine and I need someone trustworthy there. I could not think of anyone else apart from you. So, tell me, are you ready?" He smiled.

"I will go anywhere you send me, bhaiya. Thank you so much." I was drunk so getting emotional wasn't a challenging thing to do. I allowed a few teardrops to roll down my cheek to make Rajput realize what this meant to me.

Rajput and Yadav passed out after a few more pegs while I was still awake, seeping at the moment. This is exactly what I wanted, that one window of opportunity to step into this world, and it exactly came at the right time.

I took out my eighth cigarette and tapped its butt against my wristwatch before lighting it up.

A couple of drags later, I drifted down the memory lane.

Cigarette Number Eight

THE BIRTHDAY CAKE

"The accounts lecture won't be held today as ma'am is attending the teachers' meeting, she has therefore asked us to complete exercise 4.7, page number 278." Palak got back to her seat after breaking the good news to the whole class, well, you must be wondering what was so good about this news, after all, we had an exercise to complete.

The point is when there isn't a teacher lingering around you all the time, peeping into your notebook, making your life miserable, pointing out your mistakes, insulting you for your lack of common sense or knowledge, it becomes relatively easier to breathe.

"You're not completing that exercise, are you?" Bhagat had already closed his books.

We both decided to take a casual stroll down the corridors and if by any chance any teacher caught us loitering around, we had a backup reason ready – "Drinking water."

Problems had a special affinity towards both of us. Even without the slightest of intentions, we always figured out ways to invite trouble since the beginning of our school days.

As we approached the school building's exit, I saw

Shefali entering. It had been a while since I met her after the sports day. Being an all-rounder, she was always busy planning some co-curricular activity or the other along with schoolteachers.

Shefali had opted for science as a subject post 10th boards. Everyone thought she would make it to the IITs someday but deep within, I always felt that she had too big a soul to be chained down by such a small or insignificant dream.

Our eyes met, and she smiled at me as if she had been waiting for us to meet. Bhagat immediately understood the gravity of the moment and decided to leave us alone. He kept walking towards the exit.

"Hi, so we meet again." She extended her soft hands for a handshake.

"I've always been around rather it's you who is busy living the celebrity life." I chuckled as I reached to touch her palms softly.

That touch, ladies and gentlemen, was like touching an angel.

"You never treated me on your win that day and why didn't you come to collect your medal?" Shefali held my hands gently.

"Were there medals handed out to winners? I wasn't aware and for the treat, going by your extensive list of achievements, you should throw a gala dinner." I gently withdrew my palm ensuring she did not get conscious about holding my hands for too long.

"I collected the medal on your behalf but it's at my place. By evening six thirty, I'll leave for the math tuition.

I will get your medal. Please collect it from me after my tuition is over?" Shefali looked at me for an answer.

"Abhay?" she interrupted again.

"No No, I mean.. yes… I will come down to your place, sorry tuition." I fumbled out of nervousness.

"Great, I will see you at seven."

"Where are you both going by the way?" Shefali wanted the conversation to continue a bit longer.

"Accounts teacher didn't turn up so loitering around," I replied.

"Wow, you guys are professionals in bunking classes." She giggled.

I was about to invite her for a stroll around the school campus when suddenly I saw Angad walking towards the lobby.

Angad, my dear readers, was part of the elite group of students led by Rohit. He was the official bully cum bouncer of their group and his KRA (Key Responsibility Area) was that other students were always reminded of their proper place.

Angad also was good friends with Shefali and did everything possible to impress her.

"I'll see you later." I did not want Angad to have a piece of me in front of Shefali. Angad on the other hand kept staring at me wondering how the hell did I dare to talk to Shefali.

"Pandey. Come here. Why are you running?" Angad called my name from behind. He walked right across Shefali as she nervously looked at me. She was aware of Angad's credentials as a bully.

Always remember this one thing, getting bullied or insulted in front of a girl to the point that she feels sorry for you and herself intervening to stop the bully is the worst thing that can happen to you as a guy.

Maybe it was Angad's luck or sheer bad timing of deciding to mess with me, but I decided to give it back to him. It wasn't because he picked on me in front of Shefali, but because he was part of Rohit's group and my hate towards them had crossed all known boundaries.

"Listen, you melon-shaped ass holder, try calling me anything apart from Abhay and I'll ensure that everyone in school is made aware of your real name, TARBOOZA." TARBOOZA by the way is the Hindi name for the fruit watermelon.

Angad was still staring at me in disbelief when our heads turned towards Shefali who was holding her stomach and laughing her heart out. I had just landed the most lethal blow on Angad's soul. His entire aura of a bully was already in shatters.

"If I were you, I would do anything to convince her not to disclose your name in front of her friends." I walked away with a smirk on my face as Angad turned all his attention and efforts towards containing the damage I had inflicted.

Meanwhile, Anisha, Aanchal, and Neeraj had joined Bhagat outside the school campus.

"Abhay, she is totally into you." Bhagat patted me on my shoulder out of excitement.

What Bhagat did not know was that deep within me, in the darkest corners of my heart, Palak was very much there.

Days passed by and my closeness to Shefali increased. Palak was aware of these recent developments in my life. I was very good friends with Shefali but was aware of the fact that many students kept advising her against continuing her friendship with me.

As per them, I was way below her standards. People tend to become judgemental when someone else wins instead of them. I knew Shefali was way above my league and was content that she was good friends with me. Shefali on the other hand was unfazed by opinions and suggestions, that people threw at her.

It was Shefali's birthday and she had invited all her friends. The guest list had all the toppers and all-rounders coming including Rohit and his elite group. Shefali had coaxed me into attending the birthday party.

I agreed for two reasons, one, Palak would also be attending the party, and two, I knew this would mean a lot to Shefali.

Finally, all her "well-mannered" friends assembled at her place. Her father supposedly was a top official at the Tata group of companies. The interiors were spot on and I could only dream of having a room like hers.

"Wow. Look at that cake man, when do we cut it?" Bhagat elbowed one of Shefali's well-mannered friends from some other school.

He in turn gave me and Bhagat a look as if saying "Dude, don't you think you are at the wrong place? Why don't you run away and join your roadside friends?"

"Shefali you look beautiful; it's always amazing how you look so great in every dress you wear." Angad meanwhile showered Shefali with all the praise in the world.

"Thank you, Angad," Shefali replied in patent lines developed by girls over the years to keep guys hopeful and foolish enough to believe that the comment meant a lot to her.

"Abhay? Aren't you going to say something about Shefali?" Rohit dragged me into the ring. Palak stood next to Rohit and I could see in her eyes that she grew uncomfortable with her boyfriend's comment.

"Well, he is more interested in the cake. Pandey Ji, never seen anything like this before?" Mr. Angad made sure I became a laughingstock.

Everyone broke into a laugh, except for Shefali. She looked towards Angad in disgust.

"We've also never seen an ass like yours, Mr. Tarbooza." Bhagat, my wingman, my savior, my strength in the darkest of hours flew past me, bombarding Angad's castle of ego.

Everyone in the room was in splits by then, including Shefali. Rohit's guy was KIA (killed in action) and it did not go down well with him.

"Oh, so your dog bites as well?" Rohit stepped in; his comment was directed at Bhagat.

Neeraj and Bhagat immediately stood up and so did Rohit's gang of nerds. I looked at Shefali, she was almost pleading with me to not create a scene.

"Abhay, step back," Palak interrupted. She looked straight into my eyes.

"You heard her? Step back." The smirk on Rohit's face added fuel to my already burning soul. I kept my eyes fixed on Palak in disbelief.

I couldn't have lost like this. The Romeo within me had now taken up arms, turning into Rambo who was about to turn this whole party into carnage and make sure Rohit had lots of 'slaps' in dinner.

I gave a final look at Palak before losing her forever; she looked beautiful that day, just that everything evil attracts.

I only managed to say "Palak you…" when Shefali's parents stepped into the room and the Rambo within me took my fingers off the trigger.

"Why is the cake still like this? I am surprised why you people aren't making some noise?" Well, what her father didn't know was that had he been a few more seconds late, he would have been witness to the biggest carnage in history. Probably I would have cut both the cake and Rohit into pieces.

"Sorry uncle, I will have to leave, there is some important work that has come up at home and I need to get back, thanks for inviting me, Shefali." I wanted to get away from that place, those people within the room, and of course Palak.

"But you can wait until Shefali cuts the cake" Shefali's mother insisted.

"Please stay," Shefali pleaded as I walked towards the door.

"Save my cake, I am for sure not leaving that. Here is your gift and you look stunning." I winked at Shefali as she managed a smile.

Bhagat, Anisha, Neeraj, and Aanchal soon decided to walk out as well. The party had already turned into a slugfest.

I walked out of Shefali's building wondering what happened to Palak. I wasn't sure if this was the same girl I knew, or if Rohit had just filled her against me.

"You know what Abhay, I have never told you anything nor intruded on your personal space but Angad needs to be taught a lesson." Neeraj interrupted my thoughts. All these years I had known Neeraj to be a quiet student who did not believe in the idea of violence. Today seemed different.

"I wanted to punch Angad so hard in his face," Anisha added.

Honestly, I wanted to do the same but picking up a fight when you are outnumbered was foolish. I was more concerned about Neeraj, Aanchal, and Anisha who would have been dragged into a brawl for no reason.

"Maybe some other day but I promise you this, a day will come when I will teach Rohit a lesson and you all will be a witness to that." I extended my arms as all five of us got into a huddle.

Shefali met me in school the next day with a tiffin box full of cake. She pulled me into an empty classroom during the short break.

"Thank you for the gift. I never imagined you would take so much trouble for me. A pen with my name on it, this is special." Shefali opened the box and stuffed a piece of cake in my mouth.

"Shefali, I am sorry for what happened the other night. Ruined your birthday party unintentionally…" I was about to say more when Shefali put a finger on my lips.

"Don't say a word further, I am no more friends with Rohit. I'd rather be happy hanging out with you." Shefali's finger was still on my lips. I knew a lot of people who would have given everything to just touch her hand and here I was, standing in an empty classroom staring at her beautiful face and deep blue eyes.

"I have to go now, see you in the evening." Shefali skipped away, leaving the box of cake behind. It had a small note lying on top of the cake. I picked up the chocolate-smudged note and opened it.

"I love you ☺" Shefali had just turned my world upside down.

THE ELECTION TEST

It was a silent Monday morning. The world looked different that day. I had decided to quit my job and enter active politics. Money was no longer an issue. I had earned enough money for the next generation to sit at home, eat, and exist comfortably.

The thing about money is that it has the power to change, transform, or affect the behavior of every human being. I had bought a house, bought a car, opened bank accounts for both my parents, and transferred enough money for them to feel secure financially. Today, I was a role model for my relatives, the same people who had once advised my parents to stop investing in me because I would eventually be a failure.

Money changes your circumstances, people, friends, enemies, and most importantly, love. I did not go to the branch that day; instead, I straight away went to the bank headquarters.

The HR department was on the fifth floor. I walked into the VP-HR cabin. She was startled to see me barge in without an appointment.

"Mr. Abhay, I am busy. Can you please make an appointment and come back later? I did not like the way you just barged into my office." The VP-HR, Simran Kaur, was a lady whose one look was enough for any bank employee to shit in his pants.

"Listen, I don't have time for this chit-chat. Here is my resignation." I threw the letter on the table and took out my cell phone.

I had a bit of a history with Simran. It went back to the days when I was a newcomer at the bank. She visited a few branches and interviewed a couple of tenured employees to understand how much they liked working for the bank. It was part of her annual KRA.

She saw me sitting quietly in a corner, staring at the lead sheet of clients I was supposed to call and pitch insurance policies to.

Later that day, I was summoned by her to the branch manager's cabin and she asked me how was I feeling working at the bank. I gave an honest opinion about how I felt being asked to sell insurance policies to random people on my second day at the job.

She heard me patiently with a smile and then said something that set my expectations to zero.

"Listen, Mr. Abhay, I've hired you to do a job. I am not going to feed you for free and that salary you get does not come easy. The day you can return me even a month's salary, we'll talk." She signaled me to leave the cabin.

I left the cabin with dejection. That was the moment I knew I had landed the wrong job.

Today was different though. I took out a five hundred-rupee bundle of notes and threw it in front of Simran.

"Here is a month's salary you paid me, remember what

you said back then? Return me a month's salary and I'll listen to you."

Simran had never encountered such behavior before. She was used to being treated like a queen, but then every generation has rebelled.

"The culture you have created within the bank is so poisonous that there would be a time when people would just hate banks or bankers. It's no more a place where someone's hard-earned money is safe; instead, you are a life insurance selling establishment. Anyways, I don't have any hard feelings."

I took out my cell phone and played a random hindi song.

I mimicked a few Anil Kapoor steps and by the time she called the security guard, I picked up the note bundle I'd thrown on her desk and dashed down the stairs.

It felt good as I finally emerged from the building, free from all the shackles this corporate culture had put on me. That feeling of finally being able to do something you have dreamt of for so long is priceless, absolutely nothing can replace that feeling.

I was walking back to my car when the regional head called me.

"What the hell Abhay? I just got a call from the VP-HR and she wants to terminate you. How dare you even try something like that?" The regional head was visibly pissed off.

"Listen, do whatever you want to, and don't call me ever again or I'll ensure you come to the office in a wheelchair." I disconnected the call.

There are moments in life when it's difficult to explain how happy a person can feel from within. Abusing my regional head was the best feeling ever in my life. Later that night, I narrated the entire sequence of events to Yadav and Rajput and both ran out of breath laughing.

A couple of weeks later, Rajput named me as the General Secretary for the Haryana state division of the party. Haryana had three major political parties and I was asked to contest the election from a seat where my party had never really won.

"Bhaiya, you know I would lose from this seat. Our party has never won from that constituency. My political career would finish even before it starts." I was pissed off at Rajput asking me to contest elections from a weak seat.

"And imagine what happens if you win from there? Your entry would be so grand that it would set you up for success from the very beginning. Listen Abhay, either you can surrender and lose right away or contest elections and win. Do whatever you have to do but win. You will always have my full support even if you lose. Success is earned Abhay, not served on a platter." Rajput handed over the call to Yadav who wished me the best of luck and disconnected the call.

I sat alone in the party office, an old, dilapidated fan rotating slowly over my head. There was no way I could have won from that seat. I was to contest elections from the Faridabad constituency and the current MLA, Hardeep Gujar, had won three consecutive elections from this seat. For a moment, I wondered if dancing in front of VP-HR was the right thing to do.

There wasn't much left to do apart from giving Hardeep the toughest fight of his life, the only question was how?

The corporate job taught me one thing, how to plan. Irrespective of whether the plan helps me hit the target or not, it would at least enable me to deliver a solid punch. When you are pitted against the best, the first thing you need to do is build an army of loyal followers, people who would die alongside you on the battlefield and not betray you during your darkest hours.

How do you build an army of loyalists? Becoming a leader is never easy, you need to win someone's trust who is a stranger. A leader sets examples for people to follow. He would put himself in harm's way so that his people would be safe.

I decided to meet my party workers the next day, people needed to know whom they were fighting for.

Over the next few weeks, I worked and spent all my time with these guys, ensuring I won their respect. I used to eat with them, sleep at their place, wear their clothes, borrow a hundred rupee note from one of them to eat street food, and later return him a five hundred rupee note, thanking him for the favor.

It was June and summer was at its peak. The sales job at the bank had taught me how to survive a field job, especially during summers. A white kurta pajama, a white cotton towel wrapped around the face to shield against the scorching summer heat, riding on a bike with party workers, campaigning door to door from one society to another, I had immersed myself in the elections.

Politics without violence is like food without salt. A few weeks away from the elections, we were planning a rally in one of the residential societies in Faridabad. People of this society had been complaining about not having proper access roads to their society, security issues because of liquor shops just fifty meters away from the society, electricity and water issues, sanitation, hygiene, and the list was endless.

Suraj was the closest among my team of party workers. The list of volunteers who were associating themselves with my election campaign kept growing by the day. The best part about our way of going about asking for votes was that we did not dress up like thugs, instead, be it a posh society or a farmer's house, we dressed up decently and tried our best to look presentable.

It matters a lot how you project yourself in front of the general population. I wanted to project myself as a neat and clean, honest, hardworking, empathetic, and educated candidate who gave solutions to their problems rather than making promises. However, Hardeep was getting nervous and impatient with my rising popularity.

I was about to leave a party worker's residence where I had stayed overnight when Suraj rushed in.

"Minister sahib wants to talk to you." He handed over his phone, gasping for breath. I was surprised that he didn't call me on my number. I signaled Suraj to take a seat.

"I have got information that Hardeep's men would also be attending your rally. There is a threat to your life, and I want you to cancel your schedule for the day." Rajput laid down the instructions loud and clear.

"Cancel and hide somewhere? Imagine how motivating that would be for Hardeep," I replied.

"Abhay, there is a difference between foolishness and bravery. Stay away from the rally today if you want to live to fight the elections." Rajput wanted me to steer clear of the lurking danger.

"This rally is very important bhaiya, if I do not turn up, people will tag me as a liar and someone who goes back on his words. Please, the rally must be conducted today." I was scared about my life but backing out of the rally would have meant losing my face as a leader in front of party workers. That was worse than losing elections.

"I will arrange for police protection, stay alive if you can." Rajput disconnected the call coming to terms with the fact that I was too fat-headed to listen to his advice.

We reached the rally venue around seven in the evening. Policemen were already stationed at the gates and everyone was being checked and scanned carefully. I tore into Hardeep and personally spoke to the society members, understanding their issues and taking suggestions from them about how to go about development work in case I was elected.

The rally was a success and a lot of people from various other societies reached out to our volunteers sharing their issues and problems. It was then I realized how it feels to carry the hopes of people on your shoulders.

It shook me from within how we as common citizens struggle every day and survive against a corrupt system that does not care about the ones who gave them power. Some senior citizens had invested all their savings to buy a house for themselves only to keep running behind a water tanker because the municipality did not care if they got clean water to drink.

Poor people were hit the worst. They were living in hell. Kids slept near gutters, no food, no money, and no medical facilities. Girls would keep getting exposed to trafficking at an early age. When I looked into their eyes, I could see hope that maybe I would drag them out of this hell.

I was walking towards the car with a couple of personnel from Haryana police accompanying me when suddenly a huge group of people marched towards us, shouting slogans and holding Hardeep's poster in their hands.

My party workers were not far behind and started shouting slogans in my support as well. Things escalated as soon as the supporters came face to face and even before I could have intervened, blows were being exchanged between them.

Soon, hockey sticks, bats, and stumps were out, and the clash now turned bloody. I too received a couple of blows, which were directed at my head but I somehow managed to take it on my hands and body rather.

I couldn't have stood there and watched my people being beaten up and snatched a hockey stick from one of the guys who looked weak. Before he could respond, I landed a well-directed blow on his ribs. He immediately fell to the ground.

The police had intervened by then and managed to disperse the mob. Police knew I was Rajput's guy, so they did not arrest me or any of my supporters. However,

Hardeep's men had inflicted some severe damage on my party workers.

Suraj had a head injury and was rushed to the hospital. I accompanied him in the ambulance. We reached the hospital and Suraj was rushed to the ICU. I sat outside the ICU ward watching others get medical attention. Some had broken ribs, bruised faces, and blood-stained, torn shirts and it filled me with anger watching my people in such a condition.

I was hurt as well but my mind was continuously fixed on Suraj's condition. I closed my eyes, resting my forehead on my fist when suddenly there was a lot of commotion in the hospital. Soon, Rajput and Yadav emerged from the crowd.

For some reason, my impatient heart and mind suddenly calmed down at the sight of these two. However, both Rajput and Yadav looked visibly upset.

"Show me." Yadav raised my kurta's sleeves to inspect my swollen arm due to the hockey hit. Rajput meanwhile inspected the deep cut on my forehead and looked around at the rest of the party workers who were standing around hanging their heads in shame.

Rajput sat next to me staring at the floor.

"I've not come here to offer advice, sympathy, or scold you. I came here because I wanted to check if you are still willing to continue. You can back out if you want to because what you just experienced Abhay is only a trailer. Power doesn't come easily, blood is shed, people die, family is left behind and you travel to the top alone. I can interfere and ensure Hardeep pays for this, but I am going to let you fight this battle and figure out your way. Never had I seen Hardeep so much troubled before. You have managed to shake the throne, now topple that bastard. Either you would emerge from this victorious or fail to never return. Best of luck son, I hope you pull this off." Rajput left the hospital as Yadav looked at me helplessly.

Rajput's words pinched me deep within. He left me out there cold and numb to fight my own battles and for a moment, the idea of returning home and taking up a normal job crossed my mind.

Then I looked at Suraj and other young boys, some in their early twenties. They had fought for me, and bled for me, and turning my back on them was the worst thing I could have done to them or myself.

I got up and signaled Rakesh and Ajay, my other two closest team members, to assemble everyone near the hospital garden. Fifteen minutes later, I was standing in front of fifty to sixty-odd party workers in the hospital garden.

"All of you shed your blood for me today and there is nothing that can describe how proud and honored I am feeling today. I promise you one thing, Hardeep Singh will now see a side of us that make him shit his pants. It's our time now, are you with me?" I pumped my fist in excitement.

I was matched with a louder 'YES' by my team. The emotions were high and each one of us was brimming with anger and emotions.

Suraj managed to beat death but needed time to recover from the head injury. Meanwhile, the campaign had picked up the pace and there were more frequent and violent clashes between both sects.

Media had grabbed the story with both hands. Hardeep and I were breathing fire against one another. My mother was following the news closely. It took me an hour daily to assure her that I was safe and healthy, and nothing would happen to her son.

Finally, the voting day arrived, and it was close to a near curfew situation in Faridabad. People turned up in vast numbers to cast their votes. Barring a few incidents, the elections finally got over.

The results were supposed to be declared in a week. I decided to spend time with my family after the elections. Four months of madness had turned me into an animal, and it felt good to be back in the comfort of my home.

The result day finally arrived. The counting began and Hardeep and I were in a neck-to-neck contest from round one. The whole country's media had their eyes fixed on the Faridabad constituency and by evening, Hardeep had a marginal lead of around a thousand votes. There was still one last round of votes left to be counted.

It all finally boiled down to that one zone in Faridabad where there were around ten to fifteen residential societies, exactly the place where all of us were attacked and Suraj was critically injured.

The counting began and after an hour, I was leading by fifteen thousand votes. A hundred percent of registered voters from that area had voted for me. There are times in your life when you end up committing to a task just because your gut said so. Even though Rajput had warned me from campaigning in this residential society, I still went ahead only to get beaten up by Hardeep's men.

Today, that gamble paid off perfectly. Getting beaten up by Hardeep's men, an injured party worker in the hospital, or listening to the problems of people and empathizing with them gave me that extra edge over Hardeep.

The results were finally declared by evening. I had won the seat by a margin of seventeen thousand votes. Hardeep was finally defeated after three terms and I had managed to pull off an impossible win. My party had won the state elections by a majority.

My supporters and party workers thronged my house. People lined up outside my house with garlands in their hands and journalists almost climbed over each other to get a statement from me.

Inside my house, away from all the media glare, I addressed a group of five men who stood by me all along the campaign.

"You guys will be my core team, my brothers whom I'd never turn my back upon and God willing, we are destined to reach greater heights. Thank you so much." I hugged each one of them personally before walking out of my home and addressing the media.

Rajput and Yadav had summoned me to the party office. With great difficulty, I managed to reach the venue on time.

"You don't realize what you've achieved. I always knew if there was one guy who could have pulled this off, it was you." Rajput hugged me tightly. Yadav followed him and got emotional about my success.

"You are now a big person Abhay." Yadav smiled proudly.

"Yadav Ji, I will never be bigger than you." I bent down to touch Yadav's feet.

I went down to Rajput's residence later that night. As usual, all three of us sat in the same dining room, and Yadav who was our designated bartender prepared drinks for the group.

We laughed, and shared our stories, Yadav disclosed how Rajput controlled not calling up Hardeep post-attack and was up all night. My relationship with Rajput and Yadav had come to a point where they did not differentiate me from their immediate family.

I left Rajput's place early morning. A red beacon ambassador car was arranged specially to drop me off as I wasn't in a condition to drive.

While on my way home, I asked the driver to take a detour to a society in Jor Bagh. He obeyed the orders and stopped the car in front of a huge, lavish bungalow. I checked my watch; it was around seven in the morning.

I was still observing the size of the property when the gates opened, and a couple walked out in their jogging gear.

The husband was on a call with someone and started walking briskly towards the park while the wife stayed behind, stretching herself and warming up.

Suddenly her eyes fell on a white ambassador across the road. I could make out that she almost froze out of shock. I pointed towards the red beacon and smiled proudly.

Nandita's face had gone pale and moments later, she finally lowered her eyes and started walking towards the park. She must have seen the news for sure, but she never expected me to be standing right in front of her house and flaunting my newly earned power in style.

To see her lower those eyes which once looked at me in pity, was so satisfying that I almost couldn't control a few tears from rolling down my cheek. I reached into my jacket's pocket and pulled out my ninth cigarette.

Cigarette Number Nine

THE BACKBENCHER'S FATE

"You never replied to the note I left in the box." Shefali caught hold of me during the lunch break.

"Shefali, I guess the note you are referring to was stuck somewhere in the piece of cake. I sort of chewed upon it. Was it something important?" I looked innocently at Shefali while lying at the same time.

Shefali was beautiful. Any guy would have died a hundred times just to live with her once. However, Shefali and I had to go our separate ways.

Being a science student, she would land up with an IIT or a top engineering college; I on the other hand was destined to follow a herd of students who were moving northwards towards Delhi University. I did not want to fall in love with Shefali and then get into a long-distance relationship.

Also, I was still not over Palak. I'd grown up loving her and no matter what happened between us, that invisible bridge between our hearts remained intact.

Even though Shefali was a perfect answer to the void that Palak created in my life, I could not afford to take the leap of faith with Shefali. There was an inferiority complex within me. Shefali was beautiful, came from a very good family background, unlike me, was intelligent, and would for sure have an illustrious career. Sooner or later, society would make her feel wrong about her choice.

I wasn't confident about my future or myself now. Even though I had put up a valiant fight against my circumstances for a very long time, it was all because of Palak. She was no more in my life and I wasn't sure if there was anything apart from her to keep me motivated.

A girl rejecting you at the beginning is a much better option than realizing later that you were the wrong choice for her prompting her to look for ways to get rid of you.

I did not want to be someone who would later become a liability for Shefali.

"Wow, how can you eat paper?" She giggled but I could see the disappointment on her face. The reason why she put a note in the box was that she could not say it to my face and I was only looking for a way to wriggle out of this situation without hurting Shefali.

Over the next few days, I stayed away from Shefali's line of sight. The twelfth class board exams were a month away and almost all students stayed back home and tried catching up on all the course material they had comfortably ignored all their life.

Finally, the exams were held. Walking into an exam hall is like entering a war zone. You never come back the same. From panic attacks to blanking out after seeing the question paper, I have seen so many students having nervous breakdowns.

The last exam was math. A subject that had tortured me all my life. I was nervous before the exams. Standing outside the exam hall, in a corner, keeping to myself, I encountered numerous thoughts and emotions racing through my mind. I had imagined possibly everything that could go wrong during exams.

On the other hand, Bhagat stood next to me, defiant as a martyr, not bothered about consequences. He was rather more excited about this being the last exam. Palak was observing me from a distance. She always knew when I wasn't doing great emotionally.

When she couldn't take it anymore, she decided to walk up to me and gripping my hands tightly, asked me to look at her. At that moment everything came to a standstill. It was like a drug addict finally getting a shot of cocaine.

"You will do just fine, stop panicking." She exchanged her pen with mine.

"Here, use this one. It's my lucky pen but I guess you need it more than I do." Palak then slipped away like a dream.

"Get inside everyone and please take your seats according to your roll number," the invigilator announced, signaling everyone to get inside the hall.

The question paper was distributed and then it began. The next two hours were like meditation. I was so focused that it felt like I was on a trip. Palak's thirty-odd seconds of pep talk was enough for me to sort out my messed-up mind.

I finished my last question and looked at the clock. Half an hour still left. Then, I looked around to find students still engrossed in fighting it out except for one guy, Bhagat.

I think he had surrendered long ago and was only waiting for me to complete my paper. He looked at me and signaled towards the exit, asking me if both of us could walk out.

I had no intention of revising my answers. Bhagat as such was more than happy to walk out of the hall as soon as possible. I turned my answer sheet upside down, got up, looked at the beautiful invigilator, passed her a smile, and walked out of the hall.

Bhagat joined me as well and suddenly I could see fifteen to twenty students standing up to leave as well. All you need is one daring soul to start a revolution.

I impatiently waited for Palak to complete her exam. I wanted to talk to her for a few moments, hear her voice again, and no matter how small the conversation might be, still managed to fall in love with her for a while.

Finally, after twenty minutes, she walked out along with Rohit. Not giving a damn about her boyfriend, I walked up to Palak and took out the pen she had given me before the exams.

"This was sure as hell lucky, thank you, Palak." I returned her pen.

"Keep it, at least it would remind you of my existence after our school lives." Palak returned the pen to my shirt's pocket.

"How do you know we will be in touch once school is over?" I looked into her eyes, seeking an answer. Rohit stood at a distance, showing the decency of not interfering between two people who were once in love.

"I just know Abhay." She opened her arms and hugged

me before leaving with Rohit. He was visibly disturbed by my audacity to hug his girlfriend in front of his eyes.

A month later, the board exam results were out. Whether it was destiny or luck, all six of us scored well. The first option for most commerce students after passing their board exams is Delhi University.

Even though I wanted to pursue mass communication, my parents decided to choose my career. They decided to follow the herd and push me into that extensive line of students who wait for colleges like SRCC, Hindu, and Hansraj, hoping against hope their kids can somehow clear the cut-off list.

It was my last week in Jamshedpur. During this time, I met Shefali almost every day. We both would chat for hours together and she would share her insecurities without holding back anything.

Shefali was awaiting her IIT JEE and AIEEE results. Unlike most of the students who were applying and appearing for different engineering colleges, she had a sense of calmness and confidence around her. Looking at her, you knew that she already was an IIT material.

"You did not eat the paper that day Abhay." Shefali looked at me and smiled calmly.

"So you knew all this while?" I was surprised she never gave me a reaction when I lied to her.

"Why?" she asked me the obvious.

I admired Shefali for her honesty, her patience, and most importantly her down-to-earth nature. She knew I lied to her but still decided to move ahead with me. It's these moments that decide the fate of a relationship. She was brutally honest with me while I had been playing the cat-and-mouse game all along.

"I am not sure about myself Shefali. What if I fail in life and end up broke or without a job? You are beautiful and I've seen the most handsome guys run behind you for your attention. I don't know what you saw in me, but I'd not drag you down along with me, not until I've figured out my life." I confessed everything in front of Shefali but held back one detail, I was still in love with Palak. I somehow felt it would hurt Shefali.

"And what if we both end up being successful?" Shefali stopped outside her apartment's entry.

"Then I would let you decide our fate." I smiled.

"I'll choose you as my fate every time then, Abhay." Shefali did not wait for my reply and walked back to her apartment. Darn these Hindi movie dialogues.

REUNION WITH NEERAJ

My life changed after winning the elections. I could sense the raw power that came along when you became part of a large, corrupt, and inefficient system. This side of the world was darker than I thought.

As a fresher in politics, all this attention and exposure to very powerful people was attractive. I was learning new things about politics each day and one of the core learnings was being ruthless.

Every person was a potential vote and whatever you did for the country or society at large had to be evaluated on the grounds of whether it helped me get more votes. The new state cabinet was in place and I had purposely decided to stay out of the limelight and continue working for Rajput, after all, he was my mentor in politics.

For the next few months, I was sanctioned multiple rounds of funds in the name of infrastructure-related development work to be done in my constituency. However, forty percent of that entire budget was shaved off as cut to Rajput and various other babus. The remaining sixty percent was totally up to me on how I use it. It was still a lot of money and all of it couldn't be misallocated, as that would have put me on the radar of multiple agencies.

I was on my way to a press conference held to question me on the rising crime rate in my constituency. I was crossing Malviya Nagar when my driver decided to take a shortcut to avoid traffic. I was looking outside the window, my mind occupied with thinking about ways to dodge any tricky or controversial questions thrown at me by journalists when suddenly we crossed a familiar-looking college gate.

I immediately asked the driver to stop the car. I walked up to the main gate and suddenly my mind was brimming with all those memories of my past. As I strolled through the campus, it was like someone had just pressed the replay button. From the playground, and canteen to the classrooms, everything seemed to suddenly come to life, as if talking to me.

I walked up to a table in the canteen. I pulled a chair and decided to sit there for a couple of minutes. Students in the canteen kept looking at me like an alien but for me, that table carried so many memories. Palak, Aanchal, Aisha, Bhagat, Neeraj, all their faces staring at me.

The next piece missing was Neeraj. He was next on my list. I hadn't met Neeraj since college. All these years, Neeraj had worked hard in silence to build an empire for himself.

He owned a startup called 'InvestIntel'. His company advised and brokered real estate deals on behalf of large investors, corporates, etc. They enabled people to invest directly in the global real estate market. His app was a discovery and investment platform for real estate on a global level.

InvestIntel has revolutionized the real estate industry. The investors/clients of InvestIntel ranged from top CEOs and CFOs to many prominent celebrities across the globe. Neeraj's startup had raised just one round of initial funding and within three years of operations, his company had reached breakeven and was now staring at global expansion into multiple countries.

Neeraj had become one of the top entrepreneurs in the country today and his busy schedule kept him working most of the days. Neeraj was based out of Mumbai. I lost touch with Neeraj after college.

A few minutes later, I was walking towards my car calling up my assistant and asking him to send some officials from the police department instead to the press conference as I wasn't feeling well.

"Airport please." I checked the next flight from Delhi to Mumbai online as the driver took a U-turn towards the airport. Next, I dialed Bhagat's number.

"Halloo," Bhagat answered the call in his trademark Punjabi accent. He did not care if I was an MLA or Prime Minister, to him I was his childhood friend and half-brother.

"Mumbai, tonight. Book your ticket. I'll be reaching Mumbai in the next five hours." I disconnected the call even before Bhagat could say a word. I knew had I allowed him to speak, he would have come up with multiple excuses for not being able to travel.

I landed in Mumbai around evening. For a change, I wasn't accompanied by security personnel this time. Staying low profile was something I loved. Attracting too much attention to myself was never my core competency.

Neeraj's office was situated in one of the high-rise buildings in Bandra Kurla Complex. I took a taxi to his office. Clad in a normal shirt and jeans, I walked inside the building. The security guards were not aware of my current profile and asked me to step aside for a security check. It's strange how you relate to things that once irritated the hell out of you.

In a normal scenario, I could have simply barged my way to his office and no one would have dared to stop me. However, I enjoyed being treated as a normal person. It somehow made me feel good about myself.

I stepped into the lift and pressed the button for the 9th floor. There were a few more employees with InvestIntel ID cards hanging around their necks.

"Hi, is Mr. Neeraj in the office today?" I asked one of the female employees in the same lift. Other male employees were standing next to me as well, but men were men.

"Yes, you can check at the reception." She smiled and answered.

"Ok, thanks," I replied innocently, enjoying the conversation.

"I think I've seen you somewhere." One of the male employees tried recalling my face.

"Me? Guess my face is too common." I chuckled as everyone else in the lift broke into a burst of brief laughter.

I stepped out and walked towards the reception, excited about the thought of meeting my old friend. For once, the human in me had overpowered the politician in me.

Suddenly, I decided to try something weird instead. Rather than approaching the receptionist, I straightaway stepped into the office. By the time the receptionist could get up and stop me from going further, I had started strolling carelessly in the lobby, looking for Neeraj.

"Where do I find Neeraj?" I stopped in front of the same female employee whom I'd met in the lift and she innocently pointed towards a cabin that had a few people inside. There was a presentation going on, on the projector, and I could see Neeraj looking carefully at the screen.

The guards had almost reached up to me by then.

"Thanks, I owe you one." Smiling, I barged into Neeraj's office as guards followed me inside, one of them almost holding me by arms, trying to drag me away.

Everyone in the room was taken by surprise, including Neeraj who still hadn't recognized me as the lights were turned off due to the projector running.

"Neeraj, will you please switch on the lights?" I resisted two security guards who now were trying to do everything possible to shove me out of the meeting room.

One of the members in the room got up immediately to switch on the lights. By now, the entire office was looking towards the meeting room.

Neeraj got up from his seat as I stood in front of him.

"Abhay?" Neeraj couldn't believe his eyes. It had been years since we both had seen or spoken to each other.

He immediately reached out to me with open arms and we both hugged each other like brothers. To be honest, the feeling of hugging an old friend cannot be compared to anything else. Life might give you a thousand scars and a million blows, but the sight of a friend can heal even the deepest of cuts. It reassures you that everything is not wrong with the world.

"You would never improve," he chuckled as he wiped his moist eyes. Both of us got emotional after seeing each other after such a long time.

"Yeah, improve my ass." We laughed as the rest of the people in the room were still trying to figure out what exactly happened.

"Oh, so sorry people, introducing you to Mr. Abhay, respected MLA and a very dear childhood friend of mine. Please don't mind the intrusion, we were born with indecency as a major part of our character." Neeraj looked at me as he said those lines.

Perception my dear friends can change very quickly, it's all about your circumstances. A few seconds back the same set of people were judging me as a mannerless guy, who just barged into their brainstorming session. The same people now were queuing up to shake hands with me.

Many of them recognized seeing my face on television and I could see the pride on Neeraj's face. Had I been just another banker selling insurance policies, the reaction would have been very different.

Neeraj took the day off and both of us decided to head for Neeraj's place.

"So, how is life MLA saab? It's unbelievable Abhay, it took me a while to digest when I heard about your victory in the news." Neeraj signaled the driver to hand him over the keys to his car as we walked towards a black Audi in the parking lot.

"You own an Audi?" I ignored Neeraj's question and snatched the car keys from him.

"Yeah, and you own an ambassador with a red beacon asshole," Neeraj answered back.

"Not anymore sir, it's just another car without a red beacon. You tell me the directions to your place." I took the steering wheel of the car, which had interiors more lavish than my entire house when I was working for the bank.

You must be wondering why was I so excited to drive an Audi when I could have bought one for myself. Two reasons:

I had to keep a low profile or the income tax department would not leave a stone unturned to make my life hell.

Driving a friend's expensive car is a different feeling altogether.

When two old friends meet, especially unmarried bachelor guys with lots of money and absolutely no responsibilities, plans can change… quickly.

"You mean to say Bhagat is also coming and you are telling me now? Stop the car brother, I need to strangle you to death." Like me, Neeraj had also been cut off from the rest of the world for a very long time.

"Here, call him." I tossed my phone toward Neeraj.

"Where are you behenchod?" Neeraj customarily greeted Bhagat as soon as he answered the call.

"I am at the airport, flying down to Mumbai. I was cursing Abhay all this while wondering why he suddenly asked me to fly down to Mumbai and now I can't wait to meet you both. This night is going to be so sick," Bhagat replied.

"Typical Abhay, we'll pick you up from the airport." Neeraj looked towards me as I gave him a thumbs up.

Bhagat took a late flight to Mumbai the same night.

Neeraj had called up his PA and asked her to cancel all his appointments for the next two days and I was a politician, so I did not have to apply for leave as such. I could do whatever I wanted to without being answerable to anyone.

We picked up Bhagat later that night and headed for Neeraj's apartment. His apartment had the best view of Mumbai city and Neeraj, the son of a factory worker, had now become a business tycoon who owned an expensive car and a lavish house in one of the most expensive cities in India and the world. "Nice house man, you live here alone, or do any of your secretaries visit you?" Bhagat walked up to the large glass windows that opened to a huge balcony overlooking the vast landscape of concrete jungle.

"Apart from caretakers and cooks, no one." Neeraj cracked open three pints of beer as we raised a toast.

A couple of hours later and with a bottle of whisky down, Neeraj got up to show us something.

"Ladies and gentlemen, I present to you, The Bar" Neeraj slid open a wooden cabinet.

Bhagat and I took some time to digest the fact that Neeraj had a private bar. I looked at the fine collection of wine, scotches, single malts, whiskey, and rum and wondered from where we started.

"Does Aunty know about this?" I asked. Being guys hailing from small towns the very first question that comes to our mind before doing something as audacious as having a bar at home was how would parents react?

"Why do you think I have a wooden slider with a lock?" Neeraj waited for us to give him a standing ovation, we instead asked him to pull out a single malt we had just googled about.

"So Neeraj, when are you getting married?" Bhagat passed each one of us our drinks in plastic glasses. We had purposely picked up plastic glasses on the way to Neeraj's place. Old habits die hard.

"Not yet, have been working my ass off to expand my business abroad. Marriage would mean dedicating more time and bandwidth which I don't have."

Neeraj's end goal was the same as mine, to become successful. The only difference was the motivating factor to chase success.

While Neeraj wanted to chase success because it mattered to him, I chased success because I had revenge at the back of my mind. Nandita never really got out of my head. Every move, every risk, and every decision I took was with a motive to give it back to Nandita someday.

Even though my current net worth was more than Neeraj's, the difference between us was that Neeraj had earned all this money through arduous work, whereas I had compromised my ethics and manipulated my way to all this power and wealth. However, I was neither ashamed nor guilty about what I had become.

It's like training your mind to ignore all ethics and morality and look the other way. I did not want to go back to the life I once lived, working my ass off for twelve hours a day and finally managing to earn a salary.

Power is addictive, it's something that every human being wants at the end of the day. There are very few people who can handle success and power. It can turn you into a dictator or a leader, the choice is always up to you.

"Aanchal? Where is she these days?" I asked.

"She moved abroad last year. Working for an IT firm," Bhagat replied.

"Yup, spoke to her last month. She is in Adelaide and I am in any case traveling to Australia next month. Will meet her then," Neeraj replied.

"What about Palak? How is she? Where is she?" Neeraj had unintentionally but still revived my past, Palak.

"I've never been to Juhu Beach. Can we go there now?" Bhagat immediately changed the topic.

"I don't know how she is," I said.

There was an odd silence for a few minutes before finally, Neeraj realized that he had just touched the wrong wire.

My mind suddenly shifted towards the one I knew was doing pretty well.

"Do you know Nandita Singhania?" I looked at both Bhagat and Neeraj as they gave me a confused look.

"Nandita, the daughter-in-law of the Singhanias?" Neeraj replied

I nodded in agreement.

"She once ditched me for money." Alcohol took the lid off my soul. I blabbered everything to Neeraj and Bhagat and how I wanted to destroy Nandita. Both silently heard me speak my heart out and when the storm was over, I looked towards the window and held back every teardrop that wanted to flow out of my eyes.

"Damn, you dated Nandita Singhania once?" Bhagat was still in shock, least bothered about his drunk emotional friend.

"Whatever it is that you are trying to achieve Abhay, just remember, don't lose the human within you. You are much more than just a guy who is seeking revenge." Bhagat further added. He was more than a friend to me. He understood all this revenge would eventually turn me into an animal.

Neeraj remained silent. He looked at me as I picked up the liquor bottle to pour myself a drink.

"You'd need a bigger company to bring down that steel tycoon. A company that has people whom you can trust and more importantly a company capable enough to buy them out when they fall." Neeraj looked at me. He had indirectly signaled that the company was none other than InvestIntel.

"We don't need a bigger company, Neeraj, we need to make the company bigger." I handed Bhagat and Neeraj their glasses. The next move had been made. Neeraj was in the game, though his objective was more about growing the company and himself rather than helping me seek revenge on Nandita.

Bhagat looked at both of us in dejection. That night, he was the only person with a soul among the three of us.

A politician and an industrialist conspiring against someone was not actually how he had imagined his childhood friend to be.

That night we drank until sunrise before finally Bhagat and Neeraj crashed.

I stumbled my way to his balcony and felt the fresh breeze on my face. As I closed my eyes, the first face that flashed through my mind was Palak. After ages, my mind replayed an image of her.

I was happy for some reason. I had my friends back in my life, I had a plan for Nandita, and after ages, I saw Palak, I almost felt her. My dead heart had finally begun pumping emotions.

I took out the cigarette pack and pulled out my tenth cigarette.

Cigarette Number Ten

THE DELHI UNIVERSITY CHAPTER

Finally, the inevitable happened. My parents had decided on my behalf that their son should study at Delhi University because everyone else was. All my friends were applying for admissions and the typical Indian middle-class mentality kicked in, 'keep your kid in the company of known people.'

Mass Communication was not an option as I did not have enough courage to cross my parents. I did not speak my heart out and like every other kid in my school, colony, or city, I bowed my head and accepted their decision. So, commerce it is.

Shefali and I had come a long way till then. A day before I left for Delhi, we both went down a nearby lake. It was a park that had been developed around an artificial lake. The place looked beautiful around dawn. Purple skies, lots of birds chirping, and a fine breeze.

She didn't say a word the entire time, all she did was hold my hands and sob silently. I had never seen her like that before. I kept quiet; didn't know how I could have consoled her. There were those brief moments when I wanted to just hold her for a while and tell her I didn't feel like moving to Delhi as well.

"Abhay, promise me something." Shefali looked at me, her eyelashes still wet. The setting sun had splashed the last few golden sun rays on her face and by God, she looked like the last angel existing on this planet.

"Anything you say if it stops these tears." I wiped off water from her eyes.

"If you do not land up with Palak, promise me you'll come back to me." Shefali's eyes pierced through mine as she waited for a reply.

All this while, I always thought Shefali had no clue about how or what I felt for Palak. She not only proved me wrong but also proved one more thing, she was serious about us. All those fears of a long-distance relationship, cheating, and communication gaps were just too small in front of the trust she had in me.

I kept looking towards the horizon wondering what the hell was going on with my life. I wasn't happy about the place I was going to; I wasn't sure about a girl for whom guys would kill each other if they had to and I was running after a girl who was in love with somebody else.

Sometimes, it's OK to make false promises. It's OK to lie to someone because it would put a smile on the other person's face. It's Ok to tell them that everything will be fine even when you are not sure about the future yourself.

I knew that maybe a few months or years down the line, Shefali wouldn't be able to stick to her promise of waiting for me. Why should she anyways? She had a bright future, looks that would get her the best guy in the world, and a soul that was as free as a bird. Time will eventually play its role and there will be a point in her life when she will fall in love, again.

"There is no Palak, Shefali, and I am not going anywhere. Delhi is like an overnight journey. I promise I will come back to you," I said as I watched a smile appear on her face.

I left for Delhi the next day along with my father. Bhagat, Aanchal, Anisha, Palak, and Neeraj were also traveling on the same train along with their parents. It seemed to me as if they were going on a mission. Even though emotions were running high as we left the city where we'd spent all our childhood, I was insensitive to everything happening around me. What mattered to me was how would I survive Delhi over the next few months.

It did not matter which college I got into because it wasn't going to be SRCC for sure. You need to be a robot and score at least ninety-nine percent to get into SRCC. Neeraj had scored ninety-eight percent and had the best shot at the College of Demigods. For the rest of us, I wasn't sure how well an eighty-eight percent would help me get into a good college.

A day after reaching Delhi, we headed for those shortlisted colleges. Big infrastructure, and students who looked more like fashion icons as compared to us. I don't know why but the initial feeling was not comfortable. Too fast a city for too slow a person like me. I felt lost among that crowd. Long admission lines, a crowded campus, and parents running around with forms in their hands.

"I want to get back Dad; I do not like this place." I looked towards my Dad with great hope.

"It's going to be fine son, you had to grow up someday, you're a responsible guy now, and I know you will handle all this." My father made a futile attempt to boost my all-time low confidence levels.

I failed to explain to him that I felt like an alien and that continuing the journey ahead was going to be even more difficult. But then, I had grown up and was expected to handle shit on my own from now on. However, when it came to my career and future, I was an ass who couldn't decide for myself. See the irony there?

Over the next few weeks, I stood in almost every college's admission line. Soon it was clear that eighty-eight percent was still not a good enough percentage to get into a good college. To top it up, I did not even belong to SC/ST or sports quota, which further ensured students with lesser marks got admission while I faced disappointment almost every single day.

Finally, after all the struggle of filling out numerous admission forms, and standing in never-ending queues, I managed to get into a decent Delhi University college. It was situated in South Delhi a.k.a. South campus.

My father breathed a sigh of relief that at least all the investment in food and logistics he had incurred over the past seven days finally paid off.

Aanchal, Anisha, Bhagat, and Palak were still waiting for the third cut-off lists from North campus colleges. When their parents came to know that I had managed to get into a B.com Honors course, they decided to push their kids through the same college as well.

There were multiple advantages. All of us had known each other since school, were a very closely-knit group, and most importantly our families felt comfortable leaving us in an unknown environment. All of them, except Neeraj, finally got admitted into my college.

Neeraj however made it through SRCC. Even though it was the third cut-off list and he was the second last name, back in my hometown, Neeraj was the hero. He was the guy who got into SRCC while the rest of us were losers who had scored ten percent less than Neeraj.

"We are short by fifteen thousand rupees for your hostel fees, I'll see how can I arrange it. You don't worry." Neeraj's father was proud that his son had gotten through the best college but then his financial condition wasn't great. Seven days in Delhi had already strained Neeraj's father's pocket.

For the first time in my life, I realized how difficult it is for people who are not financially strong.

Comparing our parents to his father, I could see the staggering difference. His father never stood among our parent's group, a sense of inferiority complex always prevailed within him that he belonged to a lower class.

I wouldn't deny that in a few cases, he was made to realize that by our parents who felt uncomfortable with his father around. Neeraj's father would eat alone with his son in one of those cheap hotels whereas we would dine in some pleasant restaurant.

The way of dressing too was different, each parent trying his best to look the smartest around on campus, flaunting wealth at every point.

Neeraj's father on the other hand had brought two pairs of clothes with him, washed and used them alternatively. My father though was quite close to Neeraj's father. I felt proud about the fact that he acted normal, unlike other parents.

Being born into a family that can give all you ever demanded, study in the best of schools, wear the best of clothes, and eat the best food possible is a blessing. Not everyone can afford it. I looked at Neeraj and felt proud that he was my friend.

It's people like Neeraj who perform without caring about facilities. I wanted Neeraj to study in the best college, and make his father feel proud in front of our parents. Make them realize it is not always money and that talent is something that doesn't discriminate between the rich and poor.

It was somewhat past midnight. I woke up to find my father talking to someone in the lobby. I quietly sneaked up to the door and peeked out. My father and Neeraj's father were discussing something.

I decided to stay there and observe what was going on. My father took out a bundle of notes and handed it over to Neeraj's father.

"Keep this Brij, this should help you. You can ask for more, don't hesitate." He handed over the bundle to Neeraj's father.

His father quietly wiped his tears and thanking my father went back inside the room. None of them wanted Neeraj or me to see this.

I quickly jumped back to my bed and pretended to sleep. My dad quietly walked into the room and sat next to me. I tried my best to act asleep.

"Don't tell this to anyone, not even Neeraj,

understood?" my father said.

I nodded back in agreement. My father was soon asleep, but my mind kept replaying that incident again and again. How does the ego of a person respond when he stretches his hands in front of someone? How crushed the person feels from within and still does it. I can only imagine what parents go through to make their kids feel special and become a part of society.

I was very sure my father did not have that much money either, but he made a choice. Unlike others, he decided to step in and help. I was proud of him and that day he unintentionally taught me about the biggest trait a human being can have, humanity.

The next day Neeraj joined us with a new set of clothes. He looked visibly happy, flaunting his new watch and shoes. All five of us were happy to see Neeraj's new avatar. His father watched his son from a distance, my father's hand on his shoulder. I could only see the happiness in his father's eyes.

I could see the other parents putting fake smiles on their faces but the disappointment was visible. Their kids, well-fed, well-educated, well-supported, had been outdone by a factory worker's son.

I helped Neeraj move into his new hostel room, setting his luggage right. Our parents had decided to leave together, catching an evening express back to Jamshedpur.

So finally, the moment had arrived when all six of us would have to gut it out alone without our parents.

"Dad, why did you do so much for Neeraj?" I asked my father.

"Because I saw myself in Neeraj." He smiled.

My father was my first teacher and first mentor. He taught me a lesson that day – 'never forget what you are.'

THE DARK SOULED SAINT

The unavoidable press conference finally happened. A week post returning from Mumbai after the reunion with Neeraj and Bhagat, the rising crime rate issue had snowballed into a huge controversy. Things got uglier that week when a six-year-old girl child was raped and murdered.

The senior party leaders had sent their best speakers to tackle the journalists. While all this was happening, I was instructed by Rajput to visit the murdered child's parents. Until then, instead of thinking about what that kid must have gone through or what would be the condition of her parents, the entire focus was on how we saved ourselves from media trials.

I decided to visit her parents the next day. I had asked my assistant to carry a cheque of ten lakh rupees as compensation amount that would be handed over to the parents in the full media glare.

I reached their home around the afternoon. Media personnel had already flocked the grief-stricken family's house and as I walked towards the entrance, I wondered if I was the only soul-less guy on Earth. The media was more bothered about the politics around the child's death, flashing statements issued by various political party leaders in shiny fonts on the TV screen.

The father of the girl was sitting in a corner, sobbing uncontrollably. There were a lot of people, probably family, friends, and people who wanted to be on camera. It was an odd situation for me. For a moment, it felt as if this was all my fault, and it was. The crime rates in my constituency had picked up and I never bothered much because like every other citizen in the country, my default reaction was it's the government's job to control the crime. However, what I forgot was that I was part of this very government now.

As I walked towards the bereaved father, he looked at me for a moment. I could see the hate and disappointment in his eyes for me. To him, I was a bigger criminal than the guy who had raped and killed his daughter. He then turned away his gaze and kept looking in another direction, wiping his moist eyes. I'd been used to watching people hate me, but this was different. I could not take a step further.

From inside the house, I could hear the mother cry. There are these brief moments in life when no matter how hard a heart you might have or how mentally or emotionally insensitive you might be, it will move you as a human being.

Suddenly that blanket of shamelessness I had been wearing all this while was ripped apart by her loud shriek. I could sense the pain, something that I had not experienced for a while. I pulled a chair and sat next to the father. He held the kid's photograph in his hand.

I took the photograph from his hand and looked at it for a moment. She was smiling, and happy and had a shine in her eyes. There was a time in my life when I'd go to social media and write my heart out about how I felt when a girl was raped. Today, when I could do something about it, I chose to shut my eyes.

"She was just six years old. Had gone outside to play." His father looked at me, controlling his emotions as hard as he could.

"Can you please do us a favor, get everyone out, please? They are not letting us cry in peace as well." His father requested me with folded hands.

I signaled the policemen and it took fifteen minutes to get the house vacated and the media was asked to stay five hundred meters away from the place.

"I voted for you sahib and this is what I got in return. My wife hasn't had anything for the last twenty-four hours and wants to die. I don't know what to do now." He broke down again.

There wasn't much I could have said to console him. He was right, his vote to me was with this hope that maybe I would bring a change, instead what I brought for him was a ten-lakh rupee compensation cheque.

This moment shattered every bit of those false ideas I had about myself. It changed me forever. I felt ashamed as a human being that day.

All this power, authority, and money had turned me into a true politician, something that I did not plan or intend to become. Had I been more attentive towards the needs of the people who voted me to power, I guess I wouldn't have been sitting in this place trying to look for ways to conceal my embarrassment.

I got up quietly and instructed my assistant to ensure that the family faced no issues, especially monetary. I walked out of the house and took the back ally to my car, avoiding the media.

Over the next few days, I made it a point to stay in touch with the victim's family daily. It was more of an effort to get rid of the guilt but no matter what I did, I could not shake off the kid's face from my memory.

I decided to call up my father, it had been a while since I had chatted with my parents. After a couple of rings, he picked up the phone.

"Hi Dad, how are you?" I asked, feeling relieved to hear his voice after so much time.

"Not good. There is so much rubbish being said about the government and you in the news. It does not feel good when people talk bullshit about your son." He went quiet after saying those lines.

What do you do when you fall in the eyes of your parents? How do you justify that it doesn't matter what your parents think of you? Most importantly, how do you wipe that stain off your face? Many people have a simple answer to this, become shameless. I could not. He hung up without speaking further while I kept holding the phone receiver, wondering if there was any further I could have fallen.

There are times when you decide to become the law itself. Like every other common man, I did not feel like waiting for justice. I decided to use all my contacts to find out about this rapist.

A week later, I got a call from one of my contacts in the police department. The police had zeroed down on the suspect and knew where he was hiding.

"Buy out the police department if you have to but ensure that the news of his arrest does not go out in public," I instructed Suraj. The plan was simple. I wasn't sure what I'd do to him, but one thing was sure, he was dying.

Suraj, the guy who stood with me during my days of struggle, took a beating for me and risked his life to save mine. You don't let these kind of people go. Suraj was my most trusted guy, the one who knew about almost every aspect of my life.

He ensured that every single police official raiding the suspect's hideout was bought handsomely. The police officials raided the criminal's place dressed in plain normal clothes. He was arrested and escorted away at late night in a private van. No one, neither the media, neighborhood nor the top officials in the police department itself had a clue about this arrest.

The police brought him to a farmhouse owned by one of my acquaintances. I was present there with Suraj.

"Why? She was just a kid." I removed the tape from his mouth and he began crying mercy immediately.

I looked towards one of the constables who was standing ready with a loaded pistol. I had never seen a person getting shot but today was different. I nodded as he pointed the gun toward the rapist.

I could suddenly see the fear of death in his eyes. He immediately began howling and crying asking for forgiveness. The constable however did not waste much time and three well-directed shots to the chest were enough to put an end to this animal.

So possessed and blinded was I with anger that I ordered his body to be hung on the main street in the city with a billboard around his neck. The billboard carried a message – "NO MORE RAPISTS."

Building a fake encounter case wasn't a new thing for the police. A story was built that the rapist's hideout was discovered, and the police did not have time to call for backup. Thus, these four brave police personnel decided to catch hold of the rapist. However, he was armed and fired three rounds at them. The police had to shoot him down to protect themselves.

The media was all praises for the police department that brought a criminal to justice. Somehow, out of nowhere a social media post claimed that I was involved in this guy's encounter.

The media picked up the story and a week after the encounter, I was summoned by investigating agencies for an inquiry.

"Sir, if this was a fake encounter, do you feel it was the right thing to have been done by the police? Was there your involvement as well? Do you think you are above the law?" A female reporter from a Hindi news channel poked the mic into my face as I came out after a three-hour-long inquiry. I decided to send out a message and no matter how controversial it might become, I wanted to speak my heart out that day.

I stopped and looked towards the journalist who stood

there, defiant and ready to pounce upon me the moment I said anything.

"I ask all of you today, how would anyone of you feel if your five-year-old daughter was raped and strangled to death with bare hands? Try feeling the pain that a girl or woman goes through when someone rapes her. The fact is sometimes things need to be done to strike fear in the hearts of criminals. Such animals need to be killed without any mercy. This mentality needs to change that raping someone is OK in India, these animals must know that every girl or woman in India has as much right to live freely and without any fear as anyone of us. If agencies can prove this was a fake encounter and I was involved in the killing, hang me for this if you have to." I walked away as the journalists went into a frenzy.

The investigations did not reap any results. Even the investigative agencies did not poke into the case much. Every one of them knew it was a fake encounter but none of them wanted to give justice to a rapist, he didn't deserve one. I was declared innocent by the court a few months later.

A week after the judgment, I met a few civil engineers from Japan to understand more about developing planned townships. The idea was to understand how to build a fully developed and self-sustained township. I was consciously making efforts to change the way I thought as a politician.

You can change your behavior as a person but deep down inside, your core remains the same. No matter how hard you try, your default personality settings will never change. Deep down I was once a guy from a lower-middle-class family and had seen the struggle from very close quarters. The rape incident hit me so hard that my entire approach towards my role as an MLA had changed.

The happiness and satisfaction you feel when there is a smooth road to drive on, when there is clean water to drink, when you don't feel scared as a parent when your child goes to school, when a girl can walk back to her home without people staring or eve-teasing her is what describes a government's success.

The plan was simple, do not go against the system but ensure the development keeps happening at a steady pace. You cannot fight a crocodile in the water.

The engineers were busy showing me the PPT when Suraj walked in.

He handed me over his cell phone – "Someone wants to talk to you bhaiya."

"Hello," I said.

"Sahib, people call you a guy with a dark soul. If that is the case, you are a dark-souled saint to me."

The parents of the girl who was raped and killed had called to let me know that they had forgiven me.

I smiled and hung up the call. Finally, I felt like I could breathe a little better.

"The Dark Souled Saint." I smiled at the new name people had given me. Excusing myself from the meeting, I walked into the lawn and pulled out my eleventh cigarette.

Cigarette Number Eleven

THE END OF DELHI CHAPTER

Two months in Delhi had passed away in a blink. Even before any of them could realize it, Delhi changed my friends.

Neatly combed hair had now transformed to 'spike cut', T-shirts with collars were now replaced by round neck T-shirts with senseless quotations printed on them, low waist jeans with blade marks all around to give it a rugged look, deodorants instead of powder, sunglasses and a lot more to show off.

From what I could make out, Bhagat and Neeraj had embraced Delhi's culture with both hands. On the other hand, I was finding it hard to adjust or change myself. I was a fashion disaster as people called me on the campus. I dressed simply, still carrying the same hairstyle and the same pair of simple blue jeans that went well with white sports shoes.

Neeraj had gone a complete makeover and Bhagat now looked more like a member of some rock band rather than a student. His earlobes sport a stud and a tattoo on his left hand proclaiming 'KHALSA'.

He had realized that Sikhs in Delhi are style statements, a live-hearted clan that set its own rules. The girls had themselves changed a lot, short skirts, tight jeans, and even shorter T-shirts. I remember Aanchal once wearing a top to college that slightly exposed her navel. Except for a few magazines and pictures, I'd never seen a girl's navel.

I had come to college after a three-day sick leave. The weather, water, and food in Delhi made it more difficult for me to adjust. I walked up to the canteen to find Palak sitting with Rohit. This guy had managed to get himself transferred to the same college.

Palak wore a green Kurti to college that day. The bangles on her wrists, earrings, nose stud, and her hair untied but beautifully done. She outclassed every other girl on the campus that day. I looked at Rohit and passed a fake smile as Palak walked up and wrapped her arms around me.

She was one soul on Earth I could bet was happy to see me. I hugged her back gently as Rohit kept his eyes fixed on both of us.

"Abhay, at least come dressed properly to college. Look at you, seems as if you just got up and came," Palak said softly. She still owned every bit of me.

"I would have had you been my girlfriend. Don't have any motivation to dress up you see." I cloaked the truth as a joke and put up a fake smile on my face but Palak being Palak exactly knew what was going through my heart.

"I am happy with Rohit and I cannot go a day without seeing you. Maybe I'll just have an affair with both of you." Palak had a devilish grin on her face, which still defined innocence.

After five months in Delhi, one fine day I realized that

each of my friends had moved ahead in their life whereas I was still there, just existing.

Out of all six of us, I looked more like the son of a farmer, sometimes even wearing an unironed/torn t-shirt or shirt, and a pair of rubber slippers to college. I hardly paid attention to myself.

Soon the results were evident. A lot of students avoided me and a few of them had a name for me, 'Dehati' or a subtle term for the word 'villager'.

Imagine your friends turning up for a movie, all nicely dressed up and you show up in a plain brown unironed shirt, not tucked in, black full pants that had not been washed for ages, and of course, slippers. After a few more incidents when I'd turn up inappropriately dressed for some occasion or get-together, my friends started leaving me out of such plans.

Palak too would hardly bother to call me up or inform me. She'd invite her other good-looking friends. It wasn't that I couldn't afford clothes or fancy stuff, only that I had a bad dressing sense and never cared too much about how I looked in front of others. Bhagat stayed out most of the time, partying the whole night with friends. He sometimes turned up to our room after weeks.

I didn't mind, after all, having an empty room was better than having a drunk friend who'd call up his girlfriend late into the night and shout at her. Things had changed drastically in the past few months.

Palak now had her circle of friends and was involved in a lot of co-curricular activities, heading college clubs, editing college magazines, representing our college in different fests, etc. She could barely manage time and we would only meet during a few occasional lectures. She'd keep looking at her books, only to hide the guilt she felt for not having enough time for me.

Palak knew that I had been outcast by my friends and she should have been there with me, but she wasn't. She tried her best to shake off the big circle around her, but something or the other dragged her back. Her group of friends now consisted of around twenty-odd girls and boys and she had to entertain all of them.

The startling difference was that even to meet or hang out as a group together, all six of us had to plan a couple of weeks before. Each one of them was trying to prove how busy they were. I sometimes wondered what would happen once all of us started working.

I decided to stay silent and watch. There is a rule, what goes up comes down and nothing is permanent. Delhi gives you its share of experiences, when it is good, you'll love the place, but when it's bad, you'd want to end yourself at times. Delhi is a place for people possessing a tough mental and emotional level. I somehow knew all of them would need each other eventually.

After a few more months, Bhagat moved out, deciding to stay with his new group of college friends. That decision hit me hard. I knew change had arrived; only that I wasn't prepared for it. Bhagat now found his new group of friends far more happening than a simple guy from Jamshedpur.

To him, I was nothing more than a pre-historic relic from Jamshedpur that had to be done away with to move ahead. I never tried to improve my relationship with

Bhagat. In- fact, letting him go looked far more feasible to me.

He tried acting apologetic, but I knew Bhagat too well. Even after the entire communication gap between us, he was still unsure about his decision to move out. He expected me to stop him, but I didn't. I instead helped him with his luggage and packing. Bhagat tried starting a conversation but every time our male ego stopped us from sorting out issues between us.

Right after Bhagat left, the room started haunting me. It wasn't that staying alone was an issue. As such, Bhagat rarely used to show up, but then, the feeling of emptiness was even worse. I could no longer see his stuff around me, something that used to give me a feeling of my friend still being around. Suddenly, I had four empty walls around me to look at.

For the next week, I used to enter my room late at night and quickly go off to sleep. During the daytime, I'd quietly sit at some bus stop for hours, watching the traffic, grabbing an occasional burger or some rolls from a nearby street food vendor. I started bunking lectures, sometimes, not going to college for days. I would keep looking at the blank screen on my phone, expecting at least one of my five friends to give me a call, but no one had time. Even back in the room, I'd be busy watching some movie or listening to songs, I didn't want to realize the fact that Bhagat no longer stayed with me.

Soon the worse started happening. To run away from this depression, I walked the extra mile to make new friends. It so happened that a couple of months back, I had helped one of the college union guys during exams. I'd practically passed on my entire answer sheet to him. On coming out of the examination hall, he pulled me aside and said,

"Never seen you before? Hi, I am Navin Tanwar, Vice President of the Student's Union. Thanks for saving me back there, let me know if you ever need my help. I am always around."

I didn't pay much attention then and even though we had exchanged numbers, I had casually saved his contact.

As I was looking for some company that would give me a much-needed break from my self-imposed exile, one night, I bluntly dialed Navin Tanwar's number.

"Halllo." A husky voice answered the call.

"Hello, is this Navin?" I replied.

"Yes, who's this?"

"Hi Navin, I am Abhay, remember, the guy who helped you with the statistics paper?"

"Who??" Navin tried recalling.

"Tall guy, spects? Remember?" I replied, already embarrassed that he didn't recognize me.

"PHONE RAKH, C**TIYE," Navin Tanwar replied, making it clear that he didn't recognize me.

I quickly obeyed his orders, disconnecting the call instantly; poking a drunk Haryanvi is not always a great idea. Switching off the lights, I quietly lay in darkness, wondering the whole time if helping people these days was a bad idea.

I was looking towards the ceiling fan, thinking about Palak, Anisha, Bhagat, old times, etc., when my phone rang. Five months since I had heard my phone ring more than once a day (one call came from my parents).

I looked at my cell phone, it was Navin Tanwar. Confused and scared, I finally pressed the green button.

"Are you the same guy who'd helped me pass the statistics exam?" Navin's tongue fumbled as he spoke.

"Yes sir," I replied, not sure if he was drinking whiskey or some memory-improving syrup.

"*Arey Bhai*, where are you? I missed you so much. You are Bond, James Bond. Thanks for helping *bhai*. Where are you now?"

"Ok, so it's some brand of whiskey and not memory-improving drugs." I quietly said to myself after hearing a heartwarming speech from Navin.

"I am at my place," I replied.

"And where is that?" Navin wanted the address.

Like a parrot, I blabbered out the entire address to Navin. Within the next half an hour, an open Jeep stood outside the building where I used to live.

Navin walked into my room with two bottles of whiskey and three more guys. Till then, I was a guy who'd never tasted alcohol in his life and smoking was still evil.

When he left, the next evening, I had puked twice, smoked seven cigarettes, and had finished half a bottle of whiskey. The devil himself had baptized me.

Navin and his group soon accepted me as a part of their league. The only difference was, that all of them were heavy smokers and drinkers. Therefore, I swam across oceans of whiskey, beer, rum, weed, and cigarettes to seek peace for my weak soul.

Intoxication substituted Neeraj, Bhagat, Anisha, Aanchal, and Palak.

For weeks, I would disappear, most of the time roaming around with this new circle of friends I had. We didn't have a word called plan in our life. Sometimes I'd wake up in some hotel situated on a mountain in Uttarakhand.

Navin would then inform me that I passed out in some bar the previous night and they were too drunk to realize that Gangotri was some odd six hundred kilometers from New Delhi. They would drive through the night while I would lie senseless in the backseat of their car.

Once we reached there, the order of the day would be rolling cigarettes, drinking beer, enjoying the scenic beauty around, and driving up those zig-zag roads leading to the top of the mountain. I only used to attend my family's phone calls; the rest did not matter to me at all.

Such was the schedule that sometimes when I woke up, the sun had risen and set two times. I generally used to stay more in Navin's car as compared to my room.

I was in the bad company of good souls, forgetting my existence. There is though one fact about such guys, they stick together. They stand for each other, sharing feelings and problems, even if that means driving down thirty kilometers on a pitch-black night, just to pick up a heavily drunk friend from a disco or a bar.

Soon, I became one of them, picking up fights at the bar, vomiting on the streets after drinking heavily, working out heavily in the gym, and dressing up like them.

Navin stood for the post of the Student's Union President the same year and I along with the rest of his friends campaigned for Navin with all our might. Soon, I was an active and important part of university politics. From organizing campaigns and rallies to beating up the opposition party's candidate and supporters, I did everything.

I went to jail sometimes as well with Navin. He had by then become like a brotherly figure to me. I enjoyed power and respect from a large mass of students. What I avoided was going back to my college or going back to my past.

Finally, the results were declared, and Navin Tanwar was voted to power by a huge margin. I was the next in line to Navin, the one who would listen to the problems of students and communicate the same to Navin who'd take up the matter with higher authorities at the university. I continued living my life as an influential guy at the university, enjoying the newly tasted power.

Even before I realized it, Delhi had one more spoilt brat added to its endless list.

Reality hits you at some point in your life. It was a Sunday morning. I was back in my room after almost fifteen days. I woke up around the afternoon and stood in front of the mirror. It had been around four months since I had seen myself in a mirror.

It wasn't a good sight. Long hair and a full-fledged beard. I took off my shirt and carefully observed myself. A lean muscular physique and a tattoo on my neck. I didn't even remember when I got it for myself.

Dark circles below my eyes and a heart that hardly cared about feelings. It had been more than six months since I had been to college or attended a lecture. Navin was lying flat on the sofa.

For a change, I decided to go to college that day. I wanted to see Palak. I walked into the college campus, looking around, searching for the same old faces.

For the first time I managed to get some attention, people looking at me as if a fresh style statement just walked into the campus. Long hair, a beard, a leather jacket, low-waist jeans, and a pair of sunglasses made it hard to be recognized.

I checked the classroom but didn't find anyone, library – was empty, roamed around the campus for a while but found none of my old friends. I decided to grab something to eat from the canteen.

As I walked into the canteen, my eyes scanned for an empty table. I quietly walked up to the counter and pointed towards the orange juice pack kept for display in the fridge. Grabbing a sandwich, I occupied a corner table.

Suddenly my eyes fell upon a girl who looked familiar. She looked pale, with dark circles below her eyes as if she had been crying for weeks. It was Palak, around her sat a bunch of guys and girls busy joking and laughing, while she could hardly manage to put up a smile.

I just knew she was in pain and irrespective of whatever might have happened between us, Palak was religion to me, still. I felt some water on my cheeks, I didn't realize but just the very sight of Palak had moistened my eyes.

Next to her sat Rohit. He frequently kept touching Palak all the time. He would keep his hands on her thighs, touch her waist while talking, and play with her hair, and Palak quietly allowed him to do so, as if she had surrendered, hardly responding. Watching someone else touch Palak was like watching your flesh being eaten away by vultures.

My blood reached its boiling point, picking up a fight and performing well in it was now more of a daily job for me. I looked around, hoping to find a stick, bat, hockey stick, or anything I could use to smash his head with. I still didn't get up, fearing I might murder this guy. Soon, Palak got up and began leaving when this guy held her hands, signaling her to sit. She shook off his hands and began walking towards the exit when he came running, holding her waist from behind and pulling her towards himself.

"Leave me, Rohit," Palak shouted.

"Shut up and stop acting as if I never touched you before, we will leave together, and you are staying with me tonight. Do you understand?" Rohit shouted back.

"Why don't you let me go, Rohit, please I beg you." Palak folded her hands in front of him, crying.

I recalled the time when Palak walked into our class crying when we were kids. I have been in love with her since then. I kept looking like a spectator, like many others.

Palak looked around for help, her so-called friends not interfering as well. Rohit too had changed. He had managed to become the joint secretary of the same student party that we had managed to defeat when Navin was contesting elections.

I never had a faceoff with Rohit even though I had been searching for an opportunity ever since school. Today, God finally handed over to me that one opportunity to knock the hell out of this guy.

Palak was still looking around when her eyes met mine and everything went blank for a moment. She took no time to recognize me. After six months, this was the first time we were seeing each other. We both had stopped calling or texting each other long ago.

Palak's face immediately lit up. There are moments when you just know that things would just fall into place now. I'd never realized how much we both meant to each other but at that moment there, I could hear Palak's heartbeat.

Pushing Rohit aside, she walked up to my table and stood right in front of me. Wiping off tears from her eyes, she smiled.

"Where were you? Six months Abhay, you were gone for six months," said Palak.

I got up and held her hands gently. To see Palak like this, weak, numb, scared; and emotional wreckage was beyond something I could stand.

"Where is Bhagat? What about Anisha and Aanchal?" I asked, trying to act as if I was hardly bothered about what had just happened.

"Oh man, Abhay, you look so different. Been gymming and all? Excuse me, but I need to talk to Palak. She is so upset with me," Rohit interrupted from behind.

"Sure," I said, signaling him to go ahead.

Palak could not believe how much I had changed. There was a time I would have protected her as my own and now, I was allowing a dog to drag her away.

She turned to leave, tears rolling down her eyes, a feeling of helplessness visible on her face.

I looked at her and smiled.

Palak stopped. After ages, we spoke again, without speaking. She smiled back, knowing what I meant.

I walked out of the canteen, Palak still sitting with Rohit. She kept looking at me with hopeful eyes and I saw a sense of relief in her eyes. That was more than enough for me to go against the world for her if I had to.

She knew me too well, I had everything planned and yes, Rohit would be paying severely. I was surprised by the level of trust Palak always had in me, irrespective of how bad things were between us. We never shared what we felt for each other, but our feelings were too loud to go unheard.

Outside the canteen stood Bhagat, Anisha, and Aanchal, all of them had been witnesses to what had just happened and maybe must have seen worse before. As I walked past Bhagat, I noticed a plaster on his left hand.

His roommates for some reason had beaten up Bhagat. Bhagat had become a laughing stock and a punching bag for his friends due to his nature. After all, how could someone understand that innocent emotional fool he was?

They used to make him cry and then enjoy watching him cry. It's hard to believe, but that's a harsh reality many guys like Bhagat still face. Slowly, the guy who becomes a laughing stock starts losing his confidence and might be beaten up as well if he protests.

From what I knew, his friends had once stripped Bhagat naked and pushed him onto the streets. He was too drunk to realize what was going on. Anisha and Aanchal too were teased; in fact, Anisha was manhandled by Bhagat's friends at some disco they had gone to together. Bhagat never managed to protest because he was too weak and tortured to raise his voice.

Neeraj was too busy studying to afford distractions like these. In addition, the fact that he studied in a far superior college disconnected him from everyone. They kept looking at me as I quietly walked out of the college gate, deeply moved by what I had seen.

As night approached, I once again submerged myself in alcohol, which by now had become my second lifeline. As other devotees of alcohol slowly surrendered, sleeping like the dead, I quietly went onto the roof of my building.

I looked towards the dark blue skies, roughly scattered with stars as sprinkles on carbon paper, thinking about Palak.

Despite Palak being caught on the wrong side of things, I had to get her out of the mess she had created for herself. Finally, I closed my eyes, dozing off on the roof itself.

It was somewhere around the afternoon when I woke up. My head ached, and my throat had gone dry. I walked downstairs to my room; others had just woken up as well.

"Navin, I need to settle some scores with a guy," I said.

Navin quickly understood I was troubled over something. He reached for a bottle of water gulping it down in one go.

"Let's do it then." Navin stood up, reaching for his shirt.

"Rakesh, get the car keys. Abhay, meet me at the college canteen at around four in the evening." Navin winked as he said those lines.

Soon, two cars packed with boys armed to the teeth with hockey sticks, baseball bats, stumps, etc., left for my college.

The plan was simple; they would hang around until I picked up a fight with Rohit. As soon as the fight started, they would join me as a backup. Rohit was all set to see his end.

"You guys wait here, let me try this the peaceful way first," I instructed Navin to wait for me outside the college gate as I stepped out of his car.

Navin gave me a disappointed look, he was already excited about the prospect of a probable fight. It was around half past four in the evening. I walked into the canteen and as expected, I saw Palak surrounded by vultures. I walked up to her table.

"Rohit, if you don't mind can I speak to Palak for a minute? Has something to do with her family." I tried acting as good as possible.

"Yes, sure you can, why would I mind? After all, you both are childhood friends," Rohit replied in the best possible manner he could.

Palak walked outside the canteen with me. I exactly did what she expected me to do, to come and get her.

"How far has your relationship gone, be clear?" I said.

Palak looked down, sobbing. She was running out of words. I took her hands and looked at her wrists; they had several blade marks on them. I could never imagine Palak in pain.

All these years, I had been very particular about not

hurting her emotionally. It's not hard to imagine what I felt looking at those wrists. I controlled my emotions and continued.

"Did you both get physical..." I still hadn't completed the sentence when she gave a slight nod. It meant yes.

How does it feel when you come to know someone else has already claimed the only girl you loved? The answer is numb. Your instant reaction would be to start crying cause if you don't, that shock might kill you. I moved a step back, turned my face away, and with all the force and courage I had held back my tears. Palak held my hand tightly as if trying to apologize because she could not say sorry. I closed my eyes, trying to get hold of myself.

"Abhay, help me or I'll die. Rohit is a butcher." That's all Palak managed to say before she finally clung to my T-shirt and cried her heart out.

I was still trying to console Palak when I saw Bhagat standing at some distance. Next to him stood Anisha. Bhagat managed a smile, trying to conceal the amount of guilt he had within him for leaving me. Anisha wiped her eyes and walked up to Palak, trying to console her.

"Look after her, I'll be right back," I instructed Bhagat and Anisha to calm down Palak.

Even before I could walk back inside, I saw Rohit coming out of the canteen towards us. Watching Palak cling to me and crying did not go down well with him.

"So, did her father ask you to hold her hands, or has he instructed you to fuck her as well?" Rohit chuckled, his friends enjoying his comment as well.

"No, but he instructed me to fuck you." I didn't give

Rohit much time after that. Soon, my other friends joined in as well. Baseball bats, stumps, hockey sticks, and rods were finally put to some other use apart from the sport they are generally used in.

Palak kept looking from a distance as I dragged Rohit in front of the entire college. Within a few minutes, the news had reached the college dean. He took no time to inform the police. I was still beating Rohit when two constables held me from behind. I didn't stop, the demon within me had lost all control. I continued beating him until I was forced into the jeep along with Navin and a few more guys. I still managed to land a few decisive kicks on Rohit's face. It took four constables and three good rifle butt hits to control me.

As I sat in the Jeep, Palak ran up to me. She reached for my hand and tried wiping off the blood seeping from my knuckles. I held her hand, still looking at an unconscious Rohit lying in a pool of blood.

"This is it, watch over yourself Palak," I shouted as the police van sped away. Rohit's friends took him to a hospital. He had a few broken bones including ribs, arms, a thighbone, a broken nose, and a bleeding forehead. We were lucky his father wasn't an influential man; otherwise, I would have been narrating this story from jail.

We were let off after a couple of hours, thanks to Navin's influential network. I was rusticated from college, but the important part was that Palak had her life back.

Palak wanted to meet me but I declined, the reason was simple, I didn't want to see Palak again. That girl I fell in love with in school, who understood and cared for me was now gone. I could not come to terms with the fact that I was not her first choice.

Even though we had so much unspoken, unsaid between us, why did Palak never tell me anything? Why did she choose to stay with Rohit even after all that he did to her? How come my love for her lost out to a guy who was ok watching her cry and bleed? I felt I had been cheated.

Palak knew that she had lost that control, authority, and respect she once commanded over me. She presented my case to the dean as well, who never allowed me to rejoin, although he allowed my character certificate to remain clean.

Once released from jail, I made up my mind to quit Delhi. This place has given me every possible experience. However, before leaving the city I had to set a few things right.

Navin and I ensured Bhagat's roommates knew he was our friend. Over the next few weeks, my only job was to scare the shit out of his roommates.

Meanwhile, I decided to restart my studies. Apart from filling out various college forms, I also started appearing for multiple entrance exams. Finally, I landed a call letter from BIT Mesra, Ranchi for their BBA course.

I booked my tickets for Jamshedpur and a couple of days before leaving Delhi, I decided to meet my school friends for one last time. We went for an outing and after ages, all of us enjoyed ourselves and laughed our hearts out. I avoided Palak as much as I could and she did not force herself upon me, she knew me too well.

The day got over and we decided to continue the party at my place. As Bhagat stepped into the flat, it hit him that moving out was his biggest mistake. Later that night, Anisha cried her heart out. She told me about how one of Bhagat's friends had manhandled her when all three of them went out for a party and when Bhagat protested, they not only beat him up but also broke his arm. The reason Bhagat was sporting a plaster.

It wasn't like I was the Batman roaming around, punching criminals, and delivering justice to the needy but Bhagat was my brother. How would you react if someone broke your brother's arms?

That night everyone stayed back at my place. When everyone else was sleeping, I tiptoed my way to the balcony and lit a cigarette, looking at the dark, overcast skies above me, wondering how life changed so fast around all of us.

Guess Palak had been waiting for this moment when we both could talk to each other in silence. She walked up to the balcony and closed the door behind her.

"Does uncle know you smoke?" Palak would just not give up exercising her right upon me.

"No," I replied, taking another drag.

"Throw it, now." She looked at me, those wide yet beautiful eyes staring right through my soul.

I threw away the cigarette without another word.

"Why do you listen to everything I say and everything I don't?" Palak asked as the moonlight fell upon her face.

I kept quiet. I wanted to tell Palak everything. How I felt for her, how much she meant to me, how my life once used to revolve around her and still does, and how it killed me watching her choose Rohit over me. Instead, I decided to divert the topic.

"Stay away from Rohit if you can, I'll not be around always to save you." I looked away, did not want to see her face as I said those lines.

"Why, where are you going?" She exactly asked me the question I wanted to avoid.

"Back to Jamshedpur, I am leaving the day after tomorrow," I informed Palak who by now was gripping the railing and looking towards the moon, trying to avoid me from watching tears in her eyes.

"Palak, I can't do this anymore. I have become something else now and how do I explain to you… anyways leave." I was about to say that I loved her when Palak cut me short.

"Don't go, please." Palak still kept looking towards the moon.

I could see teardrops roll down from her cheeks and even though I wanted to wipe away each one of them, I stopped myself.

My stay in Delhi was coming to an end and with each passing moment, I wanted to just hold Palak for a few moments and let this feeling seep in that I might not be able to hold her like this ever again.

I disobeyed Palak for the first time and holding her arms pulled her close to me. She didn't protest and simply buried her head in my chest. The next few minutes that we held each other for was something that left a mark on my soul. That was true love, those five minutes of saying absolutely nothing and simply holding each other is what every lover in this world craves.

Palak let her grip loose and walked inside. I remained outside, looking at the same moon.

The next morning Navin and I picked up Bhagat's roommate who had misbehaved with Anisha. Bhagat, Navin, and I watched him take a butt-naked lap in a park before slapping the hell out of him. The happiness and satisfaction in Bhagat's eyes were more than enough for me.

Later that evening, I left with Navin for the railway station. Even though Navin was a strong guy both physically and emotionally, he got all emotional about me leaving Delhi. I'd never seen this guy cry, but that day, he hugged me as his own, as if he knew we'd never be meeting again.

"We'll meet bro, don't worry. Delhi is in India." I tried calming down an emotional Navin.

"Can't you stay? I'll get you back into the college bro, it's a word." Navin tried his best to convince me to stay back.

It wasn't that I was happy leaving behind everything in Delhi but staying away from Palak would give me a far more peaceful life. As I occupied my window seat, Navin waved me a final goodbye. He then turned his back on me and was lost among the crowd. As the train left the platform, I kept looking at the signboard proclaiming NEW DELHI as it slowly grew smaller before I finally lost sight.

Memories of Delhi, a few I had carried along with me and the rest few, lay scattered across the narrow lanes of Malviya Nagar leading to my room, the backseat of Navin's car, that empty street in front of Palak's hostel where we'd sometimes walk together for a few minutes and a college that took away my friends and majorly, my innocence.

I had lied to Palak that my train was the day after tomorrow, and I'd meet her before going. I wanted to leave Delhi silently.

As the train left the station, I received a text from Palak; it read, "Goodbye and take care. Thanks for wearing that red jacket, keep it close, guess it's going to be the only thing keeping us connected." Palak had gifted me a red Manchester United jacket on my birthday. I still remember how excited and happy I was to see my favorite football club's logo on it.

Palak was there at the station, only that she chose to let me go…silently.

CHALLENGING NANDITA'S EGO

"Coming soon in Faridabad, first state-of-the-art steel factory by Singhania Global Steel. Chief Guest – Hon'ble Chief Minister of Haryana"

The advertisement adored the front page of every leading newspaper in the city. On the top right corner of the page was the Chief Minister's smiling photograph and on the top left corner Naman Singhania and Nandita Singhania's made-for-each-other picture. The pride in her eyes boiled my blood to the last drop.

It seemed as if she just walked into my territory and decided to claim it as if I was a nobody. Letting Nandita lay the foundation stone for her dream project in my constituency was like allowing her to dig a nail in my heart.

I was still looking at the advertisement wondering how I could have missed something this big when my cell phone rang. It was Rajput.

"Good morning Bhaiya." The banker in me still lived.

"You did not tell me about the Singhania steel plant?" Rajput came straight to the point.

"Because Chief Minister Sahib kept me out of the loop. None of the ministers knew about this as well. Not sure how the land allocation for such a big project took place without consulting the local MLA from the constituency, that too when I am part of the ruling party here." I defended myself.

"Hmm, this new Chief Minister is very good friends with the Singhanias. The project is supposed to be a cash cow and his relatives have stakes in the steel plant. This Rana guy turned out to be extra smart." Rajput fumed; he too had been kept out of the loop for the project.

"Abhay, make sure this Chief Minister realizes who rules Faridabad. I'll ensure you have enough support to do so." Rajput passed on the instructions before disconnecting the call.

However, what Rajput did not know was that it was not the Chief Minister whom I was bothered about. It was Nandita.

Being part of the system has its advantages. The five-thousand-acre project, that too when the Chief Minister was getting a cut of one percent, could not have been approved without passing some benefit to the Singhanias. The only question was how much.

The government had offered the land at discounted rates to Singhanias but that could not be made into an issue because the land belonged to the government and the government chose development over making a profit out of land prices. The project further promised large-scale employment, which was again tending to the biggest problem faced by Haryana as a state, unemployment.

I could have created small troubles near the site but that would again be dealt with by the police because a small protest or agitation is not enough to upset a multimillion-dollar project. I needed something big enough to shake an empire to its very roots.

A week later, as per protocol, I had to attend the foundation stone laying ceremony. Not attending the ceremony wasn't an option because the Chief Minister and other dignitaries would be present in the full media glare. It would take just one reporter to notice that the youngest politician in the government and the sitting MLA from the constituency was not present for the inauguration, kicking off multiple stories and theories.

Irrespective of whether your ex-girlfriend gets married to or is dating someone else, the moment you get to know that she might be meeting or seeing you soon, you will do whatever it takes to ensure that when the moment arrives, you look nothing less than the best.

It's not just restricted to letting her feel that maybe she made the wrong choice but also letting her know that you instead became more awesome after she left. Victory and justice, right there, standing beside you gentlemen.

During that one week, I went on a low-carb diet, began running, exercised till I dropped dead in the gym, had no sugar and salt, etc., and did everything humanly possible to reduce all that fat I had gained.

However, one week of effort versus one year of binging, you know the obvious winner in this case. I gave a final look in the mirror before leaving for the venue.

As I walked out toward the car, my driver walked up to open the door.

"Sahib, you look like a prince today," he said as I took the back seat.

Without wasting time, I took out a five hundred rupee note and handed it over to him. He had just given me confidence a hundred times more than what I was tipping him with.

I reached the venue fifteen minutes in advance. As per my sources, Nandita and her husband Naman had already arrived at the venue fifteen minutes back.

My supporters had assembled in the public area, very close to the media lobby. This was my chance to let everyone know that I was the king here. Rajput had ensured I had enough people waiting with posters and garlands in their hands.

It's all about how you can put up a great show in front of the masses. I was in sales once and the greatest skill set you pick up in a sales job is how to sell yourself. When you are in a position of power, people must perceive you as a humble, approachable but very strong leader. Unless you command their respect, the masses will not follow you.

Nandita and Naman were informed about my arrival and they had to wait along with other government officials at the venue entrance to greet me. I had gained huge popularity and publicity in my area because of all the work I was doing for people in general.

From beating up eve-teasers to meeting with people who used to come with their grievances, I had slowly become part of their day-to-day lives.

As my car stopped, people thronged and shouted my name as if God had arrived himself. To my surprise, apart from the staged group of supporters, there were far more people who had gathered to see me.

I was overwhelmed. You cannot buy loyalty, the crowd had familiar faces, people whom I had helped, women whom I got employed in factories, and children who were now studying because my efforts led to the reopening of a few government schools.

This was not a staged-up show, these were rather genuine people. Unlike other leaders who would just wave at their supporters, I decided to walk up to them and acknowledge the power they had given me.

The media had turned all their cameras towards me as I walked up to the people, shaking hands with as many people as I could. The cameramen ran towards me as the noise made by the crowd reached its highest level.

As Nandita stood with her husband, people began shouting slogans in my name. As I walked up to them, all that noise behind me, I could see Nandita get uncomfortable.

You know when you realize that out of two people in a relationship, who was the one responsible for its failure? When both their eyes meet each other after a long time one of them begins to avoid eye contact. That is when you know who was at fault.

I looked at Nandita as she took the garland in her hand to greet me. I am a tall guy, above six feet to be more specific and Nandita was just tall enough to reach to my chest. For her to put a garland around my neck, I had to bend in front of her.

I did not, instead, I just ignored her and walked across her to greet the other government officials. I could see the disbelief in Nandita's eyes as I ignored her existence. I was hardly bothered about how she felt, for me that moment when I slapped Nandita's ego hard was the best I had felt in a very long time.

Naman walked up to me and decided to strike up a conversation. Nandita had to stand next to both of us as the Chief Minister's arrival was expected any time soon.

"Guess I've seen you somewhere. Your face looks very familiar," Naman began.

"Yes, don't you remember him? He and I used to work in the same branch. The guy whom I told you about. Was not financially strong but was a good salesman? Sorry, I forgot your name," Nandita interrupted. Every word she spoke was like poison dripping from her tongue.

"You must be deaf then, listen to the crowd, you will know my name." I smiled. Nandita and I looked at each other with all the hate and I think we both simultaneously swore to destroy each other that day. She turned her face away even as I kept looking, wondering how beautiful she still looked. It was stunning that something so beautiful could be so dangerous.

The Chief Minister arrived a few minutes later and the whole media rushed to cover his arrival. I stayed behind, didn't want to be part of the ass-licking herd of people who thronged the Chief Minister as he stepped out of his car.

Naman and Nandita began walking along with the Chief Minister towards the main hall, which led to the six thousand acres of land dedicated to this project. As he climbed the stairs, he noticed me standing in a corner. Even though the Chief Minister kept me out of the loop for this project, one thing he still could not do was ignore me, Rajput's right-hand man.

He cut short the conversation with Naman and walked up to me, hugging me in full public glare. The supporters ensured this hug was made worth enough as the crowd once again jumped into action. Nandita and Naman kept looking at both of us, managing to keep a fake smile fixed on their faces. On the other hand, I was surprised by the sudden show of love by the Chief Minister.

The inauguration was finally over and soon all dignitaries were guided to a hall where a lavish party was organized for all the guests. The Chief Minister had to leave due to his busy schedule.

My work was done as well, so I decided to leave quietly. As I started leaving the venue, my eyes kept searching for Nandita. In a hall packed with thousands of people, I still managed to find her in a matter of seconds. She was busy talking to a group of ladies who belonged to elite business-class families. I silently looked at her for one last time and then walked out of the hall.

"Abhay," Nandita called for me from behind.

I stopped and turned, expecting the worst. I hated Nandita and she equally had the same feelings for me but when we both looked at each other, when our eyes met, there was this awkward moment of silence between us.

Even today, when I looked at her, there was a strange sense of belonging. In an ideal world scenario, if you'd just remove people, situations, society, and money, maybe she'd just walk up to me, confess that she was wrong and that maybe love after all was the only thing that mattered to her.

"You didn't congratulate me for setting up the biggest factory in YOUR Faridabad? Leaving silently as you always do?" Nandita looked at me, holding a glass of wine in her hand, the bloody Cleopatra that she always was.

There were a lot of people standing around both of us. Nandita tried getting back to me but then politics taught me one of the biggest life lessons, how to be shameless.

Walking up to Nandita, I took her glass and handed it over to Naman who was standing next to her.

"Come here my friend, congratulations." I held her waist and pulling her closer hugged her tight.

She had no other option but to hug me back so that it did not become obvious we were only trying to get back to each other.

Naman stood there smiling, happy about two old work colleagues hugging each other.

"Nandita, thank you for leaving me," I whispered in her ear before thanking Naman and leaving the venue.

As I sat in the car, I felt as if her scent had clung to me. I didn't even realize when I reached home, all the while replaying that moment when she could feel my breath on her skin and the shock with which her body trembled.

The next day there was a full-page article on the Faridabad factory launch. The highlight of the article was a line that read, "Word is Mr. Abhay was also instrumental in getting multi-million-dollar Singhania steel project to Faridabad. India needs progressive leaders like him."

I laughed my heart out after reading the article. It was evident Rajput had ensured he didn't let the Chief Minister take credit for the project. Instead, he set me up as the new future leader in Haryana state politics. I could only imagine how Nandita would feel when she read the article.

I took out my pack of cigarettes and gave it a careful look. It had been so many years since I bought it but my obsession with every cigarette kept on multiplying over the years. Had kept the packet intact ensuring I carried it with me everywhere.

It's not like I didn't buy cigarettes; I only didn't touch this packet. It was my precious and all these years, my bond with this packet only grew stronger.

I pulled out my twelfth cigarette.

Cigarette Number Twelve

THE RANCHI DIARIES

"Gentlemen, you see that girl. She will be your Bhabhi one day," Anand pointed towards the most beautiful girl walking on the Mesra campus.

Shreedhar and I looked at Anand then at Shikha and then at each other.

"Bro, eat something. You are hungry." I pushed a plate full of veg noodles towards Anand.

"You can stuff this in your ass brother and Shreedhar Mohta you better wipe that smirk off your face." Anand picked up the fork from the plate and pointed it towards us.

After dropping Delhi University, I got through BIT Mesra, Ranchi.

BIT Mesra is one of the top engineering colleges in India. They also offered management courses and I got admission into its regular three-year BBA course.

Ranchi was just a three-hour drive from Jamshedpur so I always had the option of going back home on weekends. Also, back in Jamshedpur, BIT Mesra is a huge brand. Irrespective of whatever course I was pursuing at that college, people would still think of me as a bright student who got through a very good college. It's funny how perceptions are so easily formed, especially if your hometown is a tier two or tier three city.

Far from Delhi, I had people around me who belonged to the same society and culture. No showoff, no spiked hairstyles, no T-shirts with F word, etc. Ranchi and Jamshedpur are two of the most prominent cities in Jharkhand. Both have the same culture, same people, same habits, same living style, and standards and I felt comfortable being who I was.

I had taken up accommodation in a paying guest facility close to my college. My two roommates luckily happened to be from the same college. Anand was in my course, the same batch while Kushal was in a different course but the same batch.

Out of all three of us, Kushal was the most disciplined and intelligent. Anand and I were just intelligent enough to score marks to get the first class.

While Anand and I did not belong to Ranchi, Shreedhar, whom we became friends with on our third day in college, was a local kid from Ranchi. He completed his schooling in Ranchi which gave him access to a lot of girls in college as they were his schoolmates.

While the rest of us would stand outside the college gate, looking at girls as they emerged from the campus, Shreedhar could be seen laughing, chatting, and eating with them.

Both Anand and Shreedhar belonged to well-off families and the three of us were the most formidable alliance of pranksters this college ever had. I had moved on, from Palak to Bhagat, I had wiped off everything. The best way to heal a wound is to clean it and let it get better with time.

Everything was perfect in my life and the last thing that I wanted to get into was another relationship. I was done with the love, responsibilities, and expectations that came along with it. The best part was that our college had separate batches for both girls and boys.

The morning batch was for girls and the afternoon batch was for guys. Boys and dogs were restricted from entering college premises from eight in the morning to noon.

Anand, Shreedhar, and many other guys who wore their hearts on their sleeves would however not give a rat's ass about the dean's order. They would walk inside the campus at eleven thirty, trying to look like the coolest kid on the block, their eyes searching for that one girl who would pass a smile at them. However, almost all of them would return empty-handed eventually.

Even though I had no interest in reaching college around eleven thirty, Shreedhar and Anand would drag me to an agreement.

Anand and Shreedhar would always walk ahead of me, I generally used to follow trying to avoid as much attention as possible. As the three of us would enter along with the other male students who were in search of their perfect mates, the girls would look at us as if militants had just stormed the canteen. Having been exposed to a much-advanced culture at Delhi University, I had a different opinion though.

I knew one golden rule for sure, never approach a

girl first. Observe her, be around her, let her first feel safe being around you, start a conversation, and then give it a try. If she likes you, she will eventually be yours, if she doesn't, don't take it personally on your male ego, leave with dignity.

Back in Ranchi, guys had a very different approach though. They would just not give up on a girl till the time she either called her parents, friends, or police for help. That is when Romeo would finally back off.

Shreedhar knew most of them so obviously, it was like just another day at work for him. Anand however was from a boy's school and seeing so many girls look straight at him put him in a very awkward situation. Still, he'd do his best to ensure confidence seeped out of every step he took.

We were sitting and binging on the full plate of veg noodles we had ordered when Shikha entered the canteen along with a group of seven to eight girls. I think it was love at first sight for Anand.

There are these moments when you look at someone and automatically think "Oh, there she is. I had been looking for her all this while." While Shreedhar and I kept convincing Anand to concentrate more on the noodles rather than Shikha, he was so confident about Shikha that he decided to marry her someday.

Shreedhar was in a relationship. His girlfriend, Sonam, was also part of the same group that Shikha was a part of as well.

"Mohta, why don't you ask Sonam to introduce me to Shikha?" Anand asked Shreedhar this question as if it was his birthright, which was denied to him.

"Yeah and get killed by her instead. There are so many girls in college, why the hell do you have to try on a girl who is part of my girlfriend's group?" Shreedhar's heart was already in his mouth. His girlfriend didn't like me and Anand much.

"Wow, that's a real man speaking there. So much for brotherhood." Anand clapped silently.

"Hey, don't you bring this on brotherhood and manhood?" Shreedhar shot back.

"Hey guys, stop fighting. Shree, he is right. You are goddamn committed, what about him? Look at the hope in his eyes." I pointed towards Anand's face who by then had hurled a couple of beautifully phrased abuses on me.

"Ok, I will go and tell her that Anand wants to talk to her. If Anand backs out, I'll ensure he stays single for the rest of his life."

"Ya ya asshole, I will not back out. You have my word. I dare you to go and convince Sonam about introducing me to Shikha." Anand looked at me and smiled valiantly as if he had just won a round against Shreedhar.

Shreedhar got up and looked at Anand as if giving him one last chance to think again. Anand reached for his pocket, took out his hand, and showed Shreedhar a middle finger. I quietly took a sip at the cold drink meanwhile, this was going to be fun.

"Don't let him run." Shreedhar passed me instructions as he walked towards a group of girls that consisted of Shikha and Sonam.

Anand started getting up slowly, his eyes were on Shreedhar as he reached Sonam and whispered something in her ear. She gave a puzzled look at Shreedhar and then looked at Anand who by now had got up and was about to leave.

"Where my friend, sit down? The worst is yet to come." I held Anand's arm and dragged him to remain seated.

"You guys are my roommates, my wingman bro, listen let me run away today and I promise you a lifetime supply of free beer." Anand would have shared half of his property that day.

Though free beer was a very lucrative proposal but then weighing it against an opportunity to watch Anand talk to a girl, was priceless. I decided to side with Shreedhar.

"Sit man, she is just a girl, beautiful, confident, and most importantly sought after by most guys on the campus. You are going to be just fine. Maybe a slap or two on your cheeks and that will be it. Chill buddy." I did some poisonous pep talk with Anand.

"I don't need enemies Abhay, I have you." Anand knew there was no point, I wouldn't let him run.

I was looking at Anand's expressions and laughing when we saw Shreedhar walk towards both of us along with Sonam and Shikha. My eyes turned towards Anand who was now suppressing his smile and looking for a place to hide.

"Shikha, this is Anand and he wants to talk to you." I don't know how but Shreedhar had convinced Sonam to let Anand speak to Shikha for five minutes.

"Anand, make sure it's just five minutes, and if Shikha comes back running to me crying, both you and Shreedhar will face the worst nightmare you ever did in your lives."

Sonam warned Anand and Shreedhar, while I picked up my cold drink and walked towards the counter to clear the bill.

"You wanted to talk." Shikha began the conversation, figuring out Anand had just lost his voice.

"Friends? Can we?" Anand managed to say only this much.

"No," Shikha answered to the point.

"Only friends, no other intention, I promise," Anand insisted.

"Why should I be friends with you?" Shikha was probing Anand like an intelligence officer to a terrorist.

"What's the harm? I am not proposing to you or something." Anand replied, this time more confidently.

"Ok, just friends. You ask for anything beyond this and it will be the end of it." Shikha laid down her rules very clearly.

"Agreed." Anand smiled. He knew he had put a foot in the door.

Over the next few weeks, Anand and Shikha spoke a lot over the phone. That barrier of just friends remained, only that it got weaker with time.

It was a Saturday. Kushal and I were discussing something rubbish when Anand entered the room. He was drunk and looked crestfallen.

"I proposed Shikha over the phone guys. I told her that I liked her and cannot do this friend thing anymore." Anand looked at both of us, with chewing gum in his mouth.

"And?" I asked.

"She cried, said she always was aware of my intentions, and disconnected the call."

I figured out from where exactly the crestfallen look came on his face.

"It's fine buddy, I am getting you more beer tonight." I tried consoling Anand.

"Get some juice for me please," Kushal added.

"Should I get you milk with Cerelac in it?" Anand always made fun of Kushal when it came to drinks. Kushal didn't smoke and drink and that's why we called him a saint.

I got up to leave for the liquor shop when Anand continued, "She called me after twenty minutes though and said she tried but can't stay away from me. So, guess I am officially committed guys." Anand's facial expressions transformed from crestfallen to a full-fledged celebration.

Shreedhar joined us shortly and celebrations followed shortly. We triple-rode on Anand's bike to Shikha's house later that night.

"Come near the window once please, I want to see you." Anand stood outside Shikha's house at around twelve in the night. Shreedhar and I were at some distance, sitting on the bike, laughing about the fact that the once shy Anand Agarwal had now big enough balls to stand right below his girlfriend's house and speak to her over the phone.

Shikha came to the window and waved at Anand. Both blew flying kisses at each other and she signaled Anand to leave. I started the bike, and Shreedhar sat, leaving enough space for Anand to fit. However, Anand was drunk, and as most Romeos do, he wanted to create history that day.

He shouted, "Brother, I told you, I'll marry her someday."

Anand was happy and excited beyond control and we were happy for him. We hooted and cheered for Anand. "BRAVO TIGER," I shouted when suddenly our eyes fell on the same window where Shikha had appeared a few minutes back. It was Shikha's father and he was looking at all three of us, especially Anand.

Shreedhar ran towards Anand, dragging him towards the bike. I kept looking at Shikha's father, smiling and laughing, shamelessly.

"Good evening and bye father-in-law," Anand shouted as we sandwiched him between us and vanished into the dark and silent streets of Ranchi.

A few days later, I returned to Jamshedpur for the Durga Puja vacation. It was always nostalgic coming back to Jamshedpur. There were so many memories this city carried that no matter how much you tried avoiding it, you still would end up getting nostalgic. It was a bright summer morning. I decided to take a casual stroll around my colony.

While walking towards the market, I decided to casually take a stroll down an old but familiar road leading to Shefali's apartment. I looked towards her balcony, hoping that maybe I'd find her standing there. It was empty, except for a few flowerpots and clothes hanging from the cloth line, there was no one.

I started walking back towards my home, but for some reason, decided to look back again, one last time.

Suddenly, a girl walked into the balcony with a notebook in her hand. She was busy reading and memorizing something when her eyes fell on me, standing right across the street. At first, she ignored me and walked inside her room.

I stood there, hoping that she would recognize me because I for sure could never forget that pretty face of hers. I saw her pause for a moment and suddenly rush towards the balcony again, this time with a smile on her face and a shine in her eyes.

I couldn't believe my luck. Shefali was in town as well. It had been close to two years since we both had seen and spoken to each other. She glided down her apartment's stairs and came running towards me. Shefali stood in front of me, smiling, trying hard to control herself but emotions got the better of her.

"Hi, how come you are here? It's good to see you." She extended her hands, trying hard not to hug me. I smiled, wondering if she could ever not act strong.

"Come here." I hugged Shefali warmly as she melted in my arms. Sometimes, what is more, important is to understand what the other person wants without him or her having to tell everything to you.

Shefali stepped back and looked straight into my eyes.

"One year and ten months Abhay and you did not even bother asking, how was I?" Shefali was furious at me for disappearing.

I did not have an answer, but she did not expect me to return so abruptly into her life again.

"I am sorry but trust me, these one year ten months

have not been kind to me either. Go out for a coffee with me?" I smiled as she nodded in approval.

Destiny had once again turned to the page in my life, which had Shefali's name written all over it.

FOUR BULLETS

My popularity as a new-age politician was slowly rising. Two years as a politician taught me a lot. The way I looked at people and their problems had changed. Meanwhile, I was reading a lot about public administration, trade, the economy, etc., to improve my knowledge of various subjects, which affected the population in general.

Earning money out of everything wasn't a primary goal for me anymore. I'd chosen to work honestly for the betterment of the constituency. While the Chief Minister wasn't very happy about how my name appeared in the newspaper article after the launch of the Singhania Steel Plant and the media gave me the entire credit, there were leaders in the center who were taking note of all the political developments happening in Haryana.

Nandita's project was surely something that would have created a lot of opportunities for a state that was grappling with unemployment. Irrespective of the fact that I wanted to destroy Nandita, I decided to stay away from interfering in the Singhania Steel Plant project in any form. Instead, on a couple of occasions, I even helped Naman with labor union issues and tackling red-tapism.

Everything was running smoothly until one day I got a call from Yadav.

"Where are you?" Yadav sounded nervous.

"I am leaving for the party office. Why are you sounding so nervous? Is Rajput bhaiya all right?" I asked.

"You immediately stop the car and take an auto or something to your home. Your car has been marked this morning. I am arranging police protection for you." Yadav almost shouted on the phone.

"What is the issue?" I was still not sure why Yadav was behaving in such a manner.

"Someone has paid a notorious contract killer handsomely to murder you. Do not leave your residence without police protection." Yadav Ji wanted to avoid getting into the specifics but there was no other way he could have conveyed the seriousness of the matter.

I disconnected the call and wiped the sweat off my forehead. The fear of death can make the strongest of people piss in their pants.

My heartbeat had picked up and it felt as if my end was near. My car did not have bulletproof glasses, so it meant anyone could shoot the hell out of me.

"Vikram, stop the car and hand me over the pistol from the dashboard, and take an auto home. Leave the car in the parking or something." I instructed my driver.

"Sahib, I will come with you," Vikram insisted.

"Go home." I tucked in the pistol and stepped out of the car.

Vikram parked the car in a nearby parking lot. I waited for him to take an auto and leave. Could not have trusted this guy, he would have come back for me.

Alone in the market, I looked around. There were a lot of eyes on me and everyone seemed like a contract killer to me. I waved at an autorickshaw and was about to sit inside when it finally happened. Two guys with black scarves wrapped around their faces opened fire at me.

One bullet directed towards my head was diverted by the metal rod in the auto-rickshaw while the other one struck me on my shoulder. The third bullet hit my left leg while the fourth one hit me in my back while I tried to escape.

I took out my pistol and opened fire on one of the guys. There were around three to four guys, all armed and least expecting me to carry a weapon. However, I managed to fire two rounds and hit one of the shooters. He immediately fell a few meters away from me.

Meanwhile, the crowd went into a frenzy with people running everywhere. The shooters however were hell-bent on finishing the job and decided to flank me from opposite directions. Having lost a lot of blood already, I hardly had enough strength to walk. I could hardly see or breathe much but I also wanted to live.

The shooters fired again, this time the bullet grazing past my left rib. They, however did not advance much as I was carrying a weapon as well. Also, the firing and commotion meant the police would arrive anytime soon. They had to leave soon and I wasn't dead yet.

One of them decided to risk it all. He followed me into the ally I had run towards. My body had given up on me and all that was left within me was that will to keep breathing. I could not run any further and decided to turn and face this guy rather. He pointed his gun towards me as I pointed to mine. Both fired at the same time.

Maybe I was destined to live that day. The bullet grazed my head while mine did not hit him at all. I fell to the ground and assuming I was dead, he rushed towards the street where his other partner was waiting for him on his bike.

I lay silently in a pool of blood, waiting for my end. I was finding it hard to breathe but was still in my senses. People say there are flashbacks of all the memories stored in your brain before you die.

My parents, Palak's face when she entered the classroom for the first time, Shefali's when she tended to my wounds on sports day, everything was coming back to me. I was dying.

I gathered enough strength to drag my body and lean against the wall. Taking out the pack of cigarettes, I pulled out my thirteenth cigarette and lit it with shaking and blood-drenched hands. A couple of long drags and I could feel the nicotine seep in slowly into my blood.

From a distance, I could hear a few people shouting my name and running towards me. I could not recognize them as everything had turned hazy.

"Abhay bhaiya." Suraj held me as I collapsed in his arms.

Cigarette Number Thirteen

SOMEPLACE JUST OUTSIDE HEAVEN

'CLICK,' a golden blue flame finally appeared from the lighter, flicking and fighting against the cold wind that blew past it. Holding a cigarette in between my lips, I moved it towards the flame, waiting for its tip to glow.

Then, taking a long drag, I carefully looked at the cigarette. It was the same cigarette I held before blacking out. Soaked in blood, a white stick with tobacco wrapped in between, as if 'The Reaper' himself had manufactured the cigarette.

"Wonder how this kills people?" Smiling ironically, I blew out a streak of white smoke, watching it mix with the mysterious fog surrounding the valley. I kept staring blankly at long ranges of giant green mountains diluted in thick white mist. Such was the silence that I could hear the wind whistle past my ears.

"I guess this is what heaven looks like." I took another drag at the cigarette. This wasn't like one of those regular dreams. I felt as if I had come back to life after death. It wasn't a memory from the past I was dreaming about; I was very much in the present this time around.

"So, you are leaving?" a voice interrupted from behind. It was the same six-year-old girl who had been raped and killed. She, however looked happy and different now, beautifully dressed, with neatly done hair and a satisfying smile fixed on her face.

"But you were dead." I couldn't believe what I was seeing.

"And you will be, soon." She stood there, smiling.

"So, I am not dead yet?" I asked the girl.

"Not yet, but it depends on you." She walked up to me and held my finger with her little hands.

"What do you mean?" I was confused and afraid at the same time.

"Don't you like it here? Isn't this place beautiful?" She signaled me to sit next to her.

"Yes, it's beautiful and pure. Are we in heaven?" I asked again as if I was the kid out of the two.

"No, your soul has come to a place where it always wanted to be." She kept looking towards the giant mountain ranges.

"Yes, this feels like home. Hey, I've always imagined a place like this in my head. How did you get to know about it?" I just wouldn't shut up.

"That is not important, what is though important is the decision you need to make today." She finally turned her gaze towards me.

"What is there to decide? I am dead, this place looks beautiful, maybe I'll fly down to those mountain ranges and chill." I chuckled.

"And what if you were given an option of going back?" she asked.

"Oh really, then why didn't you?" I shot back.

"Because I wasn't given this chance," she replied and fell silent, gazing at the same mountain ranges.

"You know, not many people get that chance to go back and set things right." She pointed towards a long queue of people waiting in line, all of them, looking at me.

"Who are they?" I looked at the long and never-ending queue of people.

"They are the ones with no option. He is giving you a chance to go back," she said.

"Who is this 'He' you are referring to?" I asked her.

"Whom do you think I am referring to? The one who gave you this life in the first place," she replied.

"Why did he give me a chance? I haven't done things I should be proud about." I was confused but curious.

"I don't know, that is for you to figure out. If he gave you a chance, there must be a reason." She shrugged.

"So, I've been chosen by him to do something? You really are a kid." I laughed.

"He has his ways of getting things done, either by you or someone else. I was in pain and you had a choice to ignore everything, hand over money to my parents, and walk away. You chose something else. I am in peace because of you." She smiled and got up to leave.

"Where are you going?" I asked her, concerned about the little kid.

"Home, I live with him now. Also, as far as I know, there are still six cigarettes left for you to finish." She started walking towards the long queue.

"How do I go back?" I shouted from behind.

"If you cannot walk towards that long queue, there is

a cliff behind you. I'd go for the cliff." She disappeared as I looked towards the cliff.

I stood looking down wondering if all this was a dream or reality. Closing my eyes, I jumped into the cliff.

Next, my eyes opened in an ICU surrounded by a team of doctors.

THE REBIRTH

"WE'VE GOT A PULSE, HE IS BREATHING AGAIN." I could hear the team of doctors go into a frenzy. I blacked out again for a while before finally opening my eyes a couple of days later.

"Welcome back Mr. Abhay." The doctor looked at me reassuringly while I was still trying to figure out whether I was alive or dead.

Maa sat next to me, it looked as if she had been crying for days and her eyes looked tired. I smiled at her, just so that she could believe that I was fine.

Bhagat, Neeraj, and Anisha stood near me as well. I was happy to see them again. Suraj and the other few close associates stood behind these three.

I signaled Suraj to come near me. From what I could recall, Suraj was the last guy whom I saw before collapsing.

"Thank you," I said in a feeble voice. These people who stood around me today were the ones who most probably would have cried the most if I had died.

While I was still coming to terms with the fact that I had survived four bullets, I recalled my conversation with that little girl. It was as if I could remember everything clearly and distinctly. The endless queue of the dead, the mountains, her face, that dress she wore, every bit of that memory was fresh in my mind.

The attack on me changed me as a person. I wasn't afraid of dying anymore. Lying on the hospital bed, I had two choices, either I could quit politics, move to a peaceful town, get married, and settle down, or choose to go back to hell which almost cost me my life.

Whatever decision I took would define me for the rest of my life. I closed my eyes and thanked God for giving me one more opportunity to set my acts right.

That little girl's face kept flashing in front of my eyes. I decided not to quit politics but re-enter it as an even more hardened and seasoned politician.

A few days later, Rajput visited me along with Yadav. The Chief Minister of Delhi and my mentor were emotionally overwhelmed to see me on the hospital bed.

Everyone vacated the room as Yadav closed the door behind Rajput.

"YADAV HAD ASKED YOU TO RUN, WHEN WILL YOU LEARN TO FOLLOW INSTRUCTIONS?" Rajput did not waste time venting his anger on me. I knew it was more out of the love and affection we had for each other over the years.

"I did but they got to me before that." I justified.

"Here, I have something for you." Rajput signaled Yadav to hand him over the packet, which he was carrying along with him.

"These are the four bullets doctors retrieved out of your body and here is your pack of cigarettes. Suraj knew this packet meant something to you so he had picked it up before carrying you to the hospital. I too had seen this packet with you always, so it got me curious. I checked it and found Nandita's name written on a cigarette. This got me more curious and I dug deeper. That is when I realized this Nandita was none other than Nandita Singhania." Rajput laughed.

"Did she come to visit me?" I asked with hopeful eyes, wondering if Nandita still had some feelings for me.

"Why would she, after all, she was the one who hired the contract killer in the very first place." Yadav and Rajput's faces turned serious.

I looked away, controlling my emotions. Of all the things expected out of Nandita, her killing me was the last thing I expected.

"Wow." I wasn't ready to acccpt whatever Yadav just said.

"You get well soon and then we will discuss this, Abhay. However, remember one thing, Nandita Singhania is the meanest of people I've ever come across. Times change Abhay and so do people. You should have told me about Nandita. Of all the things you told me, I still don't know why you hid Nandita's chapter from me." Rajput got up to leave.

"Why do you support me so much?" I finally asked Rajput the question, which I always had in my mind.

"Because you are family Abhay and I turned my back on family once, won't do it again." Rajput smiled and then left.

Once they left, I looked at the bullets again. Nandita had paid someone to kill me. I wondered how foolish she was. All she had to do was stand in front of me and shoot me herself and I would not have budged an inch.

Later that evening, I asked Suraj to hand me over his phone and leave the room for a while. I punched Nandita's number and pressed the call button. After a couple of rings, she finally received the call.

"Hello," said Nandita.

"I survived. Should have at least hired better people. How much did you pay them by the way?" I asked her, as if completely normal about the fact that she tried to kill me.

Nandita remained silent. I could though sense the nervousness in the pattern of her breath. I waited for her to say something.

"Get well soon!" She disconnected the call.

I remained seated, still in shock that Nandita hated me to the extent that she was ready to kill me, just so that her ego was satisfied.

The purest form of hate always comes from the people who once had the purest form of love for you. I wasn't sure about Nandita but one thing I was very sure about was the hate I had towards her.

However, my mind was still set on one question alone, "Why was I sent back from death?"

It couldn't be as trivial as taking revenge on Nandita. There had to be a bigger purpose and the only way to discover it was to step out of this hospital and find it.

I looked at the packet of cigarettes lying on the table next to me. Picking it up, I looked at the blood-stained packet. I counted the number of cigarettes left.

Sparing Nandita was something my heart wasn't allowing me to do. I could not kill her, it was against my upbringing. However, I quietly decided to once give it back to Nandita.

Forgiving her would only give her enough motivation to be obsessed with herself. She had to be brought down.

I was still engrossed in thoughts when Suraj walked in with a bundle of greeting cards. Hundreds of people had sent me their thoughts, wishing me a speedy recovery. With nothing much to do and looking for reasons to distract myself from Nandita, I decided to go through the cards.

While going through the stack, my eyes fell upon a photograph that was carefully pasted inside a card. It was an old picture of me, Palak, and Bhagat as kids, standing next to each other, holding each other's hands. Palak stood in the middle, her face was the same as I remembered her all these years as a kid.

"You will never learn to take care of yourself, will you?" Palak had scribbled those lines for me. I paused for a moment, controlling my tears. I suddenly missed her so much that for a moment everything else seemed insignificant. I would have given up anything to see her.

I kept looking at the photograph with moist eyes when Suraj knocked on the door.

"Bhaiya, someone is here to meet you," he smiled and gently pushed open the door.

Palak was standing there, looking at me. Clad in a maroon salwar kameez, thin golden bangles that dangled on her fair wrists, earrings that seemed to sparkle like diamonds, and that hair strand on her face that she was unaware of.

How do you react to this feeling? When you are in pain and exhausted, wondering how long would you be able to keep going? Just the sense of being alone, not loved, and trying to come to terms with the fact that maybe one day, you would have to die surrounded by strange faces because there is no one to cry after you are gone. And just when this feeling of hopelessness surrounds you, you see that one person standing in front of you who was your world.

I could feel something sink within me. The Abhay that I had buried away slowly crawled out of the graveyard of my memories. She kept looking at me as I tried making eye contact with her but my eyes wouldn't stop watering. I wanted to extend my arms, bury my face in her lap, and cry, pleading with her to take me away from everything and everyone else.

Palak walked towards me as if she was completely unconscious about who was around. This moment, when two people exactly know what is going on in another person's heart is difficult to define. All those scars that time had given me, everything seemed to heal by itself. Palak sat next to me and holding my hands, let a few drops finally trickle down her cheeks.

I managed a smile.

After a while, everyone else except for Palak had left. Once alone, she finally moved closer and wrapped her arms around me. Everything apart from my beating heart stopped at that moment. I kept wondering how I managed to live this long without her.

"You've come too far Abhay, let's just go back. This is not for us," Palak whispered.

There are these small odd moments in life when you are staring at a thing you've always wanted. The moment you get it, that is the end of your ambitions. You find happiness and are content with whatever you have. No more troubles, no more fear, nothing, just plain simple life.

When Palak asked me to leave everything and come with her, I wanted to say yes at that very moment. I felt like leaving everything and vanishing with her, leaving aside all this mess.

Then, there was another part of me, the part that had pulled me out of the life I was once living. I realized that I was not good at running the rat race of life that most people do.

Walking away with Palak would have meant quitting on my goal. All these years of obsessing about crushing Nandita's ego and having my revenge would mean nothing. I could not quit, not after coming so far.

"I cannot," I replied as she looked at me hopelessly. She just knew I would not leave until I won or died.

"How are you?" I asked in a feeble voice, still overcoming that emotion of meeting Palak.

"I am better now," she replied.

"Why, what happened? Something troubling you?" I asked.

"No minister saab, no one else has that skillset. Only you seem to have been blessed with it," she chuckled.

I didn't say anything, just kept looking into her eyes.

"Why Palak, why are we like this?" I finally asked her a question, which we both had always avoided.

"This is how we are and always will be. Undefined." Palak smiled.

"How is Rohit?" I asked, wondering if she still was with the same guy I beat up in college.

"The last I saw him was in college that day before you made a mess out of him." Palak giggled.

"Oh yes, that was some fight." I acted as if I had forgotten that episode. The fact was it remained etched in my memory. This girl sitting next to me today was once everything I needed or wanted from life. How can I forget that one moment which changed everything for both of us?

"I am leaving for Jamshedpur tonight Abhay. Will be waiting for your call once you get out of here." Palak smiled and got up to leave.

"And what if you do not get that call?" I asked. Palak stopped and looked back.

"Then we will talk after you have smoked that last cigarette with Nandita's name written on it." Palak picked up the cigarette packet from the table and handed it over to me. She quietly walked away after that.

I smiled and looked at the cigarette packet with my bloodstain still on it. I pulled out my fourteenth cigarette.

Cigarette Number Fourteen

LETTING SHEFALI GO

Shefali finally got through IIT. It took her a couple of years to crack the IIT exams, but she exactly landed where she was destined to be.

"ABHAY, I GOT THROUGH IIT." Shefali shirked out of joy. I could see her beaming even though we were talking over a phone call. For a girl who had always been in control of her feelings and emotions, this was the happiest I had seen her till now.

"So now you are an IITian. Congratulations Ms. Shefali." I was happy for her.

"I will be moving to Madras. I don't know anything about the place, but I am excited." She finally broke the news.

To watch her friends, post pictures of their newfound college life keep her head straight, and stay focused on a goal required superhuman effort. Shefali had always been superhuman.

I wasn't surprised at her cracking the exams. The only thing that surprised me more was that it took her so long.

"So, when are you planning to leave for Madras?" I wanted to know the timeline before Shefali started her new life.

"A month maybe." Shefali paused as realization struck her that she would be going far from me as well and not just Jamshedpur.

"Please travel and chill this whole month. It's hard work once college begins." I diverted the topic.

"I want to be with you this whole time." Shefali interrupted.

"That seems difficult. I mean your family would not allow you to stay in Ranchi for one whole month and I can't bunk college for so long." I tried putting back her expectations in place.

"Abhay, you always knew our ways would part, right?" Shefali asked.

"There are a lot of things I also did not know; one being talking to you." I chuckled.

"Shut up. You never said yes to us because you knew this day would come. Right?" Shefali was getting there slowly.

"We will sit and talk. I am coming to Jamshedpur this weekend and extracting a party out of you." I changed the topic, again.

Shefali did not say much, she understood I was not an easy catch over the phone at least. I had never confessed my love to any girl until now. Palak taught me a lot about heartbreaks very early in life. All Shefali wanted was a confession.

I traveled to Jamshedpur that weekend. Previously a trip to my hometown would make my heart skip with joy. Shefali had filled all those gaps I had created for myself.

Now, there was a weird sense of calm sadness within

me. It felt as if I always knew that I had to let her go but kept ignoring it for so long.

I reached Jamshedpur around the evening and went straight to Shefali's house. She was there on her balcony, evening skies in the background, hair strands loosely tied in a bun, a calm but beautiful face, and those eyes that could make you toss and turn the whole night.

She looked like a painting. For a few moments, I quietly took the cover of a tree and kept looking at her. It gave me a strange sense of calmness.

Finally, I walked below her apartment and waved at her. Shefali covered her face the moment she saw me. She tried her best to hide her excitement but eventually, she jumped and skipped with joy before hugging me.

After a couple of seconds, she took control of her emotions.

"Congratulations." I extended a diary to her. It was gift-wrapped.

"What is this?" Shefali looked at her present curiously.

"Open it when you are in Madras," I requested.

"Can we go somewhere, please? I hate it when everyone keeps looking at us like zoo animals." Shefali made a weird expression.

We walked to a nearby market. Shefali had held my hand all this while, not letting it go even as people watched.

Maybe she did not care or maybe she knew this was probably the last time she would be holding my hands. She knew for sure that it would not be easy for both of us to carry whatever was between us once she moved to Madras.

I stayed calm as always, letting her fight her own battles. Shefali always was that one girl who inspired me to do more than I could afford. One of the things I learned from her was to stay in control of my emotions while staring at the most heartbreaking situations.

"Two coffees." I placed the order as she kept looking at me.

"Lay it out Shefi." I wanted her to speak her heart out that day. It was the only time I would let my guard down in front of her.

"We can still be like this Abhay. I mean, it's just Madras. We can always meet once a month. I am going to call you daily and I am not letting you go," Shefali said. I could sense she was making every possible attempt to avoid the unavoidable.

"Shefi, getting to the top is easy, the hardest part is to stay there. It would take a lot of hard work to excel at IIT. Make new friends and start afresh and I am anyways always with you." I put on a fake smile.

"So you will leave, just like that?" she asked the hardest of all questions.

"Nope. I am not. But you must. I will be a distraction. Nothing more." I shrugged.

"Please, we could have a beautiful future together." Shefali was almost in tears.

"Shefi, if it is meant to be, then no one can stop it. Deep within you know that you cannot carry the burden of a relationship that is still to find its name. There is a lot at stake for you and I am always a call away when you need me." I smiled as we finished our cup of coffee.

"Abhay, I am willing to carry the burden, all I need is a yes from you." Shefali looked at me with moist and hopeful eyes.

There are times in your life when you have to let go of something you truly love. Deep within you know that eventually, you will have to part ways, but you don't have enough courage to pull the plug. So you choose the easier way, to delay the inevitable and let time slowly and painfully take that thing away from you.

It's a brave call, to choose, to be the bad one out of the two, to cut the cord so the other person can grow and blossom. I had to do it, Shefali was destined for far greater things in life.

"Love comes with a lot of expectations, sacrifices, adjustments, and trust. No matter how much you or I try, there will be times when you will have to put aside everything and focus on what is important. I don't want us to go that route. Whatever is here Shefali, between us, it is pure. Why risk messing it up?" I kept looking towards the horizon as the sun began to set slowly.

She took some time to come to terms with the fact that she had to let me go, again. And this time maybe forever.

"Ok, but I am not giving up on hope. Abhay, if it is meant to be, it will be." Shefali nodded, finally coming to terms with my decision.

We walked back to her place in silence.

"I will miss you," I said as I was about to leave.

I still remember that moment. It had started drizzling a bit, trees rustling as a gentle breeze blew past the quiet gloomy landscape.

Shefali managed a smile while still trying her best to control her emotions. She stepped closer to me and we hugged each other.

"Abhay, I will find you. In this very life and this very world. I will find you again." She silently whispered these words in my ears and slid something into my hands before turning and walking back to her apartment.

I opened my palms to find a cotton ball, the same one she had used back in school to treat my wounds on sports day.

POLITICIAN – 2.0

"ABHAY BHAIYA ZINDABAD," the party workers assembled outside the party office as I stepped out of the car. I was a hero to them now and the sympathy wave had further ensured that my follower base only increased with time.

As I thanked and hugged each one of them, Suraj stood at the office entrance with a black thread in his hands.

"This thread carries blessings of Mahadev. I especially got it for you from Kashi Vishwanath." He smiled and tied the thread on my wrist as I hugged him. Had it not been for Suraj and a few loyal men, I would have been a dead man.

I looked at the crowd, holding garlands, posters with my picture, and shouting slogans in my name. All this love, affection, and the feeling of belonging to the masses were so different. This wasn't a crowd that had been assembled to make me feel good; instead, they were those people who believed in me.

There comes a point in your life when you have an option to change, to redeem yourself of all the sins you once committed, to come out of darkness and walk towards the light. It was one of those days for me.

I stood there for a moment, seeping in all the noise.

I never realized that I had slowly completed my journey from being a banker to becoming a leader.

It wasn't like I had solved all their issues but at least I made a genuine attempt. I was approachable to people and heard their issues. I had turned down my abroad tours and instead channeled that money into more productive tasks that would help the common masses.

It wasn't like I had become honest, it was just that I kept doing the job that I was supposed to do, help people.

Until now, my reason for joining politics was revenge on Nandita, but now it changed. It was now replaced by people who voted for me.

I decided to focus on what I was doing best and work towards becoming a leader instead. As far as Nandita was concerned, it was a battle I'd pick up some other day.

The feeling of being loved, respected, and looked up to as an inspiration is something much more powerful than money itself. After years of running behind money and power, it took me four bullet hits and a fight with death to realize that this is exactly what I was sent back for, to help people and redeem myself.

For the next year, I worked like a corporate employee, setting personal targets for various development projects and achieving them much before the deadline. From new initiatives like upgrading public school infrastructures, creating better roads within housing societies, solving water and sanitation issues, introducing renewable sources of energy in government offices, etc.

What I realized was that even though the system was corrupt and needed reforms, if one had intentions of getting things done, there was no way it could be stopped. I had to warm a few pockets but then it gave me a lot of clarity about the moles within our system.

I quietly started taking note of all such names, their connections, and the people who controlled them and realized it went all the way up to very senior levels within the government.

Soon, I started making headlines.

"Faridabad 2.0," read the front-page news article in a Sunday morning newspaper edition. As compared to the last five years, my constituency had developed ten times more in infrastructure, income, schools, health institutes, and employment within three years of my tenure as an MLA.

The article carried out a detailed analysis of how I went about transforming my constituency and by just reading the article, I felt a sense of pride from within. It felt good being pure, to realize that I had been honest about my job and towards my people; that was redemption.

My cellphone rang, it was Rajput.

"He must have read the article," I said to myself as I received his call.

"Congratulations sir, you are a celebrity now. It's so brilliant Abhay, what you've done with your constituency. I am so much interested in understanding your development model but before me, there is someone else who wants to meet you."

"Who?" I wondered why Rajput would call to inform me about such a small thing.

"The Prime Minister. He has been observing your

work silently all this while. Tomorrow eleven thirty at Prime Minister's office."

"Sh… Sh… sure bhaiya. I'll be there," I replied, not sure how to react.

I hung up the call and wondered if I had heard Rajput correctly. During all these years as a member of the party, I had only seen the Prime Minister from a distance at party meetings. Never really got a chance to meet him in person.

Most of the time he was either surrounded by prominent leaders and ass lickers within the party or the SPG commandos. I was too lazy to make my way through the crowd and show him my face, so I used to give it a pass, slipping out unnoticed once the meeting was over.

The day got over quickly and by evening, I was panicking about meeting the Prime Minister. I decided to call Bhagat but instead ended up calling Palak.

"Hello." Palak's voice was like a balm to my soul. It has been ages since I'd spoken to her but still, she knew how to stop my heart.

"Why do you have to speak to me like that?" I protested.

"What did I do? It's you who is sounding troubled," she replied, this time her voice even more beautiful.

"I am meeting the Prime Minister tomorrow," I said, wondering if Palak had psychic powers. How is it that she always knew what was going on in my mind?

"You remember; I once gave you a pen before you entered the exam hall?" said Palak.

"Yes, I still carry that pen," I replied.

"You do?" Palak knew me but this was something she

didn't expect me to do, take care of things she gifted me. What she also did not know was that I had been storing all her gifts since childhood.

"Yes, I just told you." I kept my tone flat as if it was a very normal thing to do. However, here is a small piece of advice for all guys. One of the best feelings for a girl is that her guy gives importance to even the smallest of things that give her happiness. Also, just keep it simple, as if taking care of her happiness is something routine for you. She might or might not say much but deep down, I promise you this, she would be the happiest girl on the planet.

"Abhay, you have a history of panic, but you always come out as a winner. I've seen you on TV and the odd nervousness on your face when you are facing the camera, but once you start talking, it's just so magical to listen to you."

"You will be fine, keep the pen close to you and think I am there with you," Palak replied and even though I wanted her to keep talking to me, I decided to keep my throbbing heart in control.

"I need more voters like you." I chuckled.

"You already have. Take care. Bye." Palak always knew when to end the conversation.

I reached the PMO half an hour before the scheduled time. As I waited impatiently in the lobby for the Prime Minister to arrive, I recalled how nervous I was before my first job interview. This experience was almost like that.

Exactly five minutes later, the Prime Minister arrived. While walking towards his office, he noticed me sitting in the lobby. He stopped midway and called my name aloud.

"Abhay," he said as he walked towards me, the

commandos following his heels.

I got up from my seat pleasantly surprised that he knew my name.

"You don't know how wonderful it is to see youngsters like you join politics. This country needs change more than ever." He shook hands with me and asked me to walk with him towards the lawn outside his office.

"Thank you for giving me a chance to meet you in person Mr. Prime Minister. I feel so…" I was continuing the rehearsed speech I prepared the previous night when he abruptly interrupted.

"Do you believe in the idea of making India a superpower?" The Prime Minister stopped midway in the silent lobby with his bodyguards at some distance.

"Not unless we work towards it," I replied.

"So you think we are not?" he shot back.

"No sir, we are not." I decided to give him a piece of my mind. Death changes you or at least its experience surely does. It just teaches you that nothing in life is as big as we make it. The Prime Minister could have asked me to buzz off and my political career would have been over.

However, contrary to my belief, he smiled and put a hand on my shoulder.

"This is what I like about this generation, honest to the face. Abhay, my government has been plagued with scams and scandals during my stint as a Prime Minister. I hardly have a handful of very trustworthy ministers in my cabinet and you've recently been the poster boy for my party." The Prime Minister paused and looked at me.

"Our Defence Minister has not been well lately and

has been facing consistent health issues. In the meantime, I want you to take charge of the ministry and bring in a new approach." He passed the orders as if it were something normal.

"What? No sir, I cannot." I immediately declined as this was a very huge responsibility for a guy who was neither a leader nor a nationally recognized politician. I had done some good work to make my presence felt on social media but that did not qualify me to become Minister Of Defence.

"What happened? I suddenly see all that confidence vanish. Criticizing is easy Abhay, try changing something while you still can. I trusted a sixty-year-old man who was an arts graduate as the Defence Minister of this country. Change is the only constant thing in life. The perception that only old and experienced politicians can become Home Minister, Prime Minister, and Defence Minister needs to change. Take the job. I can't force you but at least give it a thought." He patted my shoulders and walked back to his office.

I stood on the lawn, not ready to accept what just happened. I was scared, excited, confused, and happy at the same time. As an MLA, I had the freedom and flexibility to meet my friends, meet people, spend time with my family, etc. All this would be gone now.

Confused and not sure how to move forward, I decided to consult my political mentor, Rajput.

"So, how did your meeting with the Prime Minister go, Mr. Defence Minister?" Rajput chuckled.

"How do you know he offered me the job?" I asked in

disbelief, wondering if he had bugged me or something.

"Who do you think recommended you for the job?" Rajput laughed on the other side of the line.

"You deserve this Abhay. I am happy as a Chief Minister and seeing you become successful is like seeing my kid become successful. Meet me tomorrow, I don't even remember last when you, I, and Yadav had a drink together." Rajput sounded happy.

"I will see you tomorrow bhaiya." I disconnected the call and walked towards my car. Somehow, I wasn't convinced by the explanation Rajput gave. He loved me but not to the point of letting go of the position of Defence Minister. Something wasn't right, and I needed to find it out.

Politics taught me one important lesson, everyone is a snake, you just need to know which one of them is poisonous.

My gut instinct wanted me to turn down the offer but then the Prime Minister himself wanted me to take over the ministry and turning down his request was impossible.

As I sat in the car, it started raining. I asked the driver to drive slowly as I lowered the side windows. It had been ages since I'd experienced raindrops hitting my face.

"Stop the car, please," I instructed the driver.

He stopped the car in front of a small tea stall.

"Tea?" I asked the driver and he nodded in agreement.

"Let me get it for you saheb, it's raining outside," my driver insisted.

"No no, stay inside." I stepped out of the car and signaled the tea vendor to make two cups of tea. I sat on a concrete bench supported by stacked bricks. There was a plastic shed he had placed overhead to shelter him from rain.

Some of the best experiences in life come from the simplest of things. Sipping a cup of tea, the sound of rain, the smell of damp Earth, and a cigarette. It's unbeatable and rare.

From joining politics to destroy Nandita to becoming the designated Defence Minister, life taught me some of the most important lessons.

Everything had changed including the person I had become. From a guy whose only priority was money to a corrupt politician to a youngster who now wanted to change the system and help his country grow, I had my share of experiences.

I was rich, I was powerful and influential, and I had my friends' back but still wasn't content for a very long time.

True happiness lies in helping people and giving back something positive to the country. I didn't belong to that league of people who made the ultimate sacrifice. I'd rather work towards the same slowly and keep making steady progress. Corrupt or wrong people have a lot of skeletons in their closets.

I was part of this corrupt system as well. You cannot defeat the king with a pawn alone. You need to become a king yourself.

Until now, I was a pawn preparing to become a king. I wasn't the king yet but was now part of his core team.

A corrupt system, Nandita, media, everything stood

in between. I'd seen honest crusaders fall in the process of trying to change the system.

All you need to do is be the dark knight with a white soul. When the right time comes, fight the ultimate battle and give it your everything to win. That is how truth wins.

I had to weed out the corrupt by being corrupt.

"Saheb, tea." He handed me a plastic cup with shaking hands.

I looked at him. A sixty-year-old man whose face still had pride and humbleness on it even though a lifetime of struggle had left scars on his face.

"How much baba?" I asked.

"Twenty rupees saheb." The old man smiled humbly.

I finished my tea and walked up to the old man.

"Baba, here, keep this money. Think your son gave it to you." I handed him a couple of five hundred rupee notes.

Before the old man could understand anything, I smiled and walked back towards the car.

"Where to sir?" my driver asked.

"Let's just roam around for a while Gopal, it's been long since I felt the human in me," I replied, pulling out my fifteenth cigarette.

Cigarette Number Fifteen

THE FIRST JOB

"Class 2 B, which floor?" I asked the security guard sitting at the reception desk. It was my first day at the B-school. After graduating from BIT Mesra, I decided to do what everyone does, an MBA.

CAT, MAT, XAT, IBSAT, etc., you name it, I'd applied for the entrance examinations. My parents expected me to make a mature decision after I graduated. Even though I'd got the first class with distinction, I had lost interest in my studies.

I applied for a few jobs but Ranchi as a city doesn't give you a lot of employment opportunities. Finally, I decided to take the safer route and pursue post-graduation. It would give me a real shot to at least get placed.

I smoked weed before the CAT exam and tripped on one question for almost three hours. I got that question right eventually, but the train of opportunity had already left the station.

The same happened in XAT, SNAP, etc., wherein I boozed or smoked my way to the exam hall, only to doze off in the car and not even turn up for exams.

While Neeraj got through IIM, Aanchal decided to move abroad. Bhagat went on to join his father's business and Anisha moved to Chandigarh for further studies.

I on the other hand was getting calls from some of the worst B schools in India. My CAT scores were too bad to be even called scores. I decided to take one final entrance exam for a decent private MBA college. If I still couldn't get through, I would consider it as my fate and try out my luck in some other field, like mass communication, etc.

However, luck finally smiled on me and I managed to score in higher ninety percentiles. I got admitted into a fairly good B-school in Gurgaon. Private MBA colleges are like expensive showrooms. You can enter them and feel good about yourself, but at the end of the day, you'll always come out with the cheapest thing on the shelf because that is what you can afford.

The companies that come for campus placements in these colleges offer packages that are just enough for you to pay your education loan installments and buy groceries. It's a big scam and the owners of these colleges send their kids to Oxford and Harvard. That so much explains how much they believe in the quality of education in their colleges.

I was probably the first few people to enter a relatively empty class 2 B. Fifteen minutes later, we still were just fifteen odd students in the class. Our first lecture of the day was Finance and a lady professor in her mid-thirties walked into the class.

Behind her entered a bunch of students who probably must have gone through the same trouble of locating our classroom. The lecture finally began and the moment she started speaking, I knew finance either wasn't the subject I should have opted for or maybe she took it for granted that everyone knew everything.

Forty-five minutes later, she finally paused.

"Any questions? Please ask if you have any doubts. The basics need to be correct," she said.

"Is she for real?" I mumbled, wondering if opting for an MBA was even the right decision in the first place. Once again, being part of the herd mentality didn't add up to anything productive.

"I want to fuck her." I heard someone say those lines from behind me.

I looked back to find a guy smiling and winking at me as if I had appreciated his comments.

"This cannot be happening to me. School, college, and now post-graduation. How do I always manage to find the worst people in the batch and later become friends with them?" I cursed my luck.

I needed a respectable job with a decent package at least. Unless I wasn't the best student of the batch, getting a decent job was out of the question, leaving aside a decent package.

Once the class was over, I got up to leave, still trying to make sense of the finance lecture.

"What is your name? You don't look like you are from Delhi." The same guy sitting behind me was now standing in front of me with a smirk on his face.

"He is a criminal, stay away from this guy." Said my gut.

"Abhay, and yes, I am basically from Jamshedpur, Jharkhand." I smiled and started walking towards the exit.

"I am Abhishek from Bihar. I just noticed your title

is Pandey, so you are a Brahmin?" He laughed as if he cracked a joke.

"Yeah, how does that matter?" I felt irritated because of his constant pestering.

"This is my friend, Ranveer. He is a Rajput though but from Bihar. Jharkhand was also Bihar once." This time Ranveer and Abhishek laughed as if these two were the ones responsible for creating Bihar and the Rajput clan in the first place.

Not trying to look or sound rude, I smiled and left wondering if I'd come to the right place.

Two weeks passed, and things had changed.

"Is this much fine or should I pour more?" Abhishek asked as I signaled him to pour more whiskey into my glass. We were drinking at his place in Chattarpur. It was a secluded rented accommodation wherein two more families lived in the same building.

Abhishek Rathor had ensured that they were terrorized and aligned enough to not interfere when he was partying, playing loud music, drinking, creating a nuisance, etc. His place was absolute heaven for a bachelor.

Things continued at their own pace and before I realized it, the first semester was over. Because of all the drinking, partying, and probably doing everything apart from studying, I barely managed to get average scores. Meanwhile, Abhishek Rathor had scored good grades.

I decided to get hold of things. While I was still in the process of recovering from the damage I had caused to myself academically, I got voted on by the student council. I thought the student council would be one of the most influential and to-be councils at the college, instead, it turned out to be a bunch of people trying to superimpose themselves on one another. Soon, I lost interest in that too.

I had begun thinking seriously about what would happen if I went unplaced. My grades didn't support me and the only thing that could have worked in my favor was the natural orator and creativity within me.

Anyway, one and a half years passed into my post-graduation, and the reality finally struck me hard. I looked at my mark sheet. What surprised me was that even after all the shit I could have possibly done to screw up my chances of passing examinations, I still managed a six GPA.

To be eligible for placements, a student must have at least six GPAs. I had just managed to snuggle to six.

A week later, I was sitting inside a room packed with prospective candidates for the job. It was my first job interview and saying that I was nervous would be an understatement. I felt like calling up someone and sharing how I felt but the question was whom?

I had not spoken to Bhagat, Neeraj, Aanchal, Anisha, or Palak since I dropped a year at Delhi University. Shefali was a distant past and I did not make any friends in post-graduation. Abhishek and I remained close acquaintances, but he wasn't a friend I could share my feelings.

Whatever I did share with him was more over drinks or under the influence of alcohol.

Finally, I decided to call up my Dad. I took out my phone and typed Dad in the contact list on my phone.

It was then that I realized I hadn't even saved his number after I bought a new phone post-admission to

MBA, while my parents used to call me every second or third day to check on me. Something sank within me that day. Feeling ashamed about not having my father's number was small compared to the guilt I felt about never bothering to consider them so important.

It's strange how we forget our parents while running after our careers, money, girls, etc.

I searched the recently received call log and found his number finally. Before I could dial his number, the placement coordinator called out my name. Missing the chance to call the only person who could have given me confidence, I walked inside the room where group discussions were being held.

Given an opportunity to speak, I stammered and said things that didn't make sense. As a result, for the first time in my life, I flunked a group discussion. The only skillset I was banking upon had left me in the time of my need.

Post a couple of more failed rounds of group discussions and interviews, I finally understood the reality that I wasn't as good as I thought and that maybe I had to make a few corrections.

It was the last company for campus placements that year. A private bank that had come to hire from our college for the first time. There were still a lot of students left unplaced. In a room full of students desperate to get placed, I was the only one to have not cleared a group discussion even once.

Finally, before stepping into the group discussion, I decided to call up my father. He picked up my call after a couple of rings.

"Hello," he answered in a weak voice.

"Are you fine?" I replied.

"Yes, just the changing weather. How are your placements going?" He brushed aside his ill health with ease as if it was nothing.

"I am about to enter the group discussion. Dad, can I ask you a question?" I paused for his reply.

"What's wrong son?" he said.

"Do you think I am good enough to get a job?" I asked my father a question whose answer was something I had been now searching for almost a month.

"Son, you don't know this but I do. When it's your day, you are unbeatable," he replied.

Those words dug in deep. Before speaking to my father, all I was thinking about was what if I failed; now, after speaking to him, even if the bank hired only one guy student from our college, that would be me.

"Thanks, Dad, I'll let you know whatever happens here." I hung up the call with a smile on my face. The biggest change you create for yourself to be successful is when you are not afraid of failure.

The group discussion room had odd twenty people sitting around a large wooden table. The setup was more like a corporate board meeting.

"What would you prefer becoming at work – A bull or a fox? Remember, you can't be both." The moderator began.

From the beginning till the end of the group discussion, there were only two people who spoke. One was me and the other was the moderator.

I cleared the group discussion and later fared very well in the interview. Finally, post multiple rounds of interviews, there were some thirty-odd people left in the room.

I sat patiently for the placement coordinator to come up with the results. It was already seven in the evening and I hadn't had anything to eat since morning.

Finally, the coordinator walked into the room with a list in her hand.

"There are ten students who have been placed. I am calling out their names one by one. Please walk to room number seven once your name is called out to collect your offer letters," the coordinator said in a professional voice. She already sounded like an HR.

"Jasleen, Prashant, Kartik, Arun, Saumil, Aakash, Urvashi, Angad, Divya and Abhay. Congratulations to all of you. Please follow me to the next room."

While other candidates were shouting and celebrating, I silently walked out of the room. It was like my heart had opened the floodgates for every emotion to flow out freely. I walked to room number seven like a zombie, collected the offer letter, and then headed toward the washroom.

Once I entered the washroom, I shut the door. The feeling of getting placed was so intense that I puked and cried out of happiness at the same time. My brain wasn't ready to believe that I got placed and my heart didn't want to stay in my body.

I finally calmed down after a few minutes and called up my father.

"Dad, I got placed." I broke the news.

He stayed silent for a few minutes. It seemed as if he had just been paid for years of the struggle and hardship he went through.

"Well done son. Well done," he replied.

I understood he was emotionally as overcome as me but then being a father, he did not want to go weak in front of me. I decided to let him hold onto his ever-glorious composure.

"I am coming home soon, let Maa know about the same. I'll call you in a while." I disconnected the call and walked outside the college gate. I looked up. The skies had gone dark blue and everything seemed perfectly still.

After so many years of people consistently reminding me that I am a failure, I managed to, for once prove to myself that the world was wrong, not me.

BEGINNING OF REVENGE

Sources within the party had already tipped off the media about the Prime Minister's planning to change the way people in this country look at politicians. He was known for making some very bold decisions and every time he took a decision, it created ripples across the nation.

The stage had already been set and the news about me becoming the Defence Minister of India would be out in the next couple of days. I had not discussed the news about the Prime Minister offering me the role of Defence Minister with my family. Wanted it to be a surprise for them.

While the media had gone into an overdrive to guess the name of the new Defence Minister, I was busy planning how to neutralize Nandita.

Nandita tried to kill me me once because she felt threatened by my progress in politics. I was sure the moment she will hear the news about me becoming the Defence Minister of India, she would do everything possible within her reach to remove me from that position of power.

I needed to plan Nandita's downfall. The easiest would have been to kill her but irrespective of what she did to me, my heart did not allow me to go that way.

The first rule of engagement is knowing your enemy in and out. I knew Nandita as a lover but not as a wife, daughter-in-law, boss, etc. Nandita guarded her personal space like a lioness. From media people to her best friends, only a selected set of people has access to her personal space.

It all began by planting a mole inside Nandita's house. I had put Suraj on a job to get information about Nandita.

Suraj was like my shadow. I loved Suraj as my own and my family would treat him as the other son. Suraj knew my darkest of secrets and I ensured he was kept away from all the limelight, just so that he remained away from all the mess that comes along with it.

"Neeta is Nandita's most loyal maid. She is the one who heads a team of twenty servants and Nandita simply would believe her eyes closed." Suraj had managed to get one of Nandita's maids to fall for him. Over the next few days, he was able to get every possible detail out of this girl.

Nandita's husband used to travel a lot. However, they seemed to be an average couple, nothing over-the-top kind of love.

Nandita used to keep herself occupied in the day-to-day running of the company while Naman would keep meeting bigger clients and plan expansion.

"There is absolutely nothing wrong between the two, everything seems normal," replied Suraj.

"Nothing is normal with Nandita, Suraj, these guys are hiding something." I was confident about Nandita's nature. She would just not let the people she liked leave her side for a moment and here was her husband traveling several times a month on a business trip. What was more troubling was Nandita allowing him to do so.

I picked up the phone and dialed Neeraj's number.

"Minister Saab," Neeraj answered the call.

"It's time." I waited for his answer.

"So, when do we begin?" Neeraj asked.

"Take a flight to Delhi, I'll meet you at the airport once you land," I replied.

"Ok, I'll leave in the next hour."

I walked into the lawn outside my house. A guy who once lived in a rented BHK apartment with his family now owned a sprawling farmhouse.

The full moon beamed gloriously, and the gentle breeze further added to the calmness of the night. Suraj observed me from a distance and understood I was busy fighting my restless heart.

I was going after one of the biggest business tycoons in India. One mistake and I wouldn't get another chance to defend myself. My plan had to work perfectly, there was no backup.

***

It was four a.m. in the morning. Bhagat and I waited for Neeraj outside Delhi International Airport.

Suraj and I waited for Neeraj to arrive at the airport. I wanted this to be a low-key affair and thus had sneaked out with Suraj. Too much security would have attracted undue attention.

While waiting for Neeraj, I wondered why he agreed to be a part of a plan that had the potential to destroy everything that he had created if we missed out on the target. I guess the answer was simple, the returns outweighed the risks.

Neeraj and I had planned a hostile takeover of Singhania's business. Over the last few years, we both had silently worked toward placing our most trusted associates on Singhania's Board of Directors.

While Nandita thought that I would exact my revenge by attempting to kill her, I had different plans.

I would never kill anyone, this was against my principles. Nandita's wealth was what gave her that power, ego, and confidence. Take that away and her pride would collapse like a house of cards.

Over the next few months, Neeraj's base would be Delhi. He would set up his company operations and expand into all those major business segments where Singhanias was present. This would be through either strategic business tie-ups and partnerships or creating wholly-owned companies.

The money and resources needed for such rapid expansion were where I came into the picture. While Neeraj would set himself up for a hostile takeover of the Singhania group, my job was to ensure that all upcoming projects and big bets of the Singhania group did not see daylight.

Meanwhile, Naman was in England to bag a contract from one of the largest defense equipment manufacturers in the world. He had heavily invested in setting up a separate business arm for the same and this contract was crucial for his new setup to take off.

Using his contacts in the government, he had placed the lowest bid, and this meeting in London to announce the supplier was only a formality for him.

What he did not know was that being part of the system, getting the quotes was a cakewalk for me. I disclosed the quotes to his nearest rival for a five percent cut of the overall contract value.

The next morning, as planned, Naman lost the bid. With millions of dollars in debt, Naman returned to India and within a week had to shut down the new venture.

The next few days were even tougher for Naman as he lost some major clients to the Chinese and other competitors due to the same quality materials at better rates. Before Naman and Nandita could figure out, their steel business, which also was the biggest contributor to their topline, registered a record loss of forty-seven percent as compared to the previous year.

With Naman and Nandita grappling to keep their business afloat, the media began highlighting their company's financial situation, which further triggered panic among investors.

However, their CFO, Santosh Jhunjunwala, held the sinking ship of Singhanias with all his might. Santosh Jhunjunwala was an icon. His years of experience in pulling the worst of companies from the jaws of extinction made him close to God. With Santosh on board, the investors still saw hope.

Neeraj and I were aware of this. Santosh had very strong business ethics. We could not buy his loyalty; he had a bigger name to protect than fall for a few million dollars.

He had a clean slate, which further made it impossible for us to drag him into something illegal. He was unmarried, had no family, and did not indulge in anything that was either against the law or against his principles. I sometimes wondered if he had ever worked for RAW or CIA.

The only man now standing between Singhanias and their downfall was Santosh. He would buy Naman and Nandita just enough time to figure out moles within their company and set things back in place. We had to act and act fast.

A desperate man would do anything to get what he wants. Both Neeraj and I had a lot at stake and leaving everything to fate would mean our end.

I sat in the garden, thinking what it would take to get Jhunjunwala out of the way. Finally, I decided to use a very subtle but the best way to get rid of Jhunjunwala. Hurt an honest man's integrity and he won't ever come back.

My sources leaked false news to a section of paid media that it was Santosh who had tipped off competitors about the UK defense deal bid, which Singhanias had lost.

A couple of fake phone conversations between a few arms dealers and a few carefully planted clues were enough to act as evidence against Jhunjunwala.

The next morning, I woke up to the news that put a smile on my face. Not only was Santosh sacked, but he also was manhandled by Naman and his bodyguards.

Loyal men are dangerous men. When a loyal person decides to go against you, he will not leave a single stone unturned to ensure he has his revenge.

We decided to wait for a few days and allow all the

dust and uproar on Jhunjunwala's sacking to settle down. Immediately approaching him with an extended hand of friendship would have gotten a lot of media attention and eyeballs.

The thing about heroes is that when they are at the peak of their power, everyone worships them like a God. However, once they fall, people tend to forget them even more quickly.

Once the limelight was gone, no one even remembered Santosh Jhunjunwala. The media trials, his circle of friends, the intellectuals, everyone took a dig at him. While he remained silent and held his composure gracefully, I knew how deeply shattered he must be feeling from within.

Santosh was vulnerable and was looking for an opportunity to prove himself.

A couple of months later, Neeraj met Jhunjunwala at his residence in London. The agenda of the meeting was to get more insights on how to grow his business.

"Sir, I've always looked up to you as my mentor, and no matter what people say about you, for me, you are my guiding light." Neeraj started the conversation by feeding Jhunjunwala with small doses of pride that he had been longing for. Everyone loves a bit of recognition and flattery.

"Thank you, Neeraj, I've heard a lot about you, and the way you've expanded your startup is commendable," Santosh replied humbly, holding back all his emotions behind a perfectly calm face.

"Sir, I am planning to expand my business and enter FMCG, steel, automobiles, construction, etc., in the future. Can you help me understand the basics of how I go about it?

I've seen you expand the Singhania's and was wondering if there is any chance you can mentor me personally?" Neeraj's tone was dripping with humility as he asked Santosh the question that had yes written all over it.

"Neeraj, I would love to personally mentor and coach you, but I am sure you know about the recent events. I am not the same person anymore, not sure if I would be the right person in the first place to coach you." Santosh's pride and confidence had been dented due to his recent experiences.

"Sir, I know how it feels and honestly I have no intentions of pushing you. However, I have full trust and faith in your abilities. I have an offer and would want to discuss it with your permission." Neeraj made his move.

"Sure, please go ahead, I am listening." Santosh was curious.

"We currently are just a single line of business and with the current round of funding from our investors, we are expecting to diversify into steel manufacturing, to begin with. I know this is a new line of business for us and would require a lot of effort and expertise to turn it into a successful venture.

It would be an honor to have you on our board. In return, I am ready to offer you one percent of my total business valuation as your remuneration. The more the business grows, the more the money." Neeraj waited for Santosh's answer.

"Ok, let's do this." Jhunjunwala did not think twice. He had already envisioned how he was going to get back at Singhanias.

Neeraj stayed at Jhunjunwala's place for a while, gaining valuable insights and experiences from Santosh.

He had meanwhile texted me – *"Santosh is IN."*

I read the text and smiled, silently pulling out my sixteenth cigarette.

Cigarette Number Sixteen

THE FAILED GENIUS BIRTH OF INVESTINTEL

"I won't take up a job, come what may," said Neeraj as he passed me the half-smoked cigarette.

He hadn't been working for two years now, his parents had abandoned him because he took a wrong call and decided to start something of his own and failed miserably.

To meet his expenses and keep working towards his dream of building his own company, he took tuition. I was settling into my new job and had taken up one BHK rented accommodation.

Neeraj could not afford rent and badly needed a place in Delhi to stay. I hadn't spoken to Neeraj or any of my friends since I left Delhi University. Even though both of us were staying in Delhi, I was unaware of the whereabouts of any of my friends.

I was returning from the office when Neeraj called me from a PCO booth in Rohini. It took me a while to believe the fact that Neeraj had been on the streets for two days now and he used the last coin left with him to make a call to me. Had I not picked up the call, he would have slept hungry and on the streets that day.

"Why didn't you call me before? And do Uncle and Aunty know about this?" I was feeling guilty from within for drifting so far away from Neeraj that he had to think twice before calling me.

Neeraj would not cry, he never did. He would go silent in an emotionally overwhelming moment, but this guy would never cry. He did not say anything and stayed silent.

"Where are you? I am coming." I continued without waiting for his reply.

"I am near Rohini metro station," he said.

Three hours later, we were sitting on my balcony after gorging on a large pizza and a couple of cigarettes.

"And you've not spoken to your father for like one year?" I took a long drag at the cigarette.

"Yes, and it's not because I am angry at him. I am embarrassed for being a failure and disappointment to him." Neeraj sipped the beer can next to him.

"Take some time to figure out your mess. You can stay here as long as you want. Also, where is Aanchal? You both in touch?" I distracted Neeraj's mind, which was running like a horse, but only in the negative direction.

"I don't know. I haven't spoken to her since college." Neeraj shrugged carelessly.

Aanchal and Neeraj were close friends. Even though Aanchal was the quietest in our group, she was comfortable sharing things with Neeraj. I remember a time in college when Aanchal would wait for an hour after her classes at the bus stand for Neeraj to arrive so that they could catch up for a while during the evening.

"I borrowed money from Aanchal that I couldn't return." Neeraj finally owned up.

"So you eloped?" I was now confused if I was talking to the same guy who was once the nerd in our group. Constant failures had eroded Neeraj's confidence in himself.

"Fifty thousand rupees for business, all gone," he continued.

"What? How did she manage to give you this much money?" I was now interested in Neeraj's story.

"She took out a loan for me. Aanchal is working in Delhi. I tried setting up a small stock broking setup but it failed. I had to close it in a month. I did not have the money nor the courage to face Aanchal, so I changed my phone number and as you pointed out, eloped." Neeraj kept looking towards the dark skies as if he could relate to all that darkness in his life.

The only pole star he had, Aanchal, was now gone as well.

I wanted to help Neeraj but my financial situation wasn't great either. When you are not sure how to help a friend in need, the first thing you do is shut up and observe where he/she is struggling.

You can only cure a disease when you have the exact diagnosis. I kept quiet that night and let Neeraj speak his heart out. Dreamers have no place in this world, not until they turn their dreams into reality.

Neeraj had a lot of dreams, but which one to follow was the toughest call. His last few dreams did not even see daylight. Things continued the usual way for another month and Neeraj's frustration with himself kept growing.

I finally decided to intervene. Watching your friend

struggle every day isn't a great sight.

"Do you know real estate is the newest kid on the block for investments?" I threw the lighter towards him.

"Yes, the returns are very impressive." Neeraj lit his cigarette and took a long drag at it. He had started smoking up a lot and no matter how much I convinced him, he just wouldn't quit.

"You are good with numbers; can you help me organize my client's portfolio?" I handed him over a few pages, which carried a messed up portfolio of an HNI client. As bankers, we had high targets for insurance selling. To meet our targets, we would pitch insurance to a client as a five-year mutual fund investment.

"His entire investments are locked in ULIPS. He should have invested thirty percent of his revenue in real estate which would have set off losses suffered on a short-term basis in equity." After ages, Neeraj had found something where he was using his brain actively. I didn't give a rat's ass about the client or the return he would get on his portfolio but what was satisfying was that my fluke worked. I hadn't listened to a single sentence that Neeraj had said but what I did do was hand him over an idea.

"You are right. We should do this. Why don't you do something like this in your free time?" I nudged him. I was confident, Neeraj would build something out of it.

Over the next few weeks, Neeraj built a website through which people could invest in shares, bonds, and real estate (both directly as well as indirectly). I printed out my bank's entire portfolio and handed it over to Neeraj who would tirelessly call and ask them if they would be interested in investing using his portal.

It all started with one of the clients agreeing to invest a small amount in buying a small commercial space using his website. Neeraj brought down the final deal rates by almost fifteen percent and the deal went through in cash. He made his first cut of twenty-five thousand rupees. This was two times more than what he used to earn out of tuition.

Over the next few weeks, he spent a lot of time building his website. He spent a lot of time traveling and meeting various property owners, struggling builders who needed investment to complete their projects, and people who needed property ready to be sold in distress.

Six months later, Neeraj was able to open a small office space, hire a couple of tele-callers, and register his company under the name "InvestIntel."

I remember him getting drunk on the day he took his company's website live. He puked on the very Apple MacBook he had bought to add class to his meetings. He later had to operate with a normal laptop as the MacBook refused to start from that day onwards.

It was my birthday, Neeraj and I had gone to a pub in Hauz Khas to grab a couple of drinks and do the obvious, check out girls.

"I will be moving out next month Abhay," Neeraj finally said what I had expected to come from him for a long time.

"Why?" I did not know how else to react. With Neeraj around, I had forgotten my struggles. To see him grow and become a successful entrepreneur was even more satisfying. While we both used to only catch up on weekends as Neeraj remained working most of the time, we still developed a bond as two friends who were trying to create a life for themselves.

"I have been putting up with you for a year now Abhay. Never have you asked me for rent, money for food/ expenses, nothing. Now that I have fairly done well for myself, it's time I leave and carry on the rest of my journey alone." Neeraj slid an envelope full of cash towards me.

I carefully looked at the envelope and wondered if human emotions could ever be quantified in terms of money.

"How much is this?" I picked up the envelope.

"Not much but a lakh rupee, for all the trouble and expenses you paid for on my behalf. I know this is less, but this is all I could manage currently." Neeraj shrugged.

"Let's go," I replied, picking up the envelope and keeping it in my pocket.

"Where?" Neeraj asked, confused by the sudden change in plans of leaving a jam-packed ladies' night party.

I took out my bike and the next thing, we were both riding toward Noida.

"Where are we going? And why Noida man? Neeraj could not make any sense of what was happening.

An hour later, we both were standing in front of flat number 307, Amrapali Housing Society. Neeraj stood behind me as I pressed the doorbell.

A few seconds later, Aanchal opened the door.

"Hi," I smiled.

Aanchal was shocked to see both Neeraj and me

standing outside her flat at one a.m. in the night. She couldn't react to my 'Hi'.

I turned towards Neeraj and quietly slid the envelope back into his hands and whispered in his ears as I left.

"This is exactly where you say sorry to her. Do not let this moment go. Goodbye and best of luck." I walked away as Neeraj and Aanchal kept looking at each other.

Neeraj moved out a few weeks later. He and Aanchal had gotten back to talking and meeting each other regularly.

I remained out of the radar for the majority of those few weeks, returning home very late or when Neeraj was traveling. My job was done and Neeraj now could fly on his own. Moreover, the money episode made me realizc that times and people change, and you have to change along with them.

A month after he moved out, my parents and family moved in. While reading the newspaper one day, I came across the headline, "Neeraj Kumar's venture InvestIntel raises funding worth fifty crores."

Just then, my cell phone beeped. I checked the text message, which read "Your salary of Rs. 50,000 has been credited to your account number XXXXXX1851. The updated balance in your account is Rs. 55,600."

STRIKE ONE

It was a Tuesday morning. The sun shone brightly after three days of heavy rainfall. Delhi looks different after rainfall. Apart from the waterlogging and heavy traffic, there is a hidden beauty about this place, which seldom people observe.

A normally grey sky, covered with smoke suddenly looks blue. The roads seem washed and fresh while the leaves look greener. It seems as if a forgotten beauty queen returned to her original self.

There had been rapid developments over the last few months after Santosh joined InvestIntel's board. The company had set up its first steel plant on the outskirts of Ranchi by taking over an ailing steel company that was partially funded by the government.

Vikram Steels was once a brand name and a public sector giant. However, like most other government-run companies, this company too was run irresponsibly, driving it into losses. The Singhanias had an option almost a year back to buy out Vikram Steels; however, buying Vikram Steels was more of a loss-making proposition back then and even today.

The entire company needed a restructuring, right from

the senior management to the state-of-the-art equipment, recovering bad debts from clients, etc. It needed a lot of effort and money to get Vikram Steels up and running. However, with Jhunjunwala and Neeraj's brains behind the company, there was still hope.

While the company was bought over at a throwaway price, I arranged for a bailout package from the government using my political contacts. After the takeover, Jhunjunwala began by firing a lot of senior members from Vikram Steels. Post a few controversial high-profile exits and hiring, the top management looked in shape.

The biggest challenge was tackling union leaders who went on strikes every quarter demanding a pay hike. I left the responsibility of ensuring people fall in line with Suraj. A few weeks later, the old labor union was dismantled and crushed.

Within three months of the takeover, the company had managed to recover more than seventy percent of its bad debts and had won a few important clients who migrated from Singhania Steels due to lower rates and better products.

The Singhanias on the other hand had further slumped into losses. Our people in Singhania Steels were doing everything possible to ensure that the company did not get back on track. From supplying low-quality goods to key clients to ensuring a factory fire just before a critical consignment delivery deadline, we ensured Nandita and Naman always had their plates full of trouble.

Naman had become an alcoholic and there were now frequent fights between Nandita and him. We further planted a new intern in his company with whom Naman got romantically involved. Finally, it was time to trigger the coup as planned.

Santosh and Neeraj bought the majority of Singhania Steels shares from the open market and even before Nandita or Naman could react, the Board of Directors who held a substantial amount of the company's shares were all hired by Vikram Steels.

Singhania Steels turned into Vikram Steels overnight and the nation saw its biggest hostile takeover in decades the next morning. I carried the newspaper carrying headlines on the front page – "How David Bought Goliath." From a guy who once sat in a dark and empty parking lot, cursing himself for being poor with no money to masterminding the collapse of a steel giant, life has changed me a lot as a person.

I was on my way to the oath-taking ceremony where I would be formally sworn in as the Defence Minister of India. The battle still wasn't over. Nandita and Naman had a lot of wealth, power, and influence in the business circle. To bring down Nandita to her knees, a lot of work had to be done.

While professionally I had hit her in the right place, it was the damage on the personal front that would bring her to the ground. I was still engrossed in my thoughts when I finally arrived for the swearing-in ceremony. It was the biggest moment of my life but my mind still was on the press conference that Neeraj and Jhunjunwala would be holding the same evening.

Minutes later, I took oath as the Defence Minister of India in the full media glare. While the media went into overdrive covering my journey from a banker to the youngest Defence Minister of the nation, I quietly left for my new office in South Block. No leaves, no breaks, no rest. I took charge of the ministry thirty minutes after being sworn in.

Being the first day at the ministry, I had a lot on my plate already. From an army that needed an urgent upgrade in terms of weapons and technology to an air force that was grappling with a shortage of modern fighter aircraft, it took me an entire day just to understand the current situation.

I worked late, finally meeting the chief of staff of the armed forces. I was surprised by how mismanaged the ministry was until now. I realized something that day. Had it not been for the armed forces, which remained loyal and honest to the motherland, our national security would have been compromised long ago.

The last Defence Minister had made more money than the entire quarterly budget set aside for the army. Things had to be changed and changed fast.

I reached home around three in the morning. The first thing I did was call up Neeraj.

Surprisingly, he was still awake.

"Jai Hind Minister Saab," Neeraj chuckled.

"Mr. Tycoon, how did the press conference go?" I was curious to know.

"It went well. Also, Nandita called me today," Neeraj replied.

"I am listening," I said.

"She said she knows you are behind all of this and that she would not spare me, Jhunjunwala, and you for the damage we've caused to her." Neeraj's voice carried a hint of worry; after all, we both were fighting a woman who knew no rules.

"Hmm, don't worry, I'll take care of that. You've got a huge responsibility of running one of the biggest steel manufacturing companies in India. You need to build a mammoth from here." I distracted Neeraj from Nandita's topic, and instead let him concentrate on what he was best at doing.

I knew Nandita would come hard at Neeraj. It was time I made my final move to bring her down.

"Sure Abhay, this company will fly and so will you. It was such a moment of pride to see my childhood friend become the Defence Minister of this nation," said Neeraj, his voice carrying the happiness and excitement of a true friend.

"Thank you, brother, for everything," I replied as I hung up the phone with a smile on my face.

I checked my messages to find Bhagat's text. In all this madness, I had forgotten about my old friend.

"*I know you and Neeraj are big men now, just wanted to tell you that I am proud to have known both of you. Hope you guys will stay in touch.*" Read the text from my childhood friend.

I immediately made a Whatsapp group with me, Neeraj, and Bhagat in it.

"Bhagat got your emotional text, please shove it back in. We are here to stay, always." I sent the text and within minutes got a reply from both Neeraj and Bhagat. They had been up and celebrating my success as well.

I pulled out the pack of cigarettes and counted the number of cigarettes. It still had four cigarettes left.

FOUR CIGARETTES TO FINDING 'MYSELF'

Until now, every cigarette I smoked was when I moved a step closer to achieving my goal of becoming successful enough to beat Nandita's ego down to the ground.

Each cigarette took me back to those memories that were close to my chest, where I learned a lesson, gained an experience, realized the truth about human emotions, discovered love, and experienced heartbreak. Every memory was an important step in shaping me into the person I was.

I had become the youngest Defence Minister in the history of this nation but there were so many skeletons buried deep in my closet on my way to the top. Now and then, I fought with my inner conscience, and those times when my conscience won were the only moments when I had a peaceful sleep.

I had earned a lot of money through illegal means and it kept growing because the seeds of corruption I planted back then had now bloomed into cash trees. However, I was not at peace from within. I wanted to now get rid of all this money and use it for the common good of people. I was now trying to become a saint in a dark world.

That moment when I was oscillating between life and

death and the purpose of God giving me a second chance was still etched in my mind. Every night I tried to find this answer to why.

Nandita however was still my biggest obsession. Leaving her unattended for too long meant giving her enough time and space to plan something against me. Had that plan been restricted to me, it would not have made a lot of difference. It was the people I was close to who also stood at risk.

Nandita had to be knocked out cold to be safe.

There were four cigarettes between bringing Nandita down and finding my life's purpose. The next four chapters are about those four events, which changed my life.

Hang on tight!

Cigarette Number Seventeen

STRIKE TWO

With the steel business gone and the company running in losses, Naman was finding it hard to cope with failure. The secretary we had planted carefully in his office had slept her way to the Vice President and Nandita was aware of the growing closeness between them.

She rather chose to ignore them and concentrate on her work. This is where I made my next move, to replace Nandita with this secretary.

It was in the board's annual meeting that Jhunjunwala proposed the same. There was unanimous consent and the one who signed the decision letter was none other than Naman. He did not even protest which made it evident that he wanted the same to happen.

When the board meeting was over, everyone left the conference room, except for Nandita. Even Naman did not care that he left Nandita crying, and alone.

Money is not always the reason people are happy, sometimes, what matters is the people who complete your life. Nandita did not know where to go or whom to even approach. She just had to give up and accept the decision.

After half an hour of crying and fighting against her emotions, she got up and walked out of the office, gracefully.

That night the secretary visited Naman's farmhouse while Nandita waited for him to return. They both stayed at his farmhouse and I made sure Nandita knew about the same.

Any woman can only take her husband's infidelity to a point where it is hidden. When it starts happening in the open, it becomes shamelessness. Nandita immediately left for the farmhouse.

On reaching the farmhouse, she wasn't allowed to enter inside as instructed by Naman. She fought, screamed at guards, and tried to shove her way past the guards but was only pushed back. She finally broke in front of the gate, crying and howling out of pain. The guards picked her up and escorted her to the car.

I kept the pressure going now but was baffled as to why Nandita and Naman divorced each other. It was more than obvious now that Naman had another woman in life and she was calling shots.

Nandita would sit and keep her eyes glued to the television while her drunk husband would bring in his newly found ladylove in the same bedroom, that once belonged to her.

Then one fine day it finally happened.

Nandita confronted Naman and asked him to keep his affair outside the house. Naman instead started forcing Nandita to sign the divorce papers, which she wouldn't.

Soon it came to the point where he wanted her out of his life so badly that he began planning her murder.

Nandita was tipped off about the same by her servants who accidentally overheard Naman speaking over the phone.

I was at my residence, in a meeting with a few top officials from a leading defense equipment manufacturer. Nandita arrived at my residence where she sought an appointment with me. The protocol to meet me was lengthy and it took almost a month for people to reach me unless they had my direct line.

"Please, just call him and tell him Nandita wants to meet you," she instructed the office secretary who fixed appointments for me.

"Please wait for your turn. There are so many people already waiting to meet him," the peon replied.

Nandita did not protest and quietly returned to her seat. She somehow did not have the aggression or the confidence to tell the receptionist who she was. Three hours later, the list of people who were waiting to meet me was handed over to me.

"Nandita Singhania, what are you doing here?" I mumbled with a smile on my face.

"Please bring her in," I instructed the secretary. Even though it had been a while since we had seen each other, I rushed to the washroom, checked my hairstyle, adjusted my outfit, sprayed an expensive perfume, and walked outside onto the lawn where Nandita was quietly waiting.

She looked at me, dark circles below her eyes as if she hadn't slept for a while, weak and pale, depression and fatigue visible on her face. She, however, had a smile on her face that still reflected her strong as-ever self-respect.

For a moment, I wondered if this was what I wanted in the first place. All this revenge and the goal of bringing Nandita down to her knees suddenly felt useless.

"You look terrible Nandita," I replied.

"Why, does it bother you?" Nandita shot back, her eyes dripping with hate.

"What do you want?" I cut the conversation short.

"You must be wondering why am I not divorcing Naman. Right? Even after that secretary, you planted in his life did her job so well?"

"I am sorry; I don't understand what you are talking about," I replied.

"Yes, you do. You've finally got back to me. Hope you must be feeling like a real man," Nandita replied.

I kept silent. Politics had taught me a few lessons. One of them was how to be quiet even in the face of fierce criticism and hatred. It just helps you avoid the unnecessary mess you might get into.

"If you are done with your drama, please leave." I showed Nandita the way out.

"I don't know, I wanted to slap you. Yes, this is exactly why I had come here, to vent out my hatred for you." I could sense that Nandita meant every word she said.

"Go ahead." I understood the pain she was going through. Looking at Nandita made me feel guilty from within. Even though I had been dreaming of this day all my life, I hated myself today for doing this to a girl.

I realized that revenge is something that blinds you. It gets you to a point where you don't feel human anymore. Once you have finally had your revenge, it's the end of life's purpose for you. Whether for right or wrong reasons, revenge eventually burns your soul.

Nandita got up to leave. Her face and expressions said

it all; she had given up, on herself.

"Before I go, I am expecting Naman's child. Just a request, let me live if you can." Nandita held back her tears, as she looked right through my soul.

For a moment, I did not know how to react. No matter how hard I tried to justify whatever happened to Nandita, it still pinched watching her this way.

"Why are you saying this? Why would I kill you? Naman is to become a proud father. I will make sure you guys don't face any issues going forward. The other women in Naman's life will be taken care of as well." I meant every word I said. If there was one way of putting the revenge chapter to an end, this was it. In fact, I wanted to get rid of the guilt within me.

"No use Abhay, Naman wants me to abort this baby," Nandita replied.

"Why?" I was surprised at how calmly Nandita said that line.

"Because this baby carries the Singhania surname. Naman wants to divorce me and marry that bitch you introduced in his life. What he does not know is that I am not going to sign those papers, even if he kills me," Nandita replied.

"So it seems I did a favor on you by showing you his true colors." I chuckled shamelessly.

"No Abhay, I always knew this side of Naman. You only helped him make it more obvious to me. He has been beating and abusing me ever since he discovered that I was pregnant. From threatening my family members to trying to get me killed, he has tried everything. Two days back, I escaped from my house. His men have been searching for me ever since," Nandita replied.

While I had my revenge, the price that Nandita paid for it was far greater.

"Why do you believe I would help you?" I asked.

"Did I ask for help? I do not need your help, Abhay. I was here to accept my defeat and request you to not get me killed. Cannot fight two powerful men, at the same time." Nandita smiled helplessly.

"Why did you try to kill me?" I always wanted to hear the truth from her mouth. One would always confess to his/her darkest secrets in times of desperate need. Nandita was desperate and I needed answers to all my questions.

"But you are alive. Aren't you?" Nandita stopped and replied.

"Why did you try to kill me?" I asked the same question again.

"How do you think Suraj arrived right in the nick of time to save you?" Nandita cross-questioned me instead.

"Listen, I do not have time for your puzzles. Tell me, why did you try to kill me?" I was not interested in knowing about anything else.

"Abhay, Naman had planned it. However, it was me who had tipped off Suraj about the attack on you." Nandita finally revealed her side of the story.

"Bullshit, why would Naman try to kill me? Moreover, why would you want to save me?" I was confused.

"Naman wanted to kill you because you took away all the credit for Faridabad's factory launch. You were becoming influential and Naman took you as a threat to millions of dollars invested in the factory. Why I saved you, I still don't know." Nandita shrugged.

Nandita, a girl who once made fun of my situation, was now in a situation where she needed me to have mercy on her. I had a choice, to believe Nandita and let her fight her own battle or simply pick up the phone and inform Naman of his wife's coordinates. It would have put an end to Nandita, forever.

After thinking for a few minutes when Nandita silently waited for my decision, I replied.

"I do not want to believe you Nandita, but irrespective of whether whatever you told me is true or not, I will help you, even if you are too proud to take it." I got up and extended my hands.

"I can do this alone Abhay." Nandita's pride still had some spine left.

"I am not helping you Nandita, I am doing this for the baby. There is no reason why that thing inside you should die." I got up to leave.

"Abhay, I am sorry for treating you so badly. I was wrong. You know people call you the dark saint, I believe that now." Nandita finally said those words I waited to hear for almost a decade.

How do you react to something like that? I smiled and walked up to Suraj, signaling Nandita to remain seated.

"Suraj, take Nandita to my farmhouse. Ensure she gets all the proper care. And no one will know about this. Clear?" I instructed Suraj.

"Ok, bhaiya." Suraj humbly signaled Nandita to head towards his car.

Nandita silently sat inside the car. I kept looking at her as she was lost in her thoughts sitting in the backseat of the car.

As Suraj drove away, I reached for my pocket and pulled out my eighteenth cigarette. “Naman.” I silently whispered as I clicked the lighter burning my cigarette.

Cigarette Number Eighteen

STRIKE THREE

Politics taught me never to trust someone, even myself for that matter of fact. While I committed to helping Nandita because of the overpowering guilt conscience within me, there was no way I was going to believe her without doing my investigation.

My investigation revealed the same facts. Nandita was telling the truth.

Naman Singhania, former owner of Singhania Steels, Board of Directors of the Singhania Group of Companies, a guy who had seen success early in his life fell for Nandita when he met her for the first time at his close friend's wedding.

Nandita being ambitious didn't leave any stone unturned to ascertain Naman was in love with her. However, one of the aspects of human relationships is that unless you truly feel for someone, your feelings can always be corrupted, especially if you are a rich guy going through a tough time.

After getting married, both of them started building their own separate lives. Naman enjoyed his active social life. Nandita never bothered to stop him because she was too busy building wealth for herself. She used to give interviews, became an icon for feminists around the globe, and was hailed as one of the best female entrepreneurs

India had in recent times.

In a matter of time, both drifted apart even without realizing it, all that remained as a bond between them was money. We all know money can never keep relationships floating for long, bringing us to the present scenario.

My plan of further destroying Naman started with him being introduced to a drug supplier at a high-profile party. Within a month, Naman was snorting cocaine three times a day.

Meanwhile, the secretary we had planted in Naman's life had turned rouge. She would stay with Naman all the time and had stopped responding to our instructions. Naman had bought her loyalty with a lavish lifestyle and lots of money. Moreover, she had fallen for him over this one year.

It was Naman's birthday and like every other rich brat, he decided to celebrate it abroad. This was exactly the opportunity I was waiting for. By this time, the drug peddler had become Naman's guy.

He taught Naman how to smuggle drugs in flight. Naman tried it successfully a couple of times. With time, his confidence level kept increasing. He began carrying higher quantities of hash and weed with him on international flights.

While I was aware of all this, I decided to wait for the right moment.

Naman's birthday party was planned in Dubai. He decided to smuggle cocaine to Dubai. While Naman successfully passed the Indian immigration, thanks to some influence exercised by me, I ensured Dubai law enforcement agencies were tipped off secretly.

Now for people who don't know this fact, the punishment for getting caught smuggling drugs in an Arab nation may result in the death penalty. As soon as Naman landed at the Saudi airport, drug enforcement authorities pounced on him like hungry wolves.

Naman was taken into custody and the Indian media was tipped off within minutes about Naman Singhania and his girlfriend's arrest.

The Indian government gave every possible support to the Saudi Arabian government concerning Naman's investigation.

Naman and his girlfriend (or the secretary we had planted) were both sentenced to life imprisonment in Saudi Arabia. It could have been the death penalty but Saudi and India had some very crucial business deals signed. Executing an Indian businessman would have put billions of dollars worth of investment at risk.

I watched the headlines flash on the screen. The Indian officials from the External Affairs Ministry gave out official statements about Naman Singhania. It all became a big media drama but most importantly, Naman and the Singhania business empire were finally taken care of.

I pulled out my cell phone and dialed Neeraj's number.

"Yes, minister sahib." Neeraj chuckled as he received my call.

"Singhania group is now officially yours." I chuckled.

"You knew he smuggled drugs on the flight, didn't you," Neeraj replied.

"Nope, I did not." I disconnected the call and pulled out my nineteenth cigarette.

Cigarette Number Nineteen

THE PURIFICATION

Seven months after Naman was sentenced to life imprisonment, Nandita delivered a baby girl. She had been staying at my farmhouse for this entire duration. I had planned for Nandita's parents to stay with her during her final months of pregnancy.

I visited Nandita the same day. She lay there with the baby by her side. Motherhood changes even the toughest of women. Looking at her, I realized that every woman has a mother hidden within her.

The care, love, and affection that women can give to their children is something that cannot be matched. Nandita was looking at her baby and her eyes were letting tears flow freely. I saw so many emotions in that one moment.

I walked up to her and she looked at me with a smile on her face. I kneeled next to her bed and carefully looked at the baby.

Her eyes closed; her small fists clutched, a face so small yet so beautiful and pure. I had never felt innocence from such close quarters.

"Can I touch her?" I asked Nandita, giving her all the respect, a mother deserves.

Nandita nodded with a smile. I stretched my fingers to touch the baby but instead, she grabbed them with her tiny hand.

Everything stopped. For a few moments, my mind replayed the exact moment when I was lying unconscious in the hospital, fighting for my life.

The moment when that little girl asked me to choose between life and death and how I decided to take that second chance.

Her face lit up in front of my eyes and it felt as if it wasn't the baby but her who was holding my finger. I did not move for a while, wondering if this was my true purpose of staying alive, and giving her a second chance at life.

I was not a saint, maybe I was on the darker side of life. But sometimes you find a purpose, big enough for you to step out of the darkness and maybe leave everything behind.

I kept looking at the baby's face for a while. It felt as if she was talking to me.

"Abhay?" Nandita interrupted, seeing that I had not moved or said anything for the last fifteen minutes.

"Yaa." I looked at Nandita, eyes still moist but a face that concealed the joy and happiness within me.

"Are you OK?" she asked.

"Yes, so, what next?" I asked Nandita.

"Nothing Abhay, my life is for her now. I promise she would be a much better human being than me." Nandita lovingly slid her hands on the baby.

"We bought the entire Singhania group a few days

back, it's now yours to run." I got up to leave.

"Not again Abhay. I don't need anything," Nandita replied.

I gave a confused look at Nandita. Was she the same girl who once would have killed to get ownership of the Singhania group?

"I am done, Abhay. Have wished for a simple life for so long now. All this money, power, it's all so blinding. You just forget reality. You forget to talk to yourself. I don't want any of it," said Nandita.

"So where will you go?" I asked.

"I don't know but it would be better than all this mess for sure," Nandita replied.

I nodded in agreement. Before leaving, I bent down to kiss the baby once again. As I walked out, I instructed Suraj to stay back and ensure Nandita and her family did not face any trouble with hospital formalities.

Later that night I called Palak.

"Abhay, calling so late, all fine?" Palak answered the call.

"Yes, I usually get late because of work. This is all the time I am left with to talk to friends," I replied.

"What is it now Abhay?" Palak maintained her record of knowing things even before I said.

"Nothing, I just called to say thank you," I replied.

"So you are leaving me, again?" Palak cut straight to the point.

"I never came back, Palak. I was always gone. You are and will be my first love. Parallel lines, which is all we have always been. No matter how much I love you, that unspoken distance between us will always remain. This story of ours Palak is best when incomplete." I finally said all my feelings that I held back for Palak since childhood.

Palak hung up. She did not say a word. I understood she needed time to accept the reality that the day she let me go was the day that I was gone.

I had no answer as to why I let Palak go. Everything was so perfect for me so far yet we could not be together.

Chaos is drugs. It feeds on your need for fear, disruption, and anarchy. Everybody who wishes for a perfect life is someone who has not tasted chaos. I had tasted chaos for too long. The only time when I did not want chaos was when the baby held my hands.

For the next month, I stayed in touch with Nandita. That baby became my obsession as if she was my own. At times, Nandita had to extract the baby out of my arms for feeding. That little kid would just not leave me.

I was truly happy for the first time in my life. All this power, money, respect, everything became unattractive to me. What I longed for once was something I did not feel like going back to. It troubled me but I could not stop myself from thinking about Nandita and her kid.

When I could not take it anymore, I decided to take a break and go back to the city that brought me up, shaped my soul, and connected one end of it to the Mahadeva – Varanasi.

My grandfather hailed from Varanasi. I would often visit him during summer or winter vacations. He would make me sit on his shoulders and show me around the city. As a kid, I was mesmerized by Mahadev and his stories.

I would sit amongst the saints, priests, and '*Aghoris*', listening to stories about mythological characters.

I would roam around all day in the lanes of the city, carefree as if the entire city belonged to my friend Mahadev. Evenings used to be magical back then in Varanasi. A city older than the time itself would slowly wrap its charm around you. As I grew up, my bond with the city further grew stronger. The city and its soul stayed with me throughout.

Those Ghats have more stories to tell than someone could ever hear.

It was a Monday evening. The Ghats had slowly become quiet. I sat on one of the steps near the Manikarnika Ghat, watching a pyre burn. My heart and brain had been in a constant battle. I still had the last cigarette to smoke. I could not decide my fate.

An hour later, as darkness engulfed the ghat, I slowly got up and moved towards the river. It's believed that anyone who takes a dip in the holy waters of Maa Ganga at Varanasi breaks out of the circle of life and death.

Standing in the water, I took the first dip. As I submerged my head into the water, the first face I saw was Nandita holding the baby. Several dips and the same result. Not once did Palak or anyone else I had met in the past flash in front of my eyes.

By the time I finished my seventh dip, I was clear.

"Har Har Mahadev," I murmured slowly as I stepped out of the water.

The next day I was back in Delhi. It was around evening when I got a call from Nandita.

"Abhay, thank you for everything. I do not know if I can ever repay your debt but you are a good man." Nandita began as soon as I picked up the phone.

"You have already thanked me enough Nandita, what is the matter?" I recognized this tone of Nandita. Something was going on in her mind.

"I am moving to Australia." Nandita broke the news.

"Whh… why?" I knew this day would come but was not prepared to listen to her decision.

"I am starting a new life Abhay, blank slate. Want to give my daughter the life she deserves with no shadow of my past to haunt us," Nandita replied.

"When are you leaving?" I asked.

"I am at the airport Abhay," Nandita replied.

My heart sank. This small kid in Nandita's arms had become my life. She was the only thing that made me truly happy.

"I need to see her once. You cannot leave just like that. Is this how you have decided to repay me, Nandita?" I asked, irritated about Nandita's decision.

"Because even though I hated you all my life, I ended up falling for you again, Abhay. I cannot be a part of your life. You are too big now. Too big to associate yourself with a divorced woman who was once Naman Singhania's wife. The media, the people, the society, everyone will judge us, especially you. I cannot afford to put my daughter through all this. Had I met you, I could not have taken this decision. There are more people out there Abhay who need you. I have to go. Hope you understand. Goodbye, and thank you for everything." Nandita disconnected the call.

I leaned back on my chair. There was not much to say. Nandita was right. My name was too big for a woman searching for a peaceful and quiet life. Sometimes, the price you pay to become successful is so huge, that you end up staying alone.

Nandita and her baby deserved the chance they were so desperately seeking. On the other hand, I was helpless, trapped in my castle.

Quitting politics in search of a simple life was not an option anymore. There were far too many skeletons in my closet. Even if I wanted to, I could not go back to.

I had made more enemies than friends. It would just take one mistake from my end and they would leave no stone unturned in destroying me or anyone associated with me.

So the only option I was left with was to remain in power and keep guarding those secrets, forever.

The Final Cigarette

IGI AIRPORT

"All passengers for flight CX96, New Delhi to Australia are requested to head towards boarding gate 45. Thank you." The announcement echoed across the relatively crowded terminal 3.

Nandita put a cap on the milk bottle and stuffed it in her bag somehow. The baby had begun crying by the time. Trying to calm the baby, she tried reaching out for her suitcase, dropping her bag in the process.

"I will hold her." I extended my arms, signaling Nandita to hand over the baby.

Nandita looked at me in surprise. She could not understand how to react. After a few seconds where we both kept looking at each other, Nandita handed me over her baby with a smile. She somehow controlled her tears in the process.

When a woman hands you over her child, even for a few minutes, it means only one thing. She trusts you. Strangely, the baby had gone silent the moment I took her in my arms.

"She is such a drama queen." Nandita nodded.

"Yeah, the seed doesn't fall far from a tree." I smiled.

"You seeing me off wasn't exactly how I imagined

things ending between us," Nandita said, as we walked towards the boarding gate. I smiled and nodded, not saying much.

"I will take her from here. Thanks for coming Abhay." Nandita hugged me and for a few moments, we both stayed like that.

Taking the baby back in her arms, Nandita presented the boarding pass to the airline official.

"Thank you, ma'am. Please proceed." The airline official signaled Nandita to head towards the flight.

I stood there as Nandita walked away, the baby in her arms kept smiling at me, unaware that maybe this was the last time she was seeing me. I smiled back at her, making faces that made her laugh. Moments later, both of them disappeared into the crowd.

It was a weird feeling. Today, I did not want Nandita, the girl I once hated so much, to leave. For five minutes, I kept standing at the boarding gate, hoping she would come back.

She did not. Remember? Life is not a movie.

Walking back to my car, I quietly wiped my eyes and pulled out the cigarette packet.

Taking out the last cigarette, I closely looked at it. Nandita's name was still visible on it.

I lit the cigarette and took a long drag at it.

This was it, all my purpose, goals, and obsession to keep going even in the face of the impossible were all gone.

There was no more Nandita, there was no more anger, and all I could hear was a high-pitched noise in my ear.

All I was now staring at was a big void. Suddenly,

everything seemed pointless.

Whom do I live for? Whom do I fight for?

My heart still stood outside the boarding gate, hoping to see that baby's smiling face again.

My mind had begun thinking of ways to somehow counter this feeling of hopelessness and pain.

Taking the last few drags at the cigarette, I looked at its bud one final time before dropping it on the ground.

Then blowing the smoke in the air, I closed my eyes, as if letting go of every feeling that was ever trapped within me.

"Abhay." I heard a familiar voice.

I opened my eyes to find Palak standing in front of me.

Even before I could have reacted, I received a text from Nandita. It read – *"Best of luck, btw, she is cute ;)"*

I looked above as Nandita's flight took to the skies.